ABOUT THE AUTHOR

Paul Durston served with the Metropolitan Police in London for thirty years. Having retired, he devotes his time to creative writing and exploring the inland waterways. *If I Were Me*, about Charlie who experiences memory issues following a traumatic incident, is his debut novel.

He lives on a narrowboat in Worcester with his partner Caroline.

Published in Great Britain in 2022

By Diamond Crime

ISBN No: 978-1-915649-17-1

Copyright © 2022 Paul Durston

Diamond Crime is an imprint of Diamond Books Ltd.

Thanks to...

Former-detective and colleague Phil Murray for his help on all things investigative. Dr Robin Lawrence MRCPsych for his insight and patient explanations. My writing buddies Vicki Bradley, Vicki Jones, Fraser Massey and Jane Phillips for their support and input. Claire McGowan, William Ryan and all my fellow students from whom I learnt so much at City University London. Steve Timmins and Phil Rowlands of Diamond Books for showing faith in me. Caroline who tolerates my absence when present in a very confined space.

Cover and book design: jacksonbone.co.uk

Cover photograph:
iStockphoto and Adrian Balasoiu/Unsplash

PAUL DURSTON

For information about Diamond Crime authors
and their books, visit:

www.diamondcrime.uk

For my brother, Kevin.

IF

I

WERE

ME

PAUL DURSTON

CHAPTER ONE

It's dark by the time a detective has taken my dealer and I'm back in the car with Lavender.

"Charlie, never seen you wearing a skirt."

"Trousers were ripped fighting with that dealer."

"Assault on police or criminal damage?"

"Not bothered. Grazed knee. Part of it."

Lavender glides us out onto Walworth Road. "There *are* good detectives," I say. "I know them both."

"Don't tell me. You had to do their job for them."

The evening traffic is heavy. "Not really. More their attitude – lording it."

"Remember, Charlie, if something's more than ten minutes old, we're no longer friggin' interested. We trample the scene, kick doors in, pick our arses, contaminate evidence and upset witnesses. Then, when the teccos arrive, we all fuck off. They ain't lording it, they're friggin' jealous."

Such eloquence.

Lavender stops by a coffee shop. I take the hint and, on returning with two lattes, a call comes in. "Mike-Three, Mike-Three. Camberwell New Road, junction Vassal Road, serious RTC. Petrol tanker overturned. Mike-Three."

Tanker overturned? Shit. "Received by Mike-Three."

We open our doors, place our steaming coffees on the road, and we're off, doors slamming, blue lights flashing, sirens wailing, we're a minute away. Other units are answering up. Fire Brigade on way. Ambulance on way.

As we approach, I hear a poomph and a broiling fireball rolls up into the London sky.

Craning forward, I watch it rise as Lavender swings us around stationary vehicles.

"Did you see that?"

"See friggin' what?" Lavender brakes to avoid a pedestrian.

Everyone's running, away from where we're heading. A man clangs into a lamp post and falls. A woman looks back, stumbles but keeps going. A little girl in a red coat cries. A small dog runs with the crowd.

We're stuck. I leave the car and barge through the mass of people swarming towards me.

The crowd's thinning. Building line. From there, I'll be able to see. I push on, clear the crowd and reach the building's edge.

Flames reflect in shop windows.

I take a peep and feel the heat. The tanker, engulfed in flames, is on its side, its rear wheels turning. Nearby vehicles are consumed by the spreading fire. A burning woman collapses, her flames rise as she falls.

I break cover but a man throws himself on her and is consumed as well.

I crouch.

I've never felt heat like this. After the stampeding crowd, there's an eerie calm.

Dark mounds of bodies are clustered near the bus stop.

A burning man erupts from a building and pounds at his flames before falling. I move towards him but he's too far. I crouch again.

A car screeches backwards out of the fire, sparks across the pavement and through a shop front.

My arm is grabbed. It's Lavender.

"Charlie. Too close. We must get back."

To my left, there's movement. "Just a…" Can't speak. Cough. Spit. There's that movement again. What is it? Lavender's pulling my arm.

A car, on the edge. The driver's jerking. Flames are creeping up and around the bonnet. The front tyres burst. The car sighs.

I twist away from Lavender. "You go," I shout and sprint towards the car.

All around me is crushed thunder. Heat prickles my cheeks. Oily fingers scratch my lungs. Squinting through barely open eyes, I make it to the car. The flames reach for me from under the front wheels. I rip the driver's door open. It's a woman. The flames have her. Her face is moving. Blisters bubbling. Silent screams yaw from her blackened mouth. She moves her chin, an indication, I follow. In the back is a small boy, arms out, eyes pleading, mouth wide.

The woman's gone still. Flames are creeping from the far side towards the boy. I grab his arm. He's strapped in. The flames draw closer. I must reach into them to release the belt. I can do this. I'm in, hands following the belt down. I'm holding my breath. The catch. It's in my hand. It won't release. My eyes are scrunched. My skin's popping. Despite all my nerves and muscles pushing me away, I keep my hands there. I can do this. The catch won't release. I arch my head back. Bright stars. Must get away but my hands stay there. Pushing. Pulling. Tugging. Twisting. It won't release. I keep my mouth shut tight so my scream can't escape. Won't release. Won't release.

Strong hands grab me. One more go at the catch. I'm reeling back from the car. Flames have me. They're climbing. Nothing left. Can't move. A fire extinguisher roars. I'm dragged backwards, fast, away from the flames, away from the car and I have hold of the boy.

* * *

I'm no stranger to physical pain but my hands feel like they're being dragged around a gravel drive. "How much longer?"

My salamander tattoo no longer hides the scars on my left wrist. Both hands are wrapped in clingfilm-like dressings, skin burnt, muscles baked, tendons stewed, yellow blisters and weeping puss. "I was saving the boy."

In response, my hands fire lightning bolts at me while inciting other parts of my body to join in. My guts cramp, teeth throb, eyes pop, heart booms. My scream starts low, rising higher and higher.

Nurse Olu comes and starts removing the dressings from my right hand.

"Don't mess with them. Please." I'm pleading from arched back as my right hand, on being disturbed, opens up with a new barrage but Nurse Olu has the magic touch with her oils and ointments and my wailing subsides, only to start rising again as she moves to my left hand.

"Bad today," Nurse Olu says. My wailing subsides but I'm filled with anxiety about what will be. My salamander has lost his tail. Will I lose a finger? A thumb?

"Bad today, Charlie," Nurse Olu says, again.

"What do you mean?"

She smiles. "Some days seem better than others."

"They're all bad," I say, confused.

"You're fine." She grips my shoulder. "The burns on your face and legs will heal. Your hands are bad but we're on top of that. You held your breath so no lung damage. You'll be okay."

"Every day's a bad day," I say but she's gone.

Where did Lavender come from? He's quiet, not banging on about friggin' this and friggin' that, and Mary Cantrell, my sergeant, is with him. Something's wrong. Nurse Olu comes, not her usual smiling self. "Charlie, I'm sorry, the boy has died." Cantrell's hand is on my shoulder and Lavender takes my other arm as my scream rises.

Gradually, I calm down. Nurse Olu has gone. Cantrell's unfolding a newspaper. "Look Charlie, it's a few days old."

She holds it up. Pictures of the tanker on its side, fire crews with their hoses, ambulance crews with their casualties and a picture of me, in this hospital bed, arms up.

"I don't remember anyone taking that picture."

"Well," Lavender says as Cantrell lays the paper beside me, "you've been out of it. Pain or drugs. Another thing. Someone filmed you dragging the boy from the car. Posted on YouTube. Gone friggin' viral. You're a national hero."

"So modest," Cantrell says perching on my bed. "He didn't mention his part."

I want them to leave. They pick up on my feelings and, very soon, they're gone, Lavender's parting shot, "Hey, Charlie. The next day, our coffees were still on the road. Gone friggin' cold though."

I feel sick. I wanted them to go and now I want them back. Not just Lavender and Cantrell but all of them.

The newspaper's there. Pictures of the carnage bring crackling flames, burning flesh, searing heat and, like then, I feel so alone. A school-photo of a boy, smiling and fair. Big eyes. The same eyes as in the blistered face. Billy.

My hands wake up. Lightning forks up my arms. I arch my back and wind up my siren scream. Nurse Olu comes. My feet itch and my stomach heaves as I lose control and wet the bed. Nurse Olu calls a colleague and, together, they clean me up and sort me out while I close my eyes and wish I was dead.

* * *

Out in the country, where the sky comes down to the ground, is the Police Rehabilitation Centre. Been here since hospital discharge, ten days ago.

I need help washing, dressing, eating, working my mobile. The person I call most is Kathy Bond. I can't even wipe my... you know. Sod it. I can't even wipe my fucking arse.

"Who does wipe your arse?" That's Kathy.

She asks me this in the dining room while spoon-feeding me, all the blokes failing to avoid eyeing up this whirlwind of blonde bustiness as she thumps my back.

"Kathy, you really don't want to know that," I say coughing and shunning more food.

"I do. I want to know who wipes your arse."

"For god's sake."

"Is that what the red ceiling-cord in your bathroom's for? Calling in the arse-wiper?"

I leave the gawping faces of convalescing colleagues and head for my room.

Kathy drags along behind. "Not even much there to wipe."

Although she's older, we're best mates. When I first arrived at the Nick, she taught me everything, not about police work, about managing the male-dominated environment. She has three rules: one – don't fuck any of them; two – don't fuck any of them; and three – don't fuck any of them.

I shoulder my way into my room.

"Your hands giving you grief?"

I elbow a light switch. "They've got it in for me." White dressings have replaced the clingfilm. "Not just the pain, I can't do anything."

Kathy switches on side lights and outs the main light. "Counselling?"

"It's all I *can* do."

"How's it going?"

"They ask me how I feel. What do I say?" I slump into an armchair.

"Sorry, Charlie. Sounds like you're not facing up."

I love Kathy dearly, but she can be a pain.

"Your self-image is poor," she says, "you describe yourself as a broomstick."

"Well, look at me."

"Okay, not curvy."

"Like a broomstick."

"No. Athletic."

"I'm plain and boring."

"Charlie," she says, "the counsellors aren't interested in what it's like to have burnt hands. They want to know how you feel about them, how you feel about the boy dying, how you feel about yourself…"

She stops. I've dropped forward, hugging my knees, hiding my tears.

"Hey, mate," Kathy's kneeling beside me, arm around my shoulders. "I don't mean to upset you but if you don't face up, it'll bite you."

"Probably best," I say between sobs, "you leave."

"I'm not leaving." She's guiding me to my bathroom mirror. She wipes away my tears. "There, you see. I'm curvy, rather too curvy. You're sleek. Slim hips, long legs. Athletic."

"Kathy."

"Your hair. Short's good but…"

"Kathy."

"Make-up. Your face has never seen more than a smear of foundation…"

"Kathy. Give it a rest." She's my friend. Lavender, Cantrell. They all are. They're all I have.

"What does Lavender say?" Thank god she's moved on.

"He came yesterday, told a story."

"About Wade?"

"Yes." I laugh. What would I do without friends like Kathy?

"You impersonate Lavender so well. Go on, tell the story as if you're him."

"Okay." I'm not in the mood, but good to change subjects. "Well," I drop my voice and mimic scratching my belly, "*Chasing suspects*. It's that Wade friggin' Oliver. Doesn't know where he is. *White male, dark clothing.* Call that a description? Finally, a location. We're off, blues-and-twos. Then comes the crippler. *Why you chasing him?* Guess what he said. *Drunk and incapable*. Friggin' prat."

Kathy's creased up. "Funny thing about that story, it's true. It was me who asked the crippler."

"Lavender explained." I drop my voice again, "His problem is," and we both say, "his friggin' education."

Albert Lavender. Nobody calls him Albert, courtesy of his garlic breath and flowery language. I dragged the boy from the burning car but Lavender dragged me out. The burns on his face have smartened him up.

Regardless of what Kathy says, that story's a fabrication. Chasing suspects is something Wade is good at. He's big, fast and strong. He's also good at making an idiot of himself whenever he speaks.

"Anyone else visited you?" Kathy plonks into the other armchair.

"Wade, weirdly."

"On his own?"

"Even brought me a book." I wave my bandaged hands towards the paperback on the desk. "He's so thoughtful." He also brought the address I asked him for but I'm not telling Kathy about that. Wade's predictable, predictable in his uselessness. Like Kathy, predictable in her role as gossip-central. Handy that the address is in Brockley.

"He fancies you," Kathy says.

"No way. He's practically aristocracy. God knows why he's in this Job."

"Don't forget the three rules, Charlie."

"Kathy. I'm not interested."

"I know and you're twenty-five. Not right. You really should…"

There's a knock on my door, thank god. It's the guy from West Mids, in Rehab with an injured knee.

"We're going for a drink," he says in his Brummie accent. "Thought you'd like to come."

"Great idea," Kathy says, grabbing her coat.

I get in quick. "No. Sorry. Tough day. Knackered."

"No problem," he says. "Mind you," he winks, "not surprised after last night."

I'm confused.

"What happened last night?" Kathy's spotted intrigue.

He laughs. "Charlie was karaoke queen."

"Karaoke queen?" Kathy's egging him on. I don't like the sound of this and I wish he'd leave.

"What a voice she has. Wouldn't give up the microphone."

"Holding a microphone?"

Must intervene. "I'm sorry, not tonight."

"Not a problem," he says, retreating through my door.

"Have a great time," I say.

"We will," he says, limping down the corridor.

I shut the door.

"Never heard you sing, Charlie." Kathy's standing, hands on hips.

"He exaggerates," I say.

"Can't hold a spoon but can hold a microphone. Life and soul of the party but can't go out with your best mate." She swings her coat round her shoulders, sighs, and leaves.

"I didn't go to the karaoke," I shout after her.

Her strops never last. She'll be fine next time we're together.

I get ready for bed. Don't call for help. It's still early and, as I curl up under my duvet, fully dressed, I feel the pain – the pain of loneliness – and the dream.

Soaking, arched back, every time I wake, wailing; but this time's different. I DIDN'T GO TO THE KARAOKE.

* * *

There's nothing worse than being sick on sick leave. Lavender's here, on duty, car parked outside.

"I was passing," he explains.

"How thoughtful."

Considering he saved my life, I should be more gracious but my hands sting and I must get to the burns unit for fresh dressings.

"Good you're getting out and about," he says.

What prompted that? "Hardly. Only to the hospital and back."

"Running? Via the park?"

His mood has changed. "Can't run. Can't risk infection."

"So, you only go out for hospital appointments."

"Or shopping…" I stop. When Lavender's not swearing, it's time to listen.

"Your trainers are muddy."

They're on the shoe rack by the front door. I don't remember ever running in them. Not only are they muddy, they're wet and muddy.

Lavender's watching me.

I'm confused. I couldn't manage the laces. My breath's coming in short gasps. "Would you drive me to the hospital?" I say trying to show some inner calm.

"Sure. Be in the car," but his radio bursts into life with an urgent call. He frowns. "Sorry, Charlie. That could of been better timed."

"Not a problem." Kings College Hospital isn't far and I'd prefer to walk. "Thanks for coming," I say, pushing muddy trainers from my mind.

"No problem. Happy New Year," he says, trotting back to his car, as much as someone who's six inches too short for his weight can trot.

* * *

The Rehab staff were all smiles when they discharged me before Christmas. In the event, I spent Christmas alone and I'm alone again for New Year as all my mates are on duty.

I try cleaning my flat but, with these hands, it's hard but I do find Elly, my cuddly elephant from the children's home all those years ago, amongst the pots and pans. I take her out, wondering how she could possibly be there, and give her pride of place next to the telly. "There, you rhyme."

Cantrell suggested I should make use of my time studying for promotion but my hands are such a distraction and concentrating is hard. I'm not even interested in promotion. The books are on my desk in my bedroom and above them, on my pinboard, the business card. Nigel Slattery MRCPsych. A constant reminder. I don't need a psychiatrist.

I need to get ready for hospital. Washing, brushing teeth and dressing take a while with these hands.

* * *

Nurse Olu calls me through.

"Now, let's see," she says. "Hmmm." I grit my teeth as she removes the dressings. "Hmmmm."

Dressings changed, I get up.

"Stay indoors, Charlie."

I have stayed indoors.

"Have your dressings changed every day."

I have come every day.

"Don't risk an infection. Have shopping delivered. Have friends visit you. Use cabs."

"Cabs?"

"If you own a flat in Camberwell, you can afford cabs."

I nod on my way out.

"Charlie. Happy New Year."

I smile. "And you."

* * *

Walking home, I think about what Nurse Olu said. I moved from the children's home to fosters, Harry and Harriet and their children, when I was ten. They were great but I never felt one of the family. Not really. When I joined the police, Harry spoke to me, Harriet by his side.

"You've done well, Charlie. We're proud of you. We're giving you a deposit for a flat. With your police income, you can afford the mortgage."

Generous gift? Uh-uh. Severance pay.

* * *

I stop.

There's someone I must talk to. Not far.

On top of Kevan House, I can see for miles. The Shard, London Eye, Wembley Stadium on a clear day but I'm not here for the view.

I sit cross-legged.

"Hi, Joel. There was an incident. Petrol tanker overturned, fire, deaths, injuries. Only down the road. I was badly burnt. I'm getting better but I'm doubting my memory again. Like ages ago. I sometimes feel like I'm not all there. Like I'm disconnected. Maybe it's because

I'm on my own too much or because I don't have a routine. Anyway, look. It's cold up here. I won't be away for so long, promise. I'll be back soon. Take care, Joel. Happy New Year. Love you."

I head home.

* * *

The skipper's car is there when I get home and Cantrell, in high-viz jacket, is brightening up the stair-well. She has an Evening Standard under her arm.

"Waiting long?" I ask.

"No."

"Welfare visit?"

"Yes. You're looking okay."

"I'm good."

"Good."

Silence. I don't fill it.

"Well," she says, "that's the welfare bit done, just the visit to go."

I head into my kitchen and point at the kettle. "Would you mind?"

She fills the kettle and hands me the paper. "They're still covering the tanker incident. You get a mention – again."

The tone is moving onto the blame game and I put the paper to one side.

She sets the two mugs on my coffee table and we settle on my sofa. She doesn't remove her jacket.

"Sarge, I want to come back to work."

She's taking in my flat.

"I'm going stir-crazy. It's driving me nuts."

Even without looking at me, her eyes say I don't need to explain.

"A desk job, or something?" My voice trails off.

"Out of the question, Charlie. Police stations are not hygienic. You're not resuming until you're given the all-clear. Let me hear no more about it."

One last go. "The inspector said…"

Her eyes stop their distracted meandering and fix on me. "Don't arc me, Charlie."

It's time to stop.

Cantrell's expression softens. "You're missed. Our figures have dropped."

Should I feel flattered?

She continues. "You've been put forward for a commendation."

"I already have three."

"Commissioner's." Cantrell slips that word in so effortlessly.

"Doesn't help me now."

"I know. Don't think *reward*. Think *recognition*." She moves on, switching subjects easily. By the time she leaves, she's mentioned occupational health, the counselling service and wished me a happy New Year.

* * *

Counselling reminds me of the business card pinned above my desk. Nigel Slattery MRCPsych.

Karaoke? Muddy trainers? Elly? "I don't need a psychiatrist." Burns heal, pain fades, I'll return to work and this nonsense will end.

Karaoke? I can't sing. A prank. It was never mentioned again.

Muddy trainers? I got them just before the tanker incident and I've never worn them outdoors.

Like I said to Joel, is this my memory issues coming back?

Elly. Last I saw Elly was fifteen years ago at the children's home. Doesn't make sense.

Muddy trainers? Elly? "I don't know." More than the pain of my burns, the loneliness and disruption, it's Elly and the muddy trainers that disturb me. How could Elly have reappeared? How can my trainers be muddy? If the karaoke event is true, who was singing?

The business card. Nigel Slattery MRCPsych. "I don't need a psychiatrist."

To try distracting myself, I lay Cantrell's newspaper out flat and flip the pages. A headline catches my eye:

Fatal Stabbing near Children's Playground

Police are investigating a fatal stabbing of a middle-aged man whose body was found in a children's playground in the early hours of Thursday morning. Detective Sergeant French, Homicide, said the body was discovered on Primrose Hill by an early morning jogger. Next of kin have been informed. Prince Albert Road was sealed off this morning. Anyone with information concerning this incident is asked to call police on 101 quoting CAD 1245/31DEC or Crimestoppers anonymously via 0800 555 111.

Why is that making me uneasy? It's getting dark. I reach for my desk lamp and there's Elly bathed in a pool of light. "I put you by the telly." Underneath her is a hand-written note.

> *ATM*
> *30 Dec 20*
> *21:18*
> *E&C*
> *£100*

"What?" I log-in to my account. There's the transaction. Yesterday evening. 21:18. I have absolutely no memory of this. How can I have gone to the Elephant & Castle and withdrawn money without remembering?

My card must have been cloned.

"Wait a second." Purse. My card's there with five crisp twenty-pound notes and a receipt amongst many others. I'm lucky, I can see enough of it without having to pull it out. Elephant & Castle. 30/12/2020. 21:18. My debit card. Withdrawal £100.

I look back at the note. If I wasn't spooked before, I am now. That's my hand-writing and I can't hold a pen.

CHAPTER TWO

I've slept well but I'm anxious again. The note – the note I wrote.

I pull on my dressing gown and head for the kitchen.

Kathy Bond's on my sofa, waking up. "What the hell are you doing here?"

She says nothing intelligible. She often stays over, as I do at hers but when did she come round?

I sit beside her.

She's hung-over.

"Kathy, I'm sorry. I didn't mean to shout."

She doesn't say anything and won't even look at me.

Maybe coffee would help. Hang on. I'm not hung-over. What? Kathy came round, got pissed and I didn't?

I make coffee, easier, and take it through.

She's dressing.

"Here, drink this."

"No," she says, "I'll head off."

"Kathy, I don't know what's going on. Things happen and I remember nothing." I've grabbed her arm and, despite the pain, I'm holding on. "Kathy, please. Don't leave. I'm frightened."

She draws me into a hug. "Okay," she whispers, "I'll stay."

I burst into tears, again. I've never cried so much and so often.

Kathy dries my face. "What have you got for breakfast?"

"Muesli."

"For fuck's sake. I'll be back in fifteen."

* * *

Kathy cuts up my sausage and bacon. I can just about manage a spoon now.

Finally, I ask the burning question. "What happened?"

"Nothing, really," she says looking away.

"Kathy, please help me. Cantrell did her welfare visit and, after she left, I read the paper for a bit. I was feeling down so, although it was still early, I climbed under my duvet and…"

Kathy looks astonished.

"…woke up this morning to find you on my sofa."

Egg yolk hangs ready to drop from her fork poised in front of her mouth.

"What?" I'm reaching for her.

She puts her fork down. "Sargie visited you the day before yesterday. Thursday. New Year's Eve."

It starts in my gut, boiling, churning. My pulse pounds and heart drums. Can't breathe. Tongue swollen. I collapse off my chair. Breathe. Concentrate. Breaths come fast but no air. Push my forehead into the carpet. Heave at another breath but can't hold onto it. Next one's in but no effect. Head spinning. Movement around me. Firmness on my shoulders. A bag's held over my face. I fight, but no strength. Breathe. Easier. Kathy's voice. Calming. Breathing deeply now, in and out, in out. Bag rustles as it inflates and deflates. Kathy's talking, her voice comforting.

The room swims back and Kathy helps me onto my sofa.

A Morrisons carrier bag. "You stuck a plastic bag over my face?"

"It's all I had."

"What happened?"

"You had a panic attack."

"I don't do panic attacks."

"You were hyperventilating. It was a panic attack."

She's offering nothing more. "Kathy. No mucking about. What happened yesterday?"

When Kathy speaks, there's none of her mischievousness. "Yesterday, Friday, New Year's Day, I came round to see you after work. Wish you happy New Year. Phoned in advance. You said no problem. Got here about lunchtime. We chatted, drank. You didn't drink much but kept topping me up. Couldn't drive. Stayed over."

Sounds normal. "Why wasn't I drinking?"

"Not sure. I was crashing and you got a duvet for me. Next thing I know, it's morning and you're yelling at me."

I sit still, processing what Kathy said. I have no memory of this.

"Kathy. How was I? I mean, what was I like?"

She thinks for a while. "Different."

"What do you mean?"

"It was you but like you were someone else."

"How?"

"I don't mean to frighten." She stops. She's thinking hard. "It was you, but more."

"What do you mean, more?"

She clearly wishes she hadn't started. "We've known each other for over seven years. Been through shit together, good times too but, yesterday, you were someone else."

"What do you mean?"

"At first, I thought it was to do with your injuries but, what was so different, was that you were grilling me about the murder."

My breath starts coming in short gasps again but I'm ready for it. I push it down. "Kathy." I swallow. "What murder?"

Kathy reaches for the bag but decides it's not needed. "You were really inquisitive, prising every morsel of information out of me."

"Kathy. What murder?"

Kathy puts the bag down. "You really don't remember."

"Kathy, for god's sake. What murder?" My anger is showing. Frustration more like.

Kathy's not fazed. "Family man. Husband. Father of two. Near home. Primrose Hill near Regents Park. Stabbed."

She's described the article in the Evening Standard. "When?"

"Time of death, if known, hasn't been announced. Body found early hours on Thursday, New Year's Eve. You insisted on having the news on constantly. It was all you were interested in." She shakes her head. "So unlike you."

"Unlike me? It wasn't me."

"Charlie. It *was* you. Maybe that tanker incident, the boy dying and your burns have had more of an impact than you think. You be sure to speak to your doctor about this."

"I'm sorry. I need to be on my own."

She resists but, a few minutes later, I'm alone, with only myself for company.

* * *

I get ready to go for new dressings. Elly's still there, on the note:

> *ATM*
> *30 Dec 20*
> *21:18*
> *E&C*
> *£100*

Something's wrong. My antennae are up and buzzing. Dabbing at my keyboard, I google what was going on up the Elephant on Wednesday evening. The internet connection's weak so I give up and head out the door. I can't manipulate my phone to make that kind of search.

I ditch the note down a drain and, when I get to the hospital, they're having an emergency. A new nurse does my dressings. He's nice but I miss nurse Olu.

* * *

On the way home, I think about Elly, karaoke, muddy trainers, lost time with Kathy. Most of all, I'm thinking about the cash-withdrawal last Wednesday evening up the Elephant. It seems to coincide with the murder I was so interested in. I've had memory issues before, back in my teens. Harriet organised counselling and it was sorted.

Arriving home, I get the psychiatrist's card. Nigel Slattery MRCPsych. It's Saturday but worth a try. There's a knock at my door.

I've never been so popular. Stop. Back-up. Window. On the street is an unmarked police car I don't recognise.

Not good. Thank god I ditched that note. As I fumble through the locks, I know what's coming.

Outside are two suits and Cantrell. The smaller man speaks. "I'm DS French, Homicide. Charlotte Quinlan?"

Strange being on the receiving end. Now is not the time to say or agree with anything.

Cantrell confirms.

"We need to talk with you about a murder."

Now is the time to speak. "Will I be under caution?"

"Yes. You can have a representative, solicitor, fed-rep, friend, anyone."

I turn to the other man. "Who are you?"

"Steve Reeve, DI DPS. I'm here because you're a police officer." Department of Professional Standards, coppers who investigate coppers. Nasally voice.

"Sarge, will you sit with me?"

"Of course." Cantrell's smile is forced.

I shrug. "I'll come immediately. I'd appreciate a lift."

If they could arrest me, they would. I've no need to worry. I'm worried as hell. My only thoughts are about the note – the note I wrote.

The detectives are investigating a murder.

I realise now, so am I.

CHAPTER THREE

I keep reminding myself, I'm not arrested. I can walk out any time.

DS John French is pretty slick with pre-interview procedures but I'd expect that of a Homicide DS. DI Steve Reeve from DPS watches me through his purple-tinted specs. They're older, lot of service between them.

I'm thinking about the note I wrote. How will I know when to use it? Also my curiosity for the Primrose Hill murder. Kathy was saying…

"Charlie?"

Everyone's looking at me. "I'm sorry. What was the question?"

"No question. I was explaining the reason for interview."

"I'm sorry, my hands, they're quite distracting." I rest my hands, with their bulky dressings, on the table. Nurse Olu wasn't available so, bulkier than usual.

He points to a water jug and cups. "If you need a drink, just say."

"It's okay. Fine. Really."

I'm not fine. It's hardly a month since the tanker incident, the story's still on telly and in the papers and I'm being questioned, under caution, about a murder. I'm free to go but why me? Weird goings-on. My memory. Not fair.

"Charlie?"

"Sorry. It's not just my hands." I make an effort to concentrate.

DS French starts again. "Suspicious death. Body found Primrose Hill, early hours, Thursday morning. Estimated time of death, Wednesday evening. Body identified as Peter Daventry. Thursday morning, four-thirty-three, Crimestoppers received a call alleging you're the assailant. This interview is to inform you of that and see if you can help identify who made that call but first, I have some questions." He stops.

I'm holding my breath.

"Charlie?"

"I haven't killed anyone." My voice sounds strange.

French continues, warmth in his eyes. "Before we think about who made the call, do you know anyone called Peter Daventry?"

"No." Keep answers short, make them do the work.

"Have you ever been to Primrose Hill?"

"No."

"Where were you and what were you doing on Wednesday evening?"

The time of death seems to be lining up with the cash-withdrawal. Someone's called Crimestoppers and said I'm the killer. Must say something. "I went up the Elephant."

"Why?"

"Check out the Backyard Cinema'

"When did you leave home?"

"Early evening, sixish, sevenish."

"How did you get there?"

"Walked."

"What route?"

"Southampton Way. Thurlow Street." I describe a route knowing it could work against me. This is bad. I should come clean. My heart's racing. Must calm myself. Steady my breathing. In for four, out for six, in for four, out for six. It's working. I'm calming. My heart rate's dropping.

"How long were you there?"

I don't know why, but I'm confident about what I'm saying. "Until nine, half-nine." I know why I'm doing this – it's the note I wrote. Memory problems wouldn't go down well with the Job. Reversing what I'm doing grows more difficult the longer it goes on. Why did I mention the Backyard Cinema? I don't know if it was there or not. No. I know I was at the Elephant at the relevant time. Right or wrong, I'm going with that.

"Did you meet anyone?"

"No one I know."

"Can you prove you were there?"

Feigning sudden recollection, I say, "Made a cash-withdrawal."

"Receipt?"

"In my purse." My bag's by my feet. Cantrell lifts it onto the table.

French grips my bag but hesitates. "Go ahead," I say. "You'll be quicker than me."

He extracts my purse and empties it. Fortunately, there's nothing embarrassing. As he examines all the slips of paper, receipts, coupons and god knows what, it hits me. They're all neatly folded.

I hadn't realised the significance when I'd checked earlier.

My nervousness grows. Reeve watches me. Why don't I come clean?

Maybe it's Reeve's purple-tinted specs but he looks at all of me while looking at no particular part of me. Has he spotted the incongruity? French separates the five twenty-pound notes, debit card and receipt. Cantrell is poker-faced.

French sits. Seconds pass. My breath is catching. Reeve's scrutinising me. Breathe. In for four, out for six. It's working, I'm relaxing.

French looks up. "I'd like to take a break. Two hours. You okay with that?"

No. I'm on sick leave for god's sake. I'm not under arrest and they're investigating a murder. I nod.

"For the tape, please."

"Yes."

"I'll hang onto these." He's holding up my debit card, receipt and twenty-pound notes. "Happy to sign for them," he says.

I shake my head. He's hardly likely to nick the bloody things.

"For the tape, please."

"Okay, okay, whatever."

French continues. "Five this afternoon. Reconvene back here." He goes through the procedure with the audio and video recorders while Reeve watches me.

Cantrell leans forward and slips everything back into my purse and places it in my bag. "Coffee," she says.

"You'll be paying," I say.

As we leave, French is slipping the card, money and receipt into an exhibit bag – while Reeve watches me.

* * *

The nearby coffee shop is half empty and Cantrell buys lattes.

"Thank you," she's had mine put in a doubled-up take-away cup, "and thank you again for sitting with me."

"No probs."

"I suppose they're checking the CCTV up the Elephant."

"There's six of them. Departments like Homicide aren't short of resource." She sips her coffee. "No need to worry. If they had anything substantial, you'd be arrested."

"I'm not worried," at least not about that.

"They think you're worried."

Christ. What's she saying?

She continues. "An experienced officer like you, nodding and shaking your head in a recorded interview. They think you're hiding something."

I am hiding something but how can I tell Cantrell that? "Today's been a bad day."

"Every day must be bad."

I shake my head. "Not really but, when I got to the hospital this morning, they had a flap on. I didn't see Nurse Olu."

"I remember her. She's lovely."

"Yes. Funny how little things like that can upset me."

Cantrell smiles and moves on. "I take it you're keeping fit."

"I use an exercise bike."

"I'm told you have a punchbag in your second bedroom."

"I also have a proper bike, but it's pale green with a basket."

Cantrell has this way of demanding answers despite never asking questions. "Explains why you run everywhere I suppose."

"I do all sorts. Running's probably what you see most."

Other customers are looking our way.

Cantrell's noticed too. "You don't like your notoriety. Lavender's revelling in it, his stories are more gilded. Kathy's loving it, her best friend the hero cop."

"How does Crimestoppers work?"

She doesn't react to me changing the subject. "People call with information on the promise of anonymity. Call handlers link the information with any extant investigation and forward."

"Are calls recorded?"

"Of course." She sifts through magazines on the table.

Extant. That's a new word for me. Ongoing? I'll look it up later. "Sarge?"

"Yes, Charlie."

Is she annoyed with me? "What do you think of Reeve?"

She closes her magazine. "I know him. Top notch. He's spotted you're nervous and there's no reason for you to be. I'm putting it down to your condition. They won't be so understanding. Expect a rough ride when we reconvene. You must sharpen up."

What? She said all that so evenly. My breath's catching.

"Saying, 'Okay, okay, whatever,' is not a good way to talk to a Homicide DS who's got you under caution. Rein it in."

She's right.

"That breathing technique you were taught in the TSG..." Oh, god. She hasn't finished. "...in for four, out for six. It's for public order situations, demonstrations, riots. Not interviews. It's a dead giveaway. My advice is stop using it."

Thank god it's not Cantrell interviewing me.

"How are things? How is everyone?" I'm desperate to change the subject.

She shrugs. "It's busy. They're concerned about you. Those who've visited say you're frosty. They want to be there for you but don't want to impose."

"I don't mean to be frosty." I know I am. Always the same. Hugs. 'How are you?' 'When will you resume?' 'What's it like talking to reporters?' I wish they'd just talk to me.

"Team drink," Cantrell says. "Tonight. Half Nelson."

She's moved on, thank god. "I'd love that."

She puts her hand on my arm. "The others would love to see you."

Nearby customers have zoomed in on our conversation. They're so unsubtle. Cantrell holds up her magazine, indicating I should do the same.

Magazines and my hands don't work so I focus on the interview. What will they find on the CCTV? I said I'd walked up Southampton Way and Thurlow Street. What if they find footage of me riding a 68 bus up to the Elephant? Why am I doing this? I must come clean.

There's something going on, I can feel it and, if I'm going to get to the bottom of it, I need these detectives off my back. Weather the storm, Charlie. Weather the storm.

* * *

At five, Cantrell and I are back in the interview room. The detectives arrive shortly after.

Reeve resumes his scrutiny of me and French restarts the interview, reminds me I'm under caution and opens with, "What did you think of the Backyard Cinema?"

Christ, what do I say? "It had moved on before Christmas." I don't know where that answer came from.

French waits.

I wait. I'm confident. Like my answers about the route there and back. I don't understand, but my answers are good.

Finally, French sniffs. "The CCTV corroborates what you said."

My reaction surprises me. Not a concealed *sigh of relief*, more a concealed *what did you expect?*

French continues. "You said you left home about sixish-sevenish. Arrived Elephant eightish. Discovered the Backyard Cinema had moved on. You withdrew money at nine-eighteen. What did you do between eightish and nine-eighteen?"

What the hell do I say? From the CCTV, they'll know what I did. Would I have gone for a drink? Maybe coffee but where? There are dozens of coffee shops there, most would have been closed. I must answer. "Colombian Cockney." I don't know whether I went there or not but, similar to the Backyard Cinema, I'm confident.

"That coffee shop closes at eight," French says.

Not always and not a question. French's game-playing is annoying me.

He moves on. "What did you do after leaving the Colombian Cockney?"

I don't know how I know all this. Best not to try my luck anymore. "Don't remember." Is this what Cantrell means by sharpening up?

"You expecting us to believe that you can't remember what you were doing for an hour at the Elephant & Castle three days ago?"

"You've seen the CCTV. Remind me."

Cantrell's disapproval is clear.

Why are the detectives suspicious?

French opens his mouth to speak but changes his mind.

The silence is thicker than treacle but I'm not backing down. I can't. Right or wrong, I've started down this route. It's the note I wrote. It's the receipts I folded so neatly. There's something going on and I must find out what before these detectives do. So, right or wrong.

Seconds pass. I don't shape my breath.

Surprisingly, it's Cantrell who speaks. "I think," she says, "the tanker incident is playing a role in this."

The detectives' faces pan across to her like two radar dishes. They're annoyed.

42

"I have no training or experience in psychoanalysis," she continues. "Neither do you."

I didn't want her intervention, but the silence is now working against the detectives.

Their faces pan back to me.

"Crimestoppers," French moves on, "who made that call? Before we play it, Charlie, who might want to stitch you up?"

"No one."

"Anyone you've upset?"

"Can't do my job without upsetting people."

Again, Cantrell bristles her disapproval.

French continues. "The call was made before news of Daventry's death was in the public domain. Whoever made that call knows something about the murder. I'm going to play the call recording, maybe you can identify who it is."

He pulls out a mobile, pokes the screen and lays it on the table. Odd.

"Crimestoppers."

"That murder, Primrose Hill, Charlie Quinlan. It was her. She killed him."

"Who…"

"I am not repeating myself. You have enough."

"Who…"

The call handler stops as the line drops out, leaving the tippety-tap of a keyboard.

French re-sets his mobile. "Any ideas, Charlie?"

"Sorry. No idea." I can't take my eyes off the mobile.

"Sounds like you."

"Not me."

"I understand you're handy at impersonating people."

"You think I impersonated myself?" Neither of French's last two comments were questions. Should have kept quiet. Idiot. Must recover this. "Can I hear it again?" Another bloody question. Cantrell's probably given up on me.

French replays the recording.

"Sorry. Can't help." I want a copy but how do I ask without sounding weird.

Cantrell speaks. "Give Charlie a copy. Listening to it over and over might help."

She's brilliant.

French acknowledges her and says to me, "SD card okay?"

"Yes."

"Well, that's about it," says French.

I'm relaxing. The way he introduced the Crimestoppers call recording wasn't evidentially sound and they didn't sign for my card, receipt and money. Just how serious are they about this?

"Oh, mustn't forget." French lays the five twenty-pound notes, debit card and receipt on the table. "You can put those away in your purse now."

Cantrell doesn't move.

I give French a little smile and hoist my bag onto the table. My purse is on top. Using both hands, I lift it out and open the zipper with my teeth. With my left hand, I slide the debit card to the edge of the table, it's like I'm wearing oven gloves, and force it down into my purse. I look at French, but not in triumph. My hands are screaming.

44

The silence is crystalline.

In the same way, I scrabble the notes down into my purse. They've gone in crumpled and it's all I can do not to cry out.

Only the receipt to go.

Reeve is riding back on his chair. I can't ask Cantrell to do this for me. What have they seen on the Elephant CCTV?

I attempt the receipt. It's too flimsy. I can't manipulate it. I can't get it into my purse. Pain overcomes me and I lift my hands to my face as the receipt flutters to the floor. Tears have erupted and I'm using my dressings to mop them up.

"Take your time," French has come round the table and retrieved the receipt. "Water?"

"Please," I say through my sobbing.

I could kick up an almighty stink about this but I must allay the detectives' suspicions. I won't be able to find out what's going on with a surveillance team on my back.

French pours a cup of water and holds it to my mouth while I take a sip.

After my lapse, I'm regaining composure. I'm angry with myself, angry for losing this interview. Must recover it.

I look across at the detectives. "I'm sorry. My hands, they, you know'

"We understand," French says.

He has no idea but I know what's coming.

"Forgive me," he pauses, "what's different between today and last Wednesday?"

Who put those things so neatly into my purse and who wrote the note I wrote? God, this is crazy but I've got to get to the bottom of this myself. Right, now to get these detectives off my back. "For the past couple of weeks, my dressings have been changed by nurses at KCH burns unit, mostly Nurse Olu. When I went there today, they had an emergency. These dressings," I hold up my hands, "were done by a new nurse."

CHAPTER FOUR

New Year festivities have taken their toll and the Half Nelson isn't crowded as I arrive just before ten. My team will be here by quarter-past so I get a glass of wine and perch on a barstool. The barman's saying I don't need to pay but I won't have it.

A couple of the locals have raised their drinks towards me. I smile.

Two lads, late teens, stand further along the bar. I've nicked one of them a while back. Theft. Don't know his mate. They're whispering. The locals have stopped their chat. The barman's polishing a glass. The landlord appears, all eyes and body-language.

I have other things on my mind.

After leaving the Nick, I was tempted to head up the Elephant. I know the security personnel, I could easily get the CCTV footage and see what the detectives saw. The detectives are suspicious. I could, right this minute, be under surveillance.

"What's made them suspicious?" I wince. Bad habit. I look around. No one seems to have noticed.

Except the barman. "Sorry, Charlie. Did you say something?"

I smile. "Just talking to myself."

He laughs.

I return to my thoughts. Why are those detectives suspicious?

The voice on the Crimestoppers recording sounds like me but an audio match isn't definitive. Must read up about voice recognition evidence, voice identification, whatever.

Detectives. Evidence. It can't be much because, like Cantrell said, if they had anything concrete, I'd be nicked. I need to see the CCTV they saw but approaching the Elephant security would increase their suspicions.

Subtlety is required. I need someone to get those pictures for me. Of all my teammates, there are only three I feel I can approach.

Kathy Bond? She couldn't keep her mouth shut. Albert Lavender? He'd ask difficult questions. Mary Cantrell? Too by-the-book. There's also Wade Oliver. "Make that four." Too inexperienced. The rest of them? I'd be stretching friendships too far. Must stop talking out loud to myself.

Wade Oliver. Know-nothing probationer. I've seen people at fancy-dress parties more like coppers than him.

Can I trust Wade? I asked him to get me that address that turned out to be in Brockley. If I'd asked any of the others, it would have got back to Cantrell and she'd be asking her non-questions about it. Wade hasn't let on because he undoubtedly doesn't understand the significance of it which, of course, is why I asked him. Everything about Wade grates with me. He turns up to work looking like he's finishing the Tour de France. He's always giving his opinion and, when he does, it's always in a *doesn't everyone know that?* kind of way. Of all of them, he visited me most both in Rehab and at home. Even came round on Boxing Day. Pest. No, not a pest, it was me who was off, but I remember that visit because I learnt so much about him.

I'd instructed Alexa to play music and, thinking of my guest, requested classical which Wade obviously thought was me wanting to know everything about each classical composer Alexa played. When the coffee ran out, I found something stronger to drink.

I also found, as Wade spoke, I was warming to him.

We're both mid-twenties. I joined the Job at eighteen. He's about eighteen months in and he's unlikely to make it through his probation. I often wonder why he stays. Not a day passes without him making an idiot of himself but, during that visit, he changed from hesitant to confident and his breadth of experience is breath-taking. He's crewed a sailing ship around the Southern Ocean. He was in Tokyo during an earthquake. He's skied across Alaska. He's hiked through the Amazon and eaten an omelette made from tarantula eggs. He's lived in a Chateau in the Dordogne and knows more about French politics than I do about English. I was enthralled.

He's a walking encyclopaedia. He knows about dinosaurs and evolution. He knows about the stars and what it would be like to travel at the speed of light. He even explained why a kettle stops roaring as it boils.

I can't remember one explanation but listening to him was humbling. He wasn't patronising or condescending, just accepting that not everybody knows this stuff and they'll know stuff he doesn't. "Police work, for example."

I've spoken out loud again. One of the locals has looked my way. I study my glass of wine. I'm thinking more and more that Wade's the one.

He's forever asking about thief-takers. He reckons I'm one and, at risk of flattering myself, he's right. Wade's definitely not a thief-taker. His work-rate is piss-poor and he's always in trouble with the skippers.

Contrasting our lives makes it all the more remarkable we shared a beer in my flat.

His father's an ambassador and travels the world with his Parisian wife. They deposited their only son in an English boarding school. The closest I had to a father was a warden at the children's home.

While Wade was deciding which waistcoat to wear, I was dragging supermarket trolleys out of canals for pound coins.

While Wade was debating politics, I was scrapping with bullies.

When Wade received a parcel from home with clothing and fruitcake, I was breaking into the kitchen for food the warden held back for his own profit.

As Wade progressed with his education, I progressed onto foster parents.

"Why did you join the police?" I asked him.

"I like working with people and helping…"

"Not the formal answer. The real reason."

"To escape," he said, his voice hard. "Look, I've got to go." With that he was up and out the door before I could prise myself to my feet.

Definitely. Of all of them, Wade's the one to approach.

* * *

I emerge from my reverie when one of the lads comes over, holding his empty glass. The thief.

The landlord moves forward. I hold up my hand. He stops.

The pub's gone quiet. "Saw you on YouTube." The lad looks round to his mate, then back to me. "Respect." He leaves. His mate nods at me and follows.

Of all the compliments I've had, that one's brought a lump to my throat.

"Wasn't expecting that," the landlord says, sliding a fiver towards me. "My man here shouldn't have taken your money. Your drinks are on me."

"Thanks," I say still thinking about those two lads, "that's kind but you really don't need to."

"I really do," he says, "but don't worry, it's until further notice."

"I appreciate…"

"Don't. You're a star. How're the hands? Haven't seen you since then."

I free myself from the feeling provoked by those two lads. "Getting better. Should be back soon."

"Charlie, you could of at least lined them up by now." Lavender has burst in. "Been a month, to the day. Must be your friggin' round."

"I'll buy you a beer. Least I can do. You saved my life."

"Yeah. Well. Next time you're feeling cold, let me

know, I'll turn the heater up."

"I was distracted."

"Yeah, not every day, a tanker explodes on Camberwell New Road. You okay?"

"Yeah."

"Talking to someone about it?"

God. I hope he's not going to keep this up. "Counsellors at Rehab. I'm okay."

"You having bad dreams?"

"Not really. Well, a couple. Nothing I can't handle."

"You're doing better than me." He hoists his belt. "I had that Wade Oliver in my car today. He's a friggin' nightmare."

I've been spared. "Are the others coming?"

"They're on way. I hear you've been stabbing people. Not the usual pastime for someone on sick leave."

"Full of surprises, me."

"Interviewed by Homicide. Impressive. Wait till you're hauled up in front of HR. There'll be friggin' 'ell to pay."

He won't have forgotten about the muddy trainers and, thankfully, Kathy Bond arrives saying how good it is I've turned up. I slip off my stool and we hug.

Kathy whispers in my ear. "Not like you to stab people in the back."

"Full of surprises, me."

"Look at you. Your face. No trace of those burns."

I hold up my dressed hands. "Different story here."

"You're looking after them, aren't you? Not running and press-upping. Getting yourself all muddy."

"No running. No press ups." Has Lavender been

telling everybody about my trainers?

"What about arse wiping?"

She's moved on, so probably not.

Others arrive. It's all hugs and slaps on back and me saying, "Full of surprises, me," for the umpteenth time. I'm the centre of attention, a position I hate but, as the evening settles down, I feel more comfortable. Here, with my family, I'm home.

Kathy's back. "Have you seen a counsellor since leaving Rehab?"

I shake my head. She'll have a go at me now.

"You must, Charlie. Traumatic incident like that, the agony of your burns, the boy dying. It will have messed with your head."

"I'm fine, Kathy. Really." Apart from messages I leave telling myself about alibis for murders I'm stitching myself up for.

Wade comes in, nods my way, his hair falling over his eyes. He's deep in conversation.

Cantrell appears beside me, mysteriously. "Pleased you made it," she says and signals the barman to get a round in for everyone.

I lean in close to Cantrell, she's much shorter than me. "I reckon that's not the last I'll see of those two detectives."

"Probs," she says, taking her slim-line tonic. "They made a mistake."

"Not exhibiting the Crimestoppers recording properly?"

"Yes. I wonder whether it was actually a mistake."

"You think it was deliberate?"

"They're too experienced. Interesting."

Nothing changes. I'm answering her non-questions

with questions. "Who would have made that call?"

"They'll analyse it. Digitally."

"Is that admissible?"

"Depends on the judge. They'll need a suspect first."

"What sort of evidence is voice recognition?"

"Audible match, weak. Digital match, strong." Her words aren't comforting.

"They didn't mention in the interview how Peter Daventry was killed."

"It hasn't been disclosed. Lavender and Kathy are making it up."

"Do you know?"

"It hasn't been disclosed, Charlie."

I don't like being snubbed, especially when it's me in the hot seat. Lavender and Kathy will have heard Cantrell mention their names. There are times when Cantrell's coldness is an advantage but this isn't it. "It just seems the person who's been forgotten is Peter Daventry himself. Who was he? How are his family?"

Without moving, Cantrell steps back.

Kathy shows she's been listening in. "He was a family man heading home from work. This is the murder you were..."

She's stopped, thank god.

Cantrell's looking up at Kathy, her eyes steely. "Sounds like you have something to share."

"This is the, um," Kathy's floundering. Even Lavender's stepped closer. "You read it in the Evening Standard. You talked about it that time I came round." Good recovery but Cantrell's now looking at me.

"A detective posting wouldn't be much fun without

any friggin' victims."

Cantrell looks at Lavender.

"I was a detective once. I was a victim once as well. Came back to uniform because I couldn't tell the friggin' difference."

Cantrell shakes her head and walks over to another group. That was close. Kathy's looking suitably contrite, Lavender's moved onto some other story about how he saved the Metropolitan friggin' Police from its friggin' self and I'm thinking Wade is definitely the right choice.

I'm wondering how I'll catch Wade on his own without attracting attention, especially as he's in his high-viz cycling gear.

Lavender's moved onto the story of Wade and a breach of the peace. "After loads of rolling around like a primary school swimming lesson, Wade calls in the result. Breach of the peace assuaged. Assuaged? What's wrong with stopped? What it says in the book. Prevent or stop a breach of the peace. Assuaged. Friggin' prat."

Kathy leans in close to me. "Really sorry, Charlie. Hope I haven't made things difficult with you and Sargie."

"Could have done without it, Kathy."

She looks hurt.

"Hey, I'm sorry. Don't worry about it. Everything's a bit weird."

"Charlie, you must see a doctor about your memory. I've been reading. Big traumatic incident. It's to be expected."

Out the corner of my eye, I see Wade heading for the loo. I put my hand on Kathy's arm. "I've got it covered."

"You're looking a bit, not yourself. You sure you're

okay?"

"Kathy, it's been a hard day. My hands hurt. I'm tired. Oh, Kathy, I've missed you all so much. I know everyone's been visiting but," I hold out my arms as if to encompass the whole pub, "I've missed this and, with everything going on today, it's just a bit overwhelming."

She pulls me into a tight hug and I hug her back. "Do you want me to stay with you tonight?"

"Thanks for the offer, Kathy. It's great to link up with everyone again but, after today, I just need some quiet time to get my thoughts in order."

"You can always call me."

"Thanks. You're so good to me." The hand-dryer in the gents comes on. "Must pay a visit. Be right back," and I slip away.

Just as I reach the ladies, Wade comes out the gents.

"Hi," I say, "you're deep in conversation."

"Difficult job. Just talking about where it might go." His hair flops down over his eyes and he sweeps it back behind his ear. "You had some drama today. Everything okay?"

"I think so." Should I be doing this?

Wade's recognised, at last, that I've deliberately caught him on his own.

Come on, Charlie. Get on with it. "I need a favour."

"From me?"

"Yes. I came to notice for the Primrose Hill murder because a woman called Crimestoppers and stitched me up. 'That hero cop, she killed him.' I was up the Elephant at the time of death making a cash-withdrawal. Homicide stopped the interview to check out the CCTV.

When they came back, something weird happened. I need to see the Elephant CCTV."

"Why are you bothered? You've a bulletproof alibi."

"The weird thing is, despite the alibi, they're still suspicious. I need the CCTV to see what they saw. Will you help me?"

"You can get that yourself."

"If I do, Homicide will want to know why."

Wade goes quiet. This might have been a mistake.

Then he speaks. "So you want to get the CCTV without showing out."

I nod.

"So you're recruiting someone to get it for you."

I nod.

"You've chosen me."

I nod.

"You think I can get the CCTV without showing out because, being the problematic probationer, you would never involve me."

I can't believe it. Wade, so useless at anything police, is proving to be a diamond. I nod.

"I'm intrigued. I'll do it."

"Wade, you could get into trouble."

"I thought the idea was not to get caught." He's switched to that self-assured person I met in my flat.

"How?" I ask.

"I'll get you those images, I'll find out what's known about the caller and nobody will know."

"How will you do it?"

"Actually, someone *will* know."

"Who?"

"You."

CHAPTER FIVE

Cantrell is driving me home.

Wade's veiled threat, about who knows he's going after the Elephant CCTV, suggests he'll be avoiding proper channels. Wade, the know-nothing probationer.

I'm tired, had a glass of wine too many and I'm slumped against the window, people-watching. A cyclist on a bike with small wheels, some lads smoking and shivering outside a club entrance.

"They're fishing."

I shake myself back, Cantrell's talking, unprovoked. "What do you mean?"

"The detectives. They'd seen the CCTV before starting the interview. Explains their sloppiness."

"Why bother interviewing me?"

"Test you out with your purse."

We've stopped at red lights. The cyclist catches up.

"Of course," Cantrell's carrying on, "you don't need to see the CCTV. You know what they saw."

There's a young mum with a crying toddler. We set off again.

"The Job needs people like Wade." Cantrell changes subjects with such ease. "He needs looking after."

I close my eyes. What's Wade said? What does Cantrell know? Why did she say that I know what they saw? Is she trying to unsettle me? She turned up with the detectives. Is she with them? Both Kathy and Lavender know something's up and to think how close Kathy came to dropping the *memory* word. Now I've involved Wade and Cantrell's fitting these pieces together like a jigsaw. Half-a-dozen Homicide detectives? That's a lot for asking the Elephant security to show them some CCTV. The only thing that makes sense is that the interview was a means of getting me out of my flat so they could lay surveillance devices.

Nothing more is said and she drops me outside my flat. "If I'm supposed to be guilty of something, it would be handy to know what." I'm shouting at her receding car.

Indoors, I close the curtains.

If I'm under surveillance, and I must assume I am, everything I do, everywhere I go and everyone I meet will be scrutinised. Hope Wade's up for this. "How can you be under surveillance?" I know their tactics. "Uh-uh." They'd adjust for a surveillance-conscious target but, at this stage, probably just use digital surveillance – my accounts, e-mails, mobile. They'll plant microphones and cameras in my flat, probably already have. Explains why French wanted that break. While I was having coffee with Cantrell, the detectives were ushering their technologists in here. "Teccos and techies." I shake my head. I've always fancied myself as a detective. "I've wised up." Their games would grind me down. I'm better up front, with no time to think. "I must stop talking to myself, out loud."

I examine my electrical appliances. Nothing untoward. Wall sockets, untouched. Light switches, untouched. Ceiling roses, untouched. Around again, checking beneath for plaster or dirt. Even check for signs of cleaning. The little vents in the window frames, nothing. Every downward facing surface, nothing. Behind the bath panel, nothing. Curtains, nothing. Punchbag, nothing. I step back and fire my left foot at it, making it judder and jerk. I feel like working out. Shouldn't. Neighbours. Sod it. Left foot – front kick, side kick, round kick, heel kick, BANG, BANG, BANG, BANG. Right foot – front kick, side kick, round kick, heel kick, BANG, BANG, BANG, BANG. Right foot, again. Left foot, again. Tapping from above. Neighbours. Fair enough. Besides, my hands are complaining too.

It's all I can do to leave my muddy trainers. If I'm being watched, I don't want to draw attention to them.

After checking and rechecking, I'm still suspicious but there's nothing more I can do.

I lay on my bed. Am I being paranoid? "Too bloody right." For god's sake, stop talking out loud. I've always felt I have someone looking over my shoulder.

* * *

Lying in darkness, I resist sleep. Although my day's been an ordeal, I'm not physically drained.

Take stock.

Strange happenings. Crowned karaoke queen having not gone to the party. Trainers muddy despite never wearing them outdoors. After fifteen years, Elly turns up in my pots and pans cupboard. The note I wrote and I can't hold a pen, don't remember writing it, or going up the Elephant and withdrawing the cash. It's like I left a note for myself, a note to tell myself what I did. On top of all that, I know the route I took up there, that the Backyard Cinema had moved on and that I visited the Colombian Cockney.

Lost days. I lost Wednesday 30th December – the day I went to the Elephant & Castle and Peter Daventry was killed.

I lost Friday 1st January – the day Kathy said I was me but more.

Have there been other days I've missed?

I close my eyes. "You shouldn't have played games with the counsellors, Charlie."

Sometimes my dreams are poisoned by images of the tanker incident. It's not bad. I know it can be bad for some but I'm doing okay.

What's really getting me down is the pain of my burnt hands.

* * *

I've been asleep. That funny taste gives it away. 07:14. Sunday 3rd January.

Thank god.

Where was I? Losing days. Wednesday 30th December, the day Peter Daventry died and Friday 1st January, the day I was obsessed about his killing.

I feel guilty. I've been worried about myself with hardly a thought for poor Peter Daventry. Family man. Senselessly killed. Who was he?

There must have been other lost days. The month since the tanker incident has been a manic time. If not for Christmas and New Year, I wouldn't have a clue. How can I find out and keep track?

Must anchor myself. Today's Sunday 3rd January. Friends have visited. Wade visited Boxing Day.

Wait. Nurse Olu said I must come to have my dressings changed every day but I have been coming every day.

"Right."

Today. Get dressings changed and find out which days I've missed. Find a way of keeping a diary. Contact Doctor Slattery. "Well, tomorrow for that." Main job for today: find out who Peter Daventry is, was.

CHAPTER SIX

Nurse Olu's bustling around.

"Didn't see you yesterday, Charlie."

"You were busy."

She laughs, a carefree laugh. "Of course." She examines my dressings. "Who did these?"

"The new guy."

"Ummmmm." She turns my hands over. "You've been out again," she says.

"I admit I go out occasionally, for a walk around the park."

"I understand," she says, "but if you get an infection, you'll be back to square one."

She switches her attention to removing the dressings.

The pain doesn't come.

Having exposed my hands, Nurse Olu studies them. Many gleaming red spots.

"They're looking good." She indicates for me to turn them over and gives a nod of satisfaction. "How do they feel?"

"No pain, just hurt like hell."

"You'll be back to work soon, maybe a week, but please stay indoors."

As she starts rubbing in creams, I start my investigation.

"Olu. The nurse yesterday asked if I'd missed any dressing changes. I know I've missed some but couldn't be specific. Without my work routine, days merge. Could you help me out? You were so busy yesterday I didn't like to ask."

"Of course. Let's finish this and I'll check on the computer."

Not only is Nurse Olu beautiful, caring and an all-round-wonderful person, she doesn't ask questions.

I leave the hospital with the dates I didn't have my dressings changed:

Wednesday 23rd December.

Sunday 27th December.

Tuesday 29th December.

Wednesday 30th December – the day Peter Daventry was killed.

Friday 1st January – New Year's Day.

Five days, "FIVE DAYS," missing from my life.

I can't recall what I was doing on those missed days. All I know is that on Wednesday 30th December, I made a cash-withdrawal at the Elephant & Castle and, on New Year's Day, I was at home with Kathy, being me but more.

It's not far to Argos in Peckham and I get two big buckets of magnetic fridge letters and numerals. Fortunately, they have a suitable bag for me to carry them home.

I'm in Peckham, not far from Brockley. "Come on, Charlie, you can do this." Hoiking the bag up onto my shoulder, I head over to the address Wade found for me. As I arrive, a man and small boy come out. They're focussed only on each other. They get into a car and drive away.

Why did I just stand there like a dummy? Why didn't I approach them?

I head home.

* * *

At home, I empty letters and numerals onto my kitchen worktop and sort them out. Nurse Olu's dressings are great. I should have got more than two buckets. Abbreviations.

"Right." Fridge door starting top left.

DEC
23
27
29
30 PD RIP
31 CS NOTE
JAN
1 K MORE
2 H BUSY INT HN
3 H ARG

As well as more letters and numerals, I'll need a bigger fridge.

23rd December – lost.

27th December – lost.

29th December – lost.

30th December – Peter Daventry died.

31st December – Crimestoppers call, find note

1st January – Kathy, me but more.

2nd January – hospital for dressings change, they were busy, interview, Half Nelson.

Why did the detectives come round? They could have phoned and asked me to meet them at the Nick. "They didn't even come in."

3rd January – hospital, Argos.

Why did the detectives come to my flat?

Nurse Olu's dressings are thinner than normal. Things are better. The discomfort's nothing like it was a week ago.

The detectives must have wanted to see my reaction. Or check out my front door. "I don't know."

I put on rubber gloves and clean my flat while the Crimestoppers call plays in the background.

"Crimestoppers."

"That murder, Primrose Hill, hero cop, Charlie Quinlan. It was her. She killed him."

"Who..."

"I am not repeating myself. You have enough."

"Who..."

I don't recognise that voice. Sounds like me but why is it so familiar?

It's late. Didn't sleep well last night.

I make coffee, sit at my computer and, dabbing my keyboard, transcribe the call.

I listen and read. Again.

The more I listen, the more familiar that voice becomes. I have a reputation for mimicking people. I'm forever being asked: Do the Commissioner – Do the Superintendent – Do Lavender. Whoever called Crimestoppers sounded like she was impersonating me.

"BULLSHIT." This is bullshit.

I slam the computer lid, shutting off the Crimestoppers call.

Elly's under my desk lamp. "What do you want?"

She looks at me.

"Don't stare at me. What do you want?"

She looks at me.

I sweep my arm across my desk. Elly goes flying along with my half-drunk cup of coffee.

"Oh, god." Out to the kitchen for cleaning stuff. I slip gloves over my dressings and it's as I'm scrubbing the carpet, I notice my hands are okay. I flex my fingers. It's the first time I've done that since getting these burns. A little laugh escapes. No pain. Bit stiff, but no pain. I stretch them out straight and curl them into fists.

Elly's by the bed.

"Did you see that, Elly? My hands are getting better."

I'm rubbing the carpet wondering whether I should be dabbing it. There'll be a stain but I don't care. My fingers and palms are feeling good but, like the tide, the pain's rising.

I sit back at my desk and remove the rubber gloves. The pain's coming back with a vengeance. I push my fingers out straight and pull them back into fists. They're screaming at me.

Enough.

Relax.

What happened?

My mind goes to adrenalin.

Spilling the coffee provoked a flood of adrenalin, enough to blot out the pain, and I could work my hands. As the adrenalin subsided, the pain returned.

My hands are calming now.

I collect Elly and set her back under the desk lamp. "Looks like I'm on the mend. What d'you think of that?"

Elly looks at me.

"So, Elly, what's your story? I don't believe you've been with me all those years. I've moved too many times. No way could you have come along without me knowing."

Elly looks at me.

"D'you remember Ursula? A friend at the home? She gave you to me."

Elly looks at me.

"You don't remember, do you?" I poke her tummy. "Despite being an elephant."

Elly flops over and I sit her up.

"I wonder what happened to Ursula. We were close but, towards the end, she turned a bit funny. Maybe it was because I handed you back to her. I don't know. When I was moved out of the home, I was sad to be leaving my friends, but it was good to get away from Travis. Don't suppose you remember him either. Travis Hendry? The warden? Bent. Sadist."

I get ready for bed and make one more addition to my fridge diary:

3 H ARG COF

3rd January – hospital, Argos, coffee.

Before getting into bed, there's something I must check. I said I'd do it, so come on. Peter Daventry. Who is he? Who was he?

I type his name into Google but delay on pressing ENTER. Is there anything wrong with doing a search on

Peter Daventry? I didn't allay the detectives' suspicions. The interview probably increased their suspicions. Doing the search would provoke something like a submarine's sonar ping in a darkened room somewhere. So what? They'd expect me to do some kind of search on him, wouldn't they? What would they think if I didn't?

What was it Wade said? *You want to get this information without showing out.* Let's see how he gets on with the CCTV.

Feeling like I have someone looking over my shoulder, I close down my computer and get ready for bed. The last thing I see before switching off my light, is Elly, looking at me.

"Trust."

I'm up and out of bed. Light-headed, momentarily unbalanced. Who said that? Light on. "Who's there?" I move through my flat. "Who's there?" Lights on.

There's no one there.

Hearing things. Maybe it's because I'm nervous. I'm not nervous about being incriminated via Crimestoppers. Nor am I nervous because those two detectives are suspicious. I'm nervous because something inside tells me I really don't want to know who Peter Daventry is, was.

CHAPTER SEVEN

That's nice. Comfortable. Warm.

Panic.

What day is it?

My bedside clock says 08:23. What day? Monday. What date? I breathe out slowly. 4th January. I can't believe the relief I feel.

"Must get up, busy day ahead."

Washing's easier.

Coffee. Breakfast. All easier. I'm on the mend.

9am, time to call the shrink.

On the mend? Well, my hands are.

* * *

"Doctor Slattery."

Wow. I was expecting a defensive secretary.

"Hello."

"Hello."

"Oh. I don't know what to say."

"Would you prefer to speak to my personal assistant?"

"No, I want to talk to you."

"You're in luck."

I can't think of anything to say.

"Maybe start with who you are?"

"Sorry." His voice is confident, smooth and interested. "I'm Charlie Quinlan. Charlotte Quinlan."

No reaction from him.

"I'm a police officer. I've been advised to contact you."

"Who's advised you to do that?"

"Who hasn't? My Job, Rehab, Occupational Health."

"Actually, I've been expecting your call."

He's been briefed. I quell the urge to shut down the call. I breathe steadily and calm myself. I look at his business card, a Harley Street address. If I get involved with him, I'll be way out of my depth financially. There's been a long pause. He's still there, I can tell. "Why would they contact you in particular?"

"Joining dots. Mary Cantrell sounds nice."

I knew she'd have had a hand in this. "She's my sergeant."

"I read about that terrible crash in Camberwell."

"I was there." I regret saying that immediately. Too many people tell me how terrible it must have been. "That's not the full story."

"Never is." He pauses and I can hear clicking of a computer mouse.

He doesn't sound put out and I already feel comfortable with him.

"Shall we set an appointment?"

I hear the tippety-tap of a keyboard. "Yes," I say, "that would be good." Then I add, "I'm not sure though."

"Your Job, as you call it, will foot the bills."

He knows more about me than I do but, weirdly, I'm comfortable. He listens.

He's clearly busy with his computer but he speaks at the same time. "When's good for you?"

"Sooner the better."

"I've had a cancellation for tomorrow, at one. Any good?"

"Your place?"

"Harley Street, yes."

"Okay. 1pm, tomorrow, Tuesday." I'm just about to hang up but, "Hello, hello."

"I'm still here."

"Do I need to bring anything?"

"Just yourself."

"See you then. Bye."

"Look forward to meeting you."

I close down the call but it's a while before I stop looking at my mobile. I felt I could trust him. Now, I feel I've been had over, the feeling I get when I have a suspect in front of me. I know he's at it but I have no grounds, no evidence, nothing and he knows it.

It was something Doctor Slattery said.

I go to the kitchen and fill the kettle. It's still bugging me. Something he said.

I make coffee and add to my fridge diary:

4 PSY 5 1

4th January – Psychiatrist 5th 1pm.

Through to my living room and flop down on my sofa, nestling Elly on my lap. I think through the conversation with Doctor Slattery. I wish I'd recorded it, my mobile has that capability.

It comes to me.

I said, 'Do I need to bring anything?' and he said, 'Just yourself.'

* * *

Nurse Olu's smile is the biggest I've seen.

"Another week," she says.

Heading home, my mobile rings.

"Hi."

"It's Wade."

"I know."

"It could have been the guy who stole my telephone."

I sigh.

He carries on. "You free tomorrow?"

"My diary's not full."

"Phoenix. Sixteen-hundred."

"See you there."

"Great. Bye."

"Bye."

"Bye. Bye."

"Yes, bye."

"Bye. Bye. Bye. Bye."

I shut down the call. Jeez.

Back home, I update my fridge:

4 PSY 5 1 H W PH 5 4

4th January – Psychiatrist 5th 1pm, Hospital, Wade Phoenix 5th 4pm.

CHAPTER EIGHT

That's nice. Comfortable. Warm.

Panic.

What day is it?

My bedside clock says 07:47. What day? Wednesday. WEDNESDAY?

Date. 6th.

I'm up. Mobile. Nothing since Wade's call on Monday. GPS. Computer. Mobile didn't leave my flat. Fitbit. Not on my wrist. It's by my clock.

Fridge:

4 PSY 5 1 H W PH 5 4
5 H PSY W

I slide down the oven opposite my fridge. *5 H PSY W*. On 5th January, Tuesday, I got my dressings changed, saw the psychiatrist and saw Wade. *5 H PSY W*. What else can it mean? It also means I updated my fridge diary. Feel sick, but don't want to vomit. Want to scream, no breath. Want to cry, no tears.

The pain in my hands is irrelevant.

Retrieve mobile.

"Wade, it's Charlie." He was nights, I've woken him.

"Charlie?"

"Wade, wake up."

"Charlie? I'm off nights."

"I know. It's important."

"What? What's so important?" He's struggling.

"Did we meet yesterday? At the Phoenix?"

"Yes. I showed you the CCTV."

I'm stunned. "Wade. I don't remember." I don't know what else to say. Should I be telling him? Done it now. "Wade?"

He's quiet. There's movement. A groan and what sounds like a door slamming.

"Wade?"

"I'll be round in half an hour."

The mobile goes dead. I'm back opposite the fridge.

DEC

23

27

29

30 PD RIP

31 CS NOTE

JAN

1 K MORE

2 H BUSY INT HN

3 H ARG COF

4 PSY 5 1 H W PH 5 4

5 H PSY W

23rd December. 27th December. 29th December. 30th December 1st January. All days I know I've lost. Now the 5th January too. Whole days, gone. Must be going mad. Oh, god. Not again. I'm up and ripping at the dressings. Screaming. Yelling. "Get off. GET OFF. *GET OFF.*"

* * *

There's knocking. The cold kitchen floor is against my face. I roll onto my back and hold up my hands. The creams and ointments from under the dressings have gathered a layer of dirt. More knocking. Maybe, they'll go away.

"Charlie." The knocking's more insistent.

My mobile's ringing. I don't know where it is.

"Charlie. Open the door."

Sounds like Wade. I get up, not bothering about where I'm putting my sticky hands, the mess I'm leaving, what dirt or germs I'm picking up.

It's Wade.

I'm enveloped in a strong decisive force driving me to the kitchen sink. My hands are held under flowing water. Pain explodes but I'm numb to it. I watch nonchalantly as my hands are turned in the stream of water. Are they really mine?

"Cloths? Towels?" Wade is opening drawers and cupboards.

I nod towards one of the drawers. My hands are soon wrapped.

"Ambulance?"

Wade said something.

"Charlie, should I get an ambulance?"

I shake my head. "What time is it?"

"Nearly nine."

"Can you get me to the burns unit? Nurse Olu will be there."

"I cycled over. We'll have to walk."

I can see the pain, a swarming cloud enveloping my hands, but I'm floating above it. "Walking's good."

* * *

Nurse Olu's there and, with her huge smile and a suspicious glance at Wade, sorts out my hands. "I'm surprised you haven't ripped the dressings off before."

As Wade and I leave, she calls me back.

"You're okay, still on track."

* * *

It's gone eleven by the time Wade and I are in the Phoenix with coffee. He's dead on his feet but working hard to stay with me. "You need sleep."

"I'll manage," he says. "Can I crash at yours? I've everything I need for work tonight."

"Of course. Head back now?"

"Sleep can wait. You need to talk."

Before the tanker incident, I didn't give Wade the time of day. Since then, I've started seeing the non-police side of him. I must ask though. "How's it going? With the skippers I mean."

Shaking his head, and sweeping his hair back behind his ear, he stirs his coffee and takes a sip. "I'm not cut out for this."

I could have told him that when I first met him. I probably did. "You could do something else."

"Yes," he says, anger creeping into his voice, "I could do what my father says. I could do what my schooling has groomed me for. I could meet everyone's expectations, everyone's except my own."

I've never heard Wade speak like this, with such conviction and passion. He hasn't raised his voice but those nearby have turned towards us. "You said *escape*. Of all the things you could do, why did you choose police?"

He takes another slug of coffee. "The people," he says.

"What about the people?"

"Different people." He shudders. "Look, enough about me. You need to talk about you."

"You accusing me of prevarication?"

"Yes. You said you don't remember meeting me yesterday. What do you mean?"

Again, heads turn our way. I hear words, "Tanker," and, "Before Christmas," spilling from them.

"Do you want to leave?" Wade asks.

I shake my head. "It's okay." It's not okay but I must start dealing with this. That YouTube clip and the press coverage has made me recognisable. I change the subject. "I haven't thanked you for getting me that address. Well, not properly."

"The Brockley address? Put it to use yet?" He takes another gulp from his coffee.

"Been there. Couldn't work up the courage to…"

"Maybe go with someone. Sergeant Cantrell would be best."

"No. It's something I must do alone." Prying ears are tuning in. "Look, can we go?"

We talk on the way back to my flat. "Wade, you showed me the Elephant CCTV yesterday. I don't remember."

"Which bit?"

"All of it. As far as I'm concerned, we didn't meet yesterday. Worse still, I lost yesterday." I'm waving my hands with their new white bandages. The movement has woken them.

"You okay?" Wade's noticed.

"I'm good." The pain is subsiding.

"What do you mean? Lost yesterday?"

"I went to bed Monday evening and woke the next morning to find it's Wednesday."

"You remember nothing?" Wade stops.

I turn back. "Nothing at all. It's like yesterday didn't exist."

"We met yesterday. We spoke. I showed you the CCTV footage. We talked and laughed about it. You don't remember any of that?"

"Nothing."

We set off again. The walk back to my flat is just ten minutes. Wade is silent, deep in thought. Am I losing him?

CHAPTER NINE

Wade takes my keys and works through my front door locks.

"Charlie," he says, "you have your handcuff key on here?"

"Full of surprises, me." We haven't said a word for the rest of the walk home and he says that? Jeez.

He makes tea and we settle, him on my sofa, me on a dining chair. There's an elephant in the room as well as Elly. His head nods forward, jerks back and he rescues his hair that's fallen over his eyes.

"You need sleep. We'll talk later."

He looks down at his tea. "Have you any coffee?"

"Instant."

"Tea's fine."

"You get your head down."

"No. This is important. We'll work it through."

"Work it through? I'm losing my mind. Let's work it through."

Wade perks up. "You're not losing your mind. You're having memory issues. Hardly surprising considering the trauma of the tanker incident. Kathy said you weren't facing up. You said nothing to me yesterday about your appointment with a psychiatrist."

"What makes you think I saw a psychiatrist?"

"At 1pm. Your fridge. What else would *PSY* stand for?"

In the time it took to make tea, he'd interpreted my makeshift diary. Impressive, but he lets himself down.

"Good idea to keep a diary. Why don't you use a spreadsheet or something?"

"Wade," this time I can't keep the scorn from my voice, "try, for once, to think evidentially."

His hair flops down. He doesn't understand.

"Someone's framing me for a murder. I must find out who before the detectives, but I'm losing my mind."

He rallies. "You're not losing your mind. You're having memory issues. What did Nigel Slattery say?"

"I don't remember."

"Try."

"Hang on." I'm up and pointing, the best I can with these mittens. "How do you know his name?"

"I saw his business card in your kitchen when I was here before New Year."

"Wade. How do you see all this but are blind to anything suspicious?"

"Don't change the subject." He sits forward, rubbing his eyes. "You need to speak to him but wait until five-to-one and call him."

I don't want to call him at all but I know I must. "Why wait?"

"He saw you yesterday at one so he probably starts his appointments on the hour. Phoning him at five-to-the-hour increases your chances of actually speaking with him."

"That's in twenty minutes. You'll be asleep by then."

"Hopefully."

* * *

He's asleep, fallen sideways and I drape my spare duvet over him. He's a good-looking guy. Sporty. Keeps in shape. Shame he's such a div.

I turn my thoughts to the psychiatrist. I was lucky last time. Unlikely I'll speak with him again. What do I say? Memory? Paranoia? Apart from Wade, I feel like there's someone here with me. It's nothing. I never talk about it as I'd be called paranoid. It doesn't frighten me, it's just there, always has been.

"Come on. Focus." I run through the conversation in my head. A couple of scenarios. It's five-to, time to make the call.

"Good afternoon, Doctor Slattery's surgery."

"May I talk with Doctor Slattery, personally?"

"Good timing. He's between patients. Who may I say is calling?"

"Charlie Quinlan."

"Oh, hello Charlie. Lovely to meet you yesterday. Just putting you through."

So I was there.

"Hello, Charlie. It's Doctor Slattery. A pleasant surprise."

"I don't remember." The conversations I rehearsed have evaporated.

He doesn't respond.

"My memory's causing me problems."

Again, he doesn't respond.

"I don't feel in control."

"Charlie." He's speaking. "Firstly, don't stress about this. Memory issues are common in trauma cases and I'm surprised there was no indication of this when I spoke with you yesterday. Secondly, come and see me. I'll put you back to Beverley who'll make an appointment. The sooner the better."

After a couple of niceties, I'm back onto Beverley. *The sooner the better* is Friday, 5pm.

* * *

I want to see the CCTV footage. Wade's asleep and I must wait for him. What will it show? Now I don't want to see the bloody CCTV footage. Going for a run.

I head for Argos in Peckham to get more buckets of magnetic letters. Before heading home, I divert to the Brockley address but all I can do is stand and look at the house. I can't tell if anyone's in. No, this isn't right. Head home.

Wade's still sparko when I get back at six and he'll be leaving for work about nine.

I add another entry to my fridge diary:

6 W H PSY 8 5

6th January – Wade, Hospital, Psychiatrist 8th 5pm.

I need to speak with Wade before he goes but I'll leave him sleeping for another hour.

In my bedroom, I put on headphones and listen to the Crimestoppers call.

"Crimestoppers."

"That murder, Primrose Hill, hero cop, Charlie Quinlan. It was her. She killed him."

"Who..."

"I am not repeating myself. You have enough."

"Who..."

Again. Again. Over and over. I sense movement, I look up and it's Wade at my bedroom door. I drop the headphones around my neck.

"Sorry. Something to eat? Pizza?"

"There's stuff in the kitchen."

"The pizza's just arrived. Fancy some?"

"Great." I leave the headphones on my desk and follow Wade through to the living room.

The pizza's good. "Do you order pizza often?"

"No. I was thinking of you."

I think I've just been insulted.

"What were you listening to?" he asks.

"The Crimestoppers call."

He nods. "Want to see the CCTV footage from the Elephant?" Without waiting, he brings the telly to life with the remote. I recognise the scene, the two cash-machines by the entrance to the tube station. The camera-angle is side on, cash-machines to the left. It's dark but everything's well lit. Not crowded. The date and time stamp shows 30/12/2020 21:15.

21:16 – a woman with white hands appears from the bottom right and approaches the cash-machine nearest the camera. It's me. She searches, I search in my bag and pull out my purse. Holding the purse in her right hand, my right hand, I unzip it with my left and extract my card. I insert the card and start punching numbers, left index finger, jab jab jab.

21:18 – the card slides out and I slip it into my purse. The notes are presented and I slip them into my purse.

The receipt is presented and I slip it in too. I zip up my purse and drop it into my bag. As I walk away from the machine towards the camera, I close my bag and, just before passing from view, I look up and directly at the camera. Then I'm gone.

"Play that again. Just the last bit, as I look up at the camera."

Wade manipulates the video.

"I didn't."

He plays it again. "You did."

"Why would I do that?"

"Don't know but you did."

I close my eyes, panic rising. I feel a hand on my shoulder, firm, reassuring. "Charlie, breathe. Breathe slowly."

Vaguely aware that I'm not shirking away from him, I slip into my rhythm, in for four, out for six. I find my voice. "No wonder the detectives are suspicious."

"It's okay, Charlie. It could have been anything."

"Anything?" I turn towards Wade. "It's more than anything." I'm fighting back tears. "I bloody winked at the camera."

CHAPTER TEN

Wade's gone to work. It's past nine and I'm anxious about going to bed.

Wade didn't say how he got the CCTV footage but it can't have been legit. He flatly refused to leave a copy. His footage includes me arriving and leaving the Elephant & Castle area via Thurlow Street and visiting the Colombian Cockney. He had my technology dancing to his tune.

The images of the cash-withdrawal made me wince. I was jabbing it like a technophobe. That was a week ago. I could do that now but not then.

Then there's the image of me winking at the CCTV camera. A message? Who to? What did I think the detectives would make of that? When I met with Wade yesterday, he said we were having a laugh about it. What's to laugh about?

Wade offered to analyse the Crimestoppers call. What's to lose? The detectives will do it anyway, probably already have. Wade took the recording with him.

He also said he'd research Peter Daventry.

It's sleep that turns my memory on and off but it's so hit and miss.

I return to my fridge.

DEC
23
27
29
30 PD RIP
31 CS NOTE
JAN
1 K MORE
2 H BUSY INT HN
3 H ARG COF
4 PSY 5 1 H W PH 5 4
5 H PSY W
6 W H PSY 8 5

I lost 23rd December. A Wednesday. What was I doing the day before? I came home from Rehab.

I lost 27th December. A Sunday. What was I doing Boxing Day? Wade visited. He left in a strop over his *escape*.

I lost 29th December. 28th? Elly resurfaced. Did I sleep between the 28th and the 29th? No idea.

I lost New Year's Day. Most people do. Not funny. What was I doing New Year's Eve? I found the note about the cash-withdrawal, the note I wrote.

Also on New Year's Eve, a call was made to Crimestoppers, in the early hours, naming me as the murderer.

I sink down to the kitchen floor opposite my fridge. I've been spending a lot of time here lately.

I lost 5th January. Yesterday. What was I doing on the 4th? Made the appointment with Doctor Slattery.

This is getting me nowhere.

What can I remember of the days I lost? I look up at the fridge.

23

Nothing.

27

Nothing.

29

Nothing.

30 PD RIP

Peter Daventry killed. Nothing but I remember putting those letters up.

1 K MORE

Kathy came round and I was me but more. Nothing but I remember putting those letters up.

5 H PSY W

Hospital, Psychiatrist, Wade. I don't remember putting that up there.

At my computer, I check out news stories for those days. Nothing rings a bell. Except on the 30th. The Peter Daventry murder was well covered, not just in the Evening Standard. They all say much the same. On his way home from work, a regular route, near a children's playground, stabbed.

I said I'd find out about Peter Daventry. I've done nothing. I suppose I'm anxious about prying into something I shouldn't. If I had myself under surveillance, I'd be wondering why I hadn't checked out Peter Daventry. Okay. So, if I am under surveillance, they can see that I've done a search on Peter Daventry. So what?

My problem is, I don't know what is making me so anxious. Call it a funny feeling. I don't want to go there. Anyway. See what Wade turns up.

I can't believe I winked at the CCTV camera. Am I really leaving messages for myself? Leaving messages from the far side of my memory? How does that make any sense? I'll be seeing Doctor Slattery on Friday. It's Wednesday, well, Thursday now. How will I stay awake until 5pm Friday?

I need to be doing something. My promotion books will induce sleep better than any tranquiliser but there's something I want to find out. Wade's taken my recording of the Crimestoppers call. Homicide will have sent the original to the Lab. Although murder investigations take a high priority, it could be stuck there. Detectives are always frustrated by Lab delays.

Would they even tell me if the Lab analysis revealed anything interesting about the caller? Probably not. Maybe they have, on one of my lost days. Now I'm worried.

Books. Evidential value of voice identification.

Not much.

Google.

I'm tapping the keyboard now. Hands getting better.

Voice identification.

Audio. Digital.

Oh, god. Case law. Precedents. Experts. For every expert the prosecution presents, the defence will find an expert saying the exact opposite.

Circumstantial. Won't stand on its own.

I've got to read and understand this.

* * *

I'm woken by knocking. My computer's asleep. I touch the mouse. 6.30am. Thursday 7th January. Thank god.

It's Wade.

He doesn't speak.

"Coffee? Tea?"

He doesn't acknowledge me, just extracts his computer from his bag.

"Anything good happen last night?"

He taps at his keyboard. "Charlie, this is basic voice analysis software."

I sit next to him.

"This is the profile of the Crimestoppers caller." He shows me a black screen with a green jagged line.

"Okay." I'm nervous.

He shifts that window to the left and opens a new one alongside, another black screen with a green jagged line. "An analysis of another voice recording."

"Whose?" Pointless question. I know the answer.

"Yours."

I was right.

Wade looks at me. He's got something to say but he doesn't want to say it.

He draws a breath but I hold up my hand. "When did you take a recording of my voice?"

"Tuesday."

"The day you showed me the CCTV footage and we were having a good laugh about it. The day I lost."

"Yes."

"A meeting I don't remember."

"Yes."

Wade is uncomfortable. My anxiety level is soaring

and I control my breathing. I know where this is going.

I can delay it though. "Why were you recording my voice?"

"You asked me to."

"I asked you to?"

"Yes."

"Why would I ask you to record my voice?" Any anger I feel is crushed by my certainty of what Wade is about to tell me.

"You're prevaricating."

I sit back into the sofa. "You're right." Wade closes his computer and turns towards me. He's close but that's okay. "Go on then. Tell me."

"Audibly, the Crimestoppers voice and your voice, although sounding similar, are different. Digitally, your voices are identical."

He held my eyes, didn't shift his position in any way and kept his voice flat. He continues to hold my eyes. He's deadly serious.

My anxiety drops away. My breathing is even. I don't understand, but I feel calm.

I walk out to the kitchen, fill the kettle, place it on its stand and switch it on. Two mugs, teabags.

Wade leans against the kitchen door.

I watch the kettle.

Wade's watching me.

This kettle boils and I make tea.

Back to the living room, him on the sofa and me opposite on a dining chair.

"So, I stitched myself up to Crimestoppers."

"Looks like it."

"Looks like it? I either did or I didn't."

Wade relaxes. "Looks like it."

"Evidence? Admissibility? I tried looking it up but couldn't make much headway."

He nods. "Lot to read."

"And you read it."

"Yes."

"During the night."

"Quiet night."

"You read all that during the night?"

"I read fast."

I believe him.

He sips his tea. "It's not like DNA or fingerprints. Needs corroboration."

"Hence, looks like it."

"Yes."

CHAPTER ELEVEN

"Is it sleepwalking?"

"Don't think so."

"What was I like on Tuesday?"

Wade takes a while to answer. He's tired. "I don't know you that well but I'd say, more animated. Certainly more opinionated." He sits back and rubs his eyes.

"Not sure I should say this…" I stop. I know I shouldn't but I've got a feeling about Wade. He's a useless copper but he's bright. He's honest, sometimes too honest. Should I be exploiting that? I feel I can trust him. Anyway, it wouldn't be exploitation if he knows what I'm doing. I need help and I need it now.

He's waiting for me to finish what I've started saying.

"I need help."

"You're seeing the psychiatrist tomorrow."

"I need your help."

"I'm not placed to…"

"You are. I trust you. Kathy Bond's a rumour monger. Albert Lavender's a piss-taker. Mary Cantrell's by-the-book."

"There are others."

"They're all coppers."

"So?"

"You can't trust coppers as far as you can throw them."

"I'm a copper."

"Not really." That came out wrong. He looks away. "Sorry, Wade. We're all professional busy-bodies. You're different."

He doesn't move or say anything. Acquiescence?

"Wade. I need your help because none of the others could give it."

"What about friends outside the Job?"

"No."

"Family?"

I must explain, only fair. "I don't know my parents. I was raised in a children's home. Moved to fosters when I was ten. They cared for me but I wasn't really family. As soon as I joined the Job, we went our separate ways. We haven't been in touch since. I could try. They'd be there for me if I made contact, but that link's broken."

"So the only acquaintances you have are coppers?"

"Except you." That came out wrong too. "Wade, I'm sorry."

He waves his hand dismissively. "Don't be." Resigned?

"I'll do a deal with you." In for a penny. "If you help me, I'll help you."

He leans forward. "Go on."

"I'll show you coppering if you keep me awake until I see the psychiatrist, tomorrow, 5pm."

"That's more than thirty hours away."

"And you're going to keep me awake."

"I'm working tonight."

"Throw a sicky."

"Charlie."

"Wade, how many sick days have you taken?"

"None."

"None in eighteen months. It's your turn. Throw a sicky. I'll come round to yours in case they visit. They won't."

Wade sits forward. "I learn something new about you every day."

"Full of surprises, me."

He laughs. He's fading fast and he must sleep now as I'll need him to keep me awake until I see Doctor Slattery tomorrow at 5pm. I'll be alright today. Tonight and tomorrow will be difficult. Whatever this memory issue is, it's got something to do with sleep. I've only noticed lost days on waking up.

"So how are you going to teach me coppering?"

Wade said something. "Sorry, Wade. I drifted."

"That's okay. How will you teach me coppering?"

I knew he'd said something but I'd missed it. Is that like my lost days? I know that, on particular days, I've completely missed what went on. Is it a distraction thing? No. That's not it. Wade said I was interacting with him. Hardly distracted.

"Charlie?"

"Oh, god. Wade. I'm sorry. Teaching you coppering? I'm resuming Monday. I'll speak to Cantrell and get her to post us together. It'll provoke loads of gossip and rumour but I couldn't care less."

"You're having memory issues and you're going to resume?"

"I need to get back to work. You're my back stop. So long as we're together, we'll be able to work things out."

"You'll stand in court under oath saying you don't remember? Charlie, I can't be your minder."

"It's the incident, the pain and the struggle with my burns. I'm sure I just need to get back to normal and all this nonsense will stop."

Wade looks away. He's uncomfortable.

"You said you wanted to escape. You haven't really explained. Seems we both have skeletons in our closets."

No reaction.

"You need sleep. Use my bed. We'll speak again, this afternoon."

"Wait a minute. Wait a minute." Wade's suddenly all lively. "You're resuming because you've been discharged regarding your burns. The Job's paid for you to see a psychiatrist. The Met CMO wouldn't let you resume without a report from Doctor Slattery."

I see where Wade's going with this. I hadn't even considered it. "Doctor Slattery must have submitted a favourable report."

Wade's tiredness takes hold of him again. He heads through to my bedroom. I find some fresh bed linen and carry it through to find he's already undressed down to his boxers and looking very embarrassed. Not only is he a good-looking guy, he has a fine physique.

"Don't worry about that," he says quickly slipping under the duvet.

Shame he's such a div. Shame about a lot of things. And who, exactly, has Doctor Slattery submitted a report to the CMO on? I haven't seen him.

* * *

I'll give him eight hours, till 3.30pm. At 2am I'll be struggling to stay awake but, at that point, I'll still have fifteen hours before seeing Doctor Slattery.

"I won't make it."

Wade will struggle tomorrow morning.

It's a tall order, too tall.

I call Doctor Slattery.

"5pm's okay but inconvenient," I say to Beverley, "I have to rearrange things. Any chance you can fit me in today?"

She'll call me back.

Over to my diary.

That entry:

5 H PSY W

I remember making all the entries except that one. I've had something like this before. That last entry was made from the far side of my memory. *Far side of my memory*. I don't even have the language for this.

"What is it? Amnesia?" Christ, Charlie. If you are under surveillance, you're giving them what they want. Stop talking out loud.

I start researching on my mobile as my computer's otherwise engaged. Heavy going. Wade would pile through all this in minutes.

* * *

By lunch time, I've seen Nurse Olu and I'm back indoors after walking around Ruskin Park. The frosty air has livened me up.

Wade is up too, with his computer. He doesn't look round. "I had a shower. Hope you don't mind."

"Course not. What are you looking up?"

"Memory loss. Seems there are many causes. We can dismiss old age."

"That's reassuring." I sit next to him.

He angles his screen towards me. "Look," he says. "Losing your keys is nothing to worry about. Everybody misplaces them occasionally. It's time to start worrying when you find them in the fridge."

I look at him. "You commenting on my diary?"

"Hadn't thought of that. I still don't understand why you don't use something more fit-for-purpose."

He still doesn't get the evidential implications. "What else have you found?"

He taps through some pages. "Memory loss can be caused by head trauma."

"Had loads of trauma but no head trauma."

"Stress too."

"Had loads of stress."

"You know about medication and drugs."

"Rohypnol?"

"Midazolam's another."

"Someone's been spiking my drinks?"

"I don't think so."

"You an expert now?"

"Charlie. I'm trying to help."

I close my eyes. Why am I so prickly? It couldn't be those date-rape drugs. I'm too aware of what's going on, my bouts last too long, I'd need topping up. "Wade. I'm sorry. Go on."

"Under stress, there's something called dissociative fugue which can lead to unexpected travelling or wandering."

"Dissociative what?"

"Fugue. Losing awareness of identity often coupled with travelling or wandering."

"Dissociative fugue?" I can't believe I'm hearing this but I'm seeing it.

"Look. I can't penetrate this. Google only scrapes the surface. Drilling down into the more academic reports will take time. The psychiatrist will know about this stuff."

"I suppose that when I see him, I have to hope I remember what happens."

"I'd be happy to sit in with you."

"I'm not sure about that. Can I think about it?"

"Of course. Oh, and I don't need to throw a sicky. I telephoned Duties and took a day's annual."

"You were lucky to get that at such short notice."

"Apparently I won't be missed."

I manage not to say anything.

* * *

To kill time, Wade and I go to Morrisons. I said I didn't need to shop but he said the content of my kitchen cupboards could be better. Made me laugh. What he meant was my kitchen cupboards are full of crap.

He fills a trolley with vegetables and salad, spices, herbs, tins of beans and tomatoes, coconut oil.

"What's that?" I ask.

"A squash."

"Squashes aren't that big."

"They're squash-size."

"It's bigger than my head."

We move into another aisle.

"What are red lentils?" I ask, holding up a kilo pack he'd selected.

"Red lentils," he says.

He also adds ground coffee and, from the home section, a cafeteria.

"A cafetière," he says.

"What I said," I say.

He adds some bottles of beer and spends ages selecting two bottles of wine.

In the bread aisle, he grabs some flat bread.

"Naan bread," he says.

"What I said," I say.

He's so easy to wind up.

* * *

Back indoors, he cooks a curry. I thought curries took four days to cook.

It's delicious, not too spicy. "Coriander?" I ask.

"Cilantro," he says.

"What's that?"

"Coriander," he says, shrugging.

"So, I was right?"

"Not really."

"Smart-arse."

He bites back his explanation.

"I recognise it, from the Colombian Cockney."

"Makes sense," he says, still managing not to explain.

"Go on then. What's the difference between coriander and cilantro?"

He puts his fork down, takes a deep breath and says, "Well, if you must know…"

I burst out laughing. I'm laughing so much, I don't hear the explanation.

By the time he's finished, he's laughing too.

As I mop my plate with flat bread and he mops his with naan, I ask, "Why does the Colombian Cockney smell of cilantro?"

"Colombians, in general, aren't partial to hot spices so cilantro features frequently in their cuisine. It's quite delicate. Same plant but coriander is made from…"

"Wade," I put my hand on his arm, "don't overdo it."

I'm looking longingly at the wine.

Instead, he makes coffee. Strong coffee.

"This is like an expresso."

"Espresso. The more the better."

He really doesn't know when he's being wound up.

The coffee's so strong, it makes me shudder.

"Thought any more about me sitting in with you at the psychiatrist?"

"Jury's still out on that."

We clear the dishes, working easily around one another. He suggests we go and see a film. *Die Hard* is rerunning at the Odeon in Streatham.

I watched it over Christmas. Bruce Willis in a white vest that turns black. My Fitbit registered that I fell asleep at the beginning and woke at the end. Maybe my Fitbit has better taste in films than me.

"Maybe a film's not a good idea." He's caught my reaction. "Ten-pin bowling? If you're resuming on Monday, it'll be a good test for your hands."

He's right and I agree saying, "I'll beat you."

On seeing my bike, pale green with a basket, he agrees to leave his bike at mine and I'll drive us over to his. My car hasn't been driven since before the tanker incident.

"Your bike will be fine," he says when he hears my battery's flat.

"It's okay," I say, releasing the hand brake, rolling my car down the hill and bumping it into life after twenty yards.

"Okay if you're on a hill," he says.

"Jump-starter's in the boot."

"Most would replace the battery?"

"Thieves only like cars that work."

"Good point. Well made."

Something I like about Wade, he's so accepting.

"Do you ever clean your car?"

"Thieves like bright shiny things. A rotten banana skin draped over the steering wheel is more effective than any crook lock."

"Is this you teaching me police work?"

I don't have an answer for that but I'm revelling in my newfound dexterity and the feeling of freedom at being back behind the wheel. Even the heavy traffic's not annoying me.

* * *

Wade's place is a converted flat in a terraced house in Streatham. Finding a parking space within a hundred yards is good going, apparently. While he's making more coffee, I look around.

His flat is not tidy but organised. His coffee table is covered in newspapers and magazines. The one on top is called The Week and has a cartoon of the prime-minister on the front cover. There's a copy of The Telegraph, The Guardian and The Times. Also, The Financial Times, Spectator, Economist. All current.

"Do you read all these?" I ask as he comes in with two mugs.

"Of course. Doesn't everyone?"

"I get The Metro and The Evening Standard."

"Superficial," he says.

My mobile rings as I'm taking a sip from a coffee so strong, it's syrupy. "Hello, it's Charlie."

"It's Doctor Slattery. Charlie Quinlan?"

"Yes. Hello, Doctor."

"You wanted an earlier appointment?"

"If possible."

"May I ask why?"

I'm lost for words. I wasn't expecting this. I don't know what we've already talked about. Last time I called him, he said he was surprised that I hadn't raised memory loss with him at Tuesday's appointment. I have no memory of that appointment. Wade has looked up. I'd been expecting a call from Beverley. I hadn't expected to be talking with Doctor Slattery direct. Over the mobile is hard as I'm wary of people listening in. "My memory's playing tricks on me. I think it's something to do with sleep. I've stayed awake since I made the appointment with Beverley. There's no way I'm going to be able to stay awake for another twenty-four hours."

"I understand. If you could make it up here for seven this evening, I'll see you then."

It's 5.30pm. "I can do that. Are you sure?"

"Absolutely fine. See you at seven."

"Oh, Doctor? Is it okay if I bring a friend and could he sit in?"

"Of course. Anything that makes you feel more comfortable is fine by me."

We close down the call.

"What do you think of that?" I say to Wade.

"He must be giving up his evening to see you. We better head off straight away."

"What's the best route?"

"Train and tube."

I swing my coat round my shoulders noticing how actions that were so difficult, if not impossible, are now back to second nature.

"One thing I definitely won't forget," I say as we're heading out, "is my promise to thrash you at ten-pin bowling."

* * *

Riding the train up town, I sit opposite Wade. The train's practically empty. The tube will be packed. "Wade. Yes, I'd like you to sit in with me."

"My pleasure."

"We can talk about it afterwards."

"Why didn't you come clean with Doctor Slattery about your memory issues?"

"I've only ever spoken with Doctor Slattery over the phone. I might be under surveillance. I don't want the Job knowing about all this weirdness until I understand it, so I steered clear of the detail. I'll explain fully to him when I see him face to face."

"Trouble is, because you're not opening up on the telephone, Doctor Slattery's only assessing you on what happened when you met and he must have submitted a favourable report to the CMO. I understand your desire to be reserved about what you say on the telephone because you're concerned about who might be listening in but I think you're being a bit..." His voice trails off.

"Paranoid?"

"No. Mistrustful. There's also the reports that would have been submitted in respect of the counselling you received in Rehab, a time when you admit you weren't facing up – Kathy's words, not mine. After what you did at the tanker incident, the Job will bend over backwards to help you."

He's right, but he does mean paranoid, just doesn't want to say it. I don't even know what everybody finds so distressing about it. I've lived with the feeling of being watched all my life. I was surprised when school friends said they didn't feel it or, if they did, it really spooked them. Harriet, my foster mother, spoke about someone walking on her grave. Proverbs, superstitions. Why are people so uncomfortable with it? My mind's wandered again. "I'm with you about Doctor Slattery and Rehab but I really do believe that I've just got to get my routine back and all this nonsense will end. Getting back to work is the biggest step I can take to re-establish my routine."

"Okay. I applaud what you're saying. Changing the subject. You asked about Peter Daventry. At one of my mother's soirees, I…"

"Re-establish my routine and regain control of my life."

"Completely agree. Anyway, Peter Daventry. I met a group of…"

"My burns are sorted. I'm ready to get back and take control."

Wade stops. He's leaning forward and looking down at his feet. He's thinking, analysing. He looks up. "Charlie. You asked me to find out about Peter Daventry. I've been trying to tell you. You've interrupted me each time. Have you changed your mind on that?"

He's right. "I don't know. Gut feeling. I don't like Peter Daventry. I don't want to know about him."

"How can…"

"Wade, just stop." Christ. I shouted that. Another passenger looks over. "I'm sorry. There's how I should feel and there's how I feel. They're different." The other passenger has returned to her book. If I keep my voice down, she'll be out of earshot. "I should feel sorry for Peter Daventry and his family but I don't. His name rings alarm bells inside me and I don't know why. It's like I want to find out about him and, at the same time, I don't."

"I haven't learnt much but maybe, if you hear what I've discovered, you could put your feelings into context."

"Not now, Wade. Another time."

Wade's still leaning forwards. Our knees are rubbing. He's looking at me, his eyes keen. "You're apprehensive about seeing Doctor Slattery."

I nod.

"You're concerned about what he's going to find out."

I nod. It's not apprehension, concern or worry. I'm petrified and tears are coming.

Wade's taken hold of my hands. "I'll be right by your side."

CHAPTER TWELVE

"Wade. What the hell happened? Please call me. Please."

It's Saturday morning, the 9th, sevenish. Last thing I remember was being an idiot in front of Wade on a train. That was Thursday.

My account says my mobile was turned off at 18:04 that Thursday. My Fitbit is gone. There's a voice message from Wade later Thursday evening asking how things went.

I'm calm. Is this the new normal?

Nurse Olu. Did I see her yesterday? Maybe the fridge will say.

Last three entries:

6 W H PSY
7 H PSY W
8 O

O?

Of course. Run out of Hs. O for Olu.

So according to my own record, on the 7th, Thursday, I went to the hospital, saw Doctor Slattery and Wade. Saw Nurse Olu on the 8th. I don't remember any of that and I don't remember making those entries.

Hang on, the entry for the 6th has changed. Reference to the 5pm appointment on the 8th has gone.

Why would I have done that? Of course, the 5pm appointment on the 8th became the 7pm appointment on the 7th. If I changed it, I'd have changed it to:

6 W H PSY 7 7

I check my letters and numerals. There are enough 7s. If I'd changed it, I'd have made it accurate. "So who the hell changed it?"

My mobile rings. "Hi, Wade. Thanks for calling back. Listen. I can't remember."

"How much?"

"From when we were on the train together, I remember getting a bit weepy and emotional, through to this morning about seven."

Silence.

"Wade."

"Fridge say anything?"

"Yes, but nothing revealing." Nothing revealing? Just that someone other than me has been updating my fridge diary. Now's not the time to talk about that. "Any ideas?"

"I'm coming round."

"No. Wait. Weren't you working last night?"

"Yes."

"Is my car still at yours?"

"Hang on." Sounds like he's opening a window. "Yes."

"Okay. Listen. I must get my dressings changed and recover my car. Get your head down. See you noonish."

* * *

Nurse Olu wasn't there. Another nurse changed my dressings and confirmed I'd been discharged and could resume work. My new dressings are nothing more than light gloves, yet still offering confidence.

I get a cab straight from the hospital to Wade's.

Wade is on a call when I arrive.

"Sleep well?"

"I haven't slept since our telephone conversation."

"Oh, god. Sorry."

"No need. Have you eaten?"

"Not really."

He points to the kitchen. "Grab yourself something. There're cereals, toast and the like." He waves his mobile. "Must finish this off."

He's on to, what sounds like a bank.

I sit opposite him with some muesli. His call seems to be coming to an end.

"Successful?" I ask as he pockets his mobile.

"Don't ask. Anyway, what happened to you?"

I've been rehearsing this on the way over. "We were heading to Victoria on Thursday and I woke up this morning."

He heads out to his kitchen. I throw myself back and look up at the ceiling. I really don't need Wade being all arsy with me.

Wade comes back with a pot of coffee and mugs. Not looking at me, he pours the coffee, his movements deliberate and precise. He pushes one of the mugs towards me and sits back, cradling his coffee under his nose.

He takes a deep breath. "During that train ride, I noticed a difference. You were, I don't know. If it happens again, I'll pay more attention."

Is he with me or against me? Has he decided he doesn't want to play anymore?

"You're good at impersonating people." He's carrying on. "Since you telephoned this morning, I've been thinking about that. You seemed to be impersonating yourself."

"What?" I couldn't help that.

"It's just an impression, so please don't put any store by it."

At this moment I don't think anything can surprise me. "Please, just tell me what I said, what I did, where we went?"

"Not much to say, but there is something very interesting. You say the last thing you remember is getting all weepy and emotional. It was at that moment there was a distinct change in atmosphere."

He's nervous.

"I thought it was what I said, you know, about being with you, beside you. I said I didn't mean anything by it and sorry if I'd upset you but you said not to worry."

I would have said that.

He doesn't falter, "You became impatient but, what was most noticeable, was that..." unlike him to be searching for words, "...right at that change of atmosphere, your weepiness and emotion cleared up." He sips his coffee and looks directly at me. "How did you do that? How could anyone do that?" He looks down again. "You said nothing more until Victoria. Then you said you'd changed your mind and you wanted to see the psychiatrist on your own."

I wouldn't have said that.

He keeps going. "I offered to come with you, wait outside, but you wouldn't have it. Last I saw was you heading down into the tube. I collected my bike from outside yours. Sent you a message around eight enquiring how you got on. You didn't respond. With nothing much else to do, I went into work, saved a day's annual."

"I didn't see your message till this morning."

He shrugs.

"So you don't know whether I went to see Doctor Slattery."

He shakes his head.

I extract my mobile and ring the Harley Street office. Of course, it's Saturday. Next open Monday morning.

"How do you feel?" Wade asks.

It's a while before I answer. "I need to get back to work. You know how it is when you're off. Lose track of days, things get disordered. Add on the trauma of all those deaths, burning people writhing, the boy, his mum burning in front of him. Add to that my burns, the pain, the boy dying. I can put all this behind me by getting back to work. Getting back to work will mark the end to this episode in my life."

"Wait, wait, wait." Wade sits forward. "You seem very composed. More composed than you've been since that incident."

"Now that I don't have my hands distracting me, I can focus better."

"No. Not that. It's like you've made up your mind."

"I have made up my mind. You accuse me of prevarication." I raise my hands, "Guilty. I need to move

113

on. I don't need endless analysis. I don't need a psychiatrist. I need to get on with my life. I'm stuck in a limbo."

"Charlie, hear me out. I applaud what you're saying, but you don't know what you're dealing with. You had a memory lapse yesterday. You had a memory lapse and you wrote yourself a note. You had a memory lapse and you telephoned Crimestoppers and accused yourself of murder."

"Do you believe that?" I'm on my feet, angry.

Wade isn't fazed. "The caller's voice and yours are a digital match."

"You know full well that evidence is circumstantial at best. What corroboration have you got?"

"Well…"

"None. None what so bloody ever." I'm shouting. "I was up the Elephant at the time of the murder making a cash-withdrawal."

"And you don't even remember that." Wade's now up on his feet.

He's right. I sit down.

He's standing over me.

I look away.

He sits. "By the way. I have some info on Peter Daventry."

I turn back to him. "You have?" I did ask him for it. I suppose I should hear it.

"I heard what you said, about how you *should* feel and how you *do* feel. He's a normal bloke. Wife, two children. No previous. No police record. He has LinkedIn and Facebook profiles. Works in the City. Financial Analyst. Lives near Primrose Hill. Was on his way home when he was killed."

"How did you find out he doesn't have a police record?"

"The journalist who wrote the article in the Independent is a friend of the family. He got his information from that Homicide DS, John French. Isn't he the DS that interviewed you?"

Wade certainly is full of surprises. "Yes. Will that journalist expect anything in return?"

"No."

"Does he know why you're asking?"

"I actually found all that out overhearing a group of friends talking about the Primrose Hill murder at one of my mother's midweek soirees."

Mother's midweek soirees. He spat those words out. It must have been painful for him to go back. Anyway, what a break. "Thanks for telling me," I look away, "at least, making me listen."

He shrugs.

What is wrong with me? I expect tears but there's no such feeling. I look down at my hands. "We both have skeletons in our closets. You haven't really told me about yours. You're using the police to *escape* yours. You don't like the expectations placed on you. You're pursuing expectations you've set yourself but, if it all goes pear-shaped, you have a bolt hole. It seems I'm finding out about my skeletons and, if it all goes pear-shaped, I've nothing."

It's a while before Wade speaks. "I said I'm with you, right by your side. I mean it. There's a way through this and, together, we'll find it."

CHAPTER THIRTEEN

Sunday morning, lying in bed following frenetic checking of dates and times.

What a mess. The far side of my memory.

Karaoke, muddy trainers, cash-withdrawals, a note I wrote, additions to my fridge diary. When I'm on the far side of my memory, I leave messages for myself because I know I'll forget.

I'm on the kitchen floor, back against the oven, looking up at my fridge.

Last entry:

8 O

Lost days. I can now add the 8th to them. Also the 7th, well, some of it. So, sleep is not the trigger.

God, this is bollocks. What am I saying? That I'm deliberately hiding something from myself?

"Together."

Someone's in my living room. I'm up. Too quick. There's no one in my living room. Faintness gone. I run through my flat. "Who's there?" Out the front door. No one's there. "Who said that?"

I retreat inside, bolt and chain.

Must update my diary.

9 W

Oh, why bother? What good is it doing?

I'll be resuming tomorrow, Late Turn.

That word I heard, *together*, was it in my head? Did I say it out loud? This has happened before. The word was *trust*. When was that? The day after the interview. A Sunday too.

These need recording. Maybe I'll keep the fridge diary for a bit. Not enough letters. I add to the entry for the 3rd.

3 H ARG COF TRU

3rd January – Hospital, Argos, Coffee, TRUST.

New entry for today:

10 TOG

10th January – TOGETHER

I felt good earlier. Now I'm sick with worry and the detectives spring to mind. I talked with Wade yesterday about what will happen when the Lab returns their analysis of the voice recordings. A reasonable question is whether they'll even try matching it with my voice. Would they think it likely I'd stitch myself up?

If I were them, I'd check it against my voice. French and Reeve were not convinced. Who can blame them? The CCTV showed me poking the cash-machine and manipulating the contents of my purse with ease. They won't have missed me winking at the camera.

Then, at the end of the interview, they tested me. Of course they're suspicious. So, they'll find out, pretty soon, that the Crimestoppers caller's voice and mine are a digital match. They're suspicious and they won't let go.

Yesterday, Wade helped me explore the legislation around voice identification. We didn't find much more than we already knew – circumstantial, needs corroboration.

"They have no corroboration," Wade said.

He's right but they're suspicious. They'll call me in for another helpful chat under caution. They'll put it to me and see what I say. I wonder what stunt they'll pull when they do that?

A more serious question is who I'll ask to sit with me. Cantrell was great. She turned the silence against the detectives. The trouble with Cantrell is that she's great so long as she's on my side. How long will it be before she becomes as suspicious of me as the detectives?

A solicitor? I want to help the murder enquiry, not put up barriers. It would, however, be a reasonable request for a second interview under caution.

I don't know the victim and I don't want to know about him. That's the scary thing. Why do I feel so uneasy about someone I don't know? That could be the stunt the detectives have lined up for me. "Why haven't you been trying to find out about Peter Daventry?"

What should I say to that?

I look across at Elly sitting on my desk.

"What do you think, Elly? What should I say to that?"

She looks at me.

"You wouldn't forget, would you."

Oh, god. Is talking to myself better or worse than talking to a stuffed elephant?

CHAPTER FOURTEEN

Monday, 2pm, Late Turn, parade. My dressings are so delicate I'm wondering what purpose they serve. My leather gloves fit over them. Everybody's all smiles and awkward hugs. Kathy, over the top. Lavender, "About friggin' time."

This morning, over the phone, Beverley confirmed I attended last Thursday. She'll get back to me with another appointment. Still waiting.

Cantrell comes in and everyone stands up. "Sit down."

Parades by Cantrell are short and to the point.

My request to be posted with Wade was ignored. I'm with Lavender.

After parade, while Lavender's preparing the car, I'm in Local Intel catching up. I've been away since the beginning of December. Over six weeks of catching up.

I start wading through the files: Bulletins, Notices, Registers, Daily Briefings, Sightings, Movements, Indices, Visits, Searches. Electronic versions and their hard backups. There are loads of entries since I've been away, but nothing much has really changed. Harop's gone inside to give the locals a break from his burglary but Frazer's come out to take over. Dillon's been weighed off for dealing but James has been released on bail to continue trading. Frakes is wanted on Warrant and Symons is on remand in custody for GBH. So, Harop's in, Frazer's out, Dillon's in but James is out, Frakes is out and Symons is in. Give it a couple of months and it'll look as though the deck's been shuffled.

* * *

Lavender's waiting patiently as I jump into the passenger seat. I'm checking the radio and logging onto mobile data as Lavender glides the car out onto the main drag.

We're soon at the scene of the tanker incident.

Apart from some tell-tale marks on the road and evidence of heat damage on nearby buildings, everything's pretty much back to normal.

"This the first time you visited here since the incident?" Lavender asks.

I nod, get out and walk to the point where the rubbernecker took the video that went viral on YouTube.

Lavender follows.

"That's where the tanker was," I say, pointing to a stretch of tarmac with freshly painted lines.

I move to where I first saw the carnage. The traffic's stopped.

I point. "That's where the woman fell. If I'd got to her first, I'd have died with her."

Moving on. "This is where you first tried to drag me back."

Lavender scowls. "Come on, Charlie. Maybe this ain't such a good idea."

Further along is the bus stop. "All those people."

A bit back from that, "That's where the car was." I start walking towards that spot. Lavender grabs my arm, "Charlie, we should get back."

I look down at his hand and see flames on my arms, the smell of burning oil and flesh and the heat. Screams. Flames. Writhing bodies.

"Charlie. Come on. Snap out of it."

I'm crouched down, opposite the bus stop. Lavender's bent over me, his hands gripping my shoulders, strong hands. People have stopped.

"Everything okay, officer?"

"It's her. The one who saved the boy."

"Is she going to be alright?"

"I'm fine, I'm fine." I walk back to the car and swing into the passenger seat. Lavender is pacifying the concerned pedestrians. The traffic starts moving again, drivers staring at me as they pass. No noise. No shouts. No gestures. Lavender has dispersed the little crowd. His face is thunder as he bounces into the driver's seat. "Stupid idea," he snarls as he fires up the engine.

Passing Oval, I place my hand on Lavender's shoulder. "Thank you. That must have been hard for you."

"Yeah. It was hard."

"You've been working full on since the incident. You can't have avoided this area."

He turns off the main drag, finds a secluded spot and parks up.

"I don't mind admitting, Charlie. It's been tough. All the questions. The ins and outs of a duck's arse. What the hell can we give to the inquiry? When a petrol tanker explodes on a main road in a built up area, lots of people die." He turns and faces me. "Twenty-seven people died that night. Over a hundred hospitalised."

I know the numbers.

"And, yeah. I can't get those images out of my mind. I'm struggling, Charlie, and everybody still expects me to be the *you're avvinna friggin' larf* Lavender."

Christ. There are tears in his eyes.

"It's not fair, Charlie. Everybody on duty that night is suffering. We've just had to carry on."

All I can think of is how selfish I've been.

"Charlie." He's collecting himself back together. "I don't want to belittle what you did, the pain you suffered, the injuries, the trauma but we've all been hurting too and all we've seen is you get all the attention."

I feel like shit.

"Every one of us put our lives on the line that night. Paramedics. Fire officers. That's what we do. When everyone's running away, we're running towards."

One of Cantrell's comments springs to mind. 'You get a mention – again.' She said that on handing me the newspaper during the welfare visit. *Again*. That word carried so much and I was blind to it.

"Albert, I'm back now. Shall we do some police work?"

He fires up the engine. "Yeah. Why friggin' not?"

* * *

Police work doesn't really mean visiting a coffee shop, but that's where we are, Lavender in the car, me in the queue and, no sooner am I back in the car…

122

…we get a shout.

"Friggin' 'ell."

It's a suspects-on. "Received by Mike-Three."

We open our doors, place our coffees on the road and we're off, doors slamming, blues flashing, sirens wailing.

Lavender's all elbows.

I don't watch the road or how many motorists, cyclists or pedestrians we nearly wipe out. That's for Lavender. My attention's on the info. Anonymous informant, occupants away, white male loitering, sound of breaking glass. Local intel has nothing on the address.

There's rarely suspects on premises at a suspects-on-premises shout but, a quarter mile out, Lavender kills the blues-and-twos.

We drift past the address, an end-of-terrace. Lavender turns down the side street. There's a garden wall. I jump out, closing the door gently.

Lavender moves away for a once-round-the-block. Other units are assigned.

The top of the wall, complete with glass shards, is just within reach. Grateful for my gloves, I find purchase and pull myself up to see over.

Turns out the suspect of the suspects-on-premises is doing the same, but in the opposite direction. I don't know who's more surprised, him or me.

Funny what adrenalin can do. As the suspect falls back, lurching for the neighbouring garden, I'm up and over the wall, glass shards and all.

By the time I land, he's crossing the next garden. I'm over the fence as he's vaulting the next. He crashes through the third. I'm on his heels as he hurdles the fourth and lands in a pond.

"Unlucky," I say cuffing him. He's shivering. It is January.

My mates come bounding in saying, "Nice one, Charlie."

Despite blankets and the van's heater on full blast, my prisoner's blue when we reach the Nick.

Lavender picks up another operator and I take my prisoner to Custody. It's over two hours before I ditch burglar-bill to the CID. I hate detectives.

It's dark by the time I'm back out with Lavender.

* * *

"When I joined, all I wanted was to be a detective. Finished probation, got on the Crime Squad, but the sitting around for hours on end in a cramped vehicle with three other cops all belching and farting drove me nuts. I was fine once the GO GO GO came. Joining the Department lost its appeal."

"So you got yourself thrown out of the friggin' TSG instead."

"They couldn't handle me holding the record for the four-hundred-metre shield run."

"I applied for the Thick and Stupid Group once."

My eyebrows are up around my hairline.

"I thought I'd look good with one of them little round shields," he explains, "like the three-hundred Spartans at the Battle of Monopoly."

Dare I ask. "How did you get on?"

"Didn't get it, too friggin' fat."

Lavender releases the handbrake and we move out of the yard. Cantrell has paired me with Lavender for a reason. Taking me to the scene of the tanker incident was a test. He'll be reporting back about me, probably already has.

With his leather gloves folded down over the backs of his hands and his battered cap he never takes off, he might be showy but he's a superb driver. Rarely leaves the car. Dealing with incidents is the operator's job. If it gets tasty, he'll join in but with a derisory, 'You need a friggin' hand?'

We pass Wade skulking near a junction where motorists often turn against a no-right-turn sign.

"Drop me off," I say.

Instead of stopping he swings into a side street and pulls over. He shifts in his seat and looks at me. Oh, god. Story time.

"You know that guy who's breach of the peace was friggin' assuaged? He was charged with threatening behaviour. Pleaded not guilty. Wade and yours truly gave evidence. Chummy turned out to be loaded and the defending brief turned out to be a Silk. I was called first and I'm having a right hard time under cross-examination. Anyway, I'm sitting in back of court, aren't I, when Wade's giving evidence. Under cross-examination the Silk's going down the same lines he did with me. He's in mid-flow when Wade suddenly lifts his hand. The Silk stops. 'Officer?' he says. You won't believe what Wade said next. 'Seems we have a problem.'" Lavender's trying, unsuccessfully, to mimic

Wade's posh accent. "The Silk says, 'Really officer. Pray share with the court.' I was a bit surprised at that. Silks don't ask questions unless they know what the answers will be but the Silk doesn't know Wade. 'There's a choice to be made,' says Wade, 'and the choice is between believing us,' he waves his hand in my direction, 'or believing your client.' Friggin' 'ell. I'm thinking contempt of court, leaving through the door down to the cells rather than the one out to the foyer. The Silk flutters his gown and adjusts his wig having clearly forgotten he wasn't wearing them and says, 'Actually, that's a choice for His Worship.' Whereupon His Worship chips in with, 'Yes, you're right. That is my choice and I'm looking forward to hearing just how believable your client is.' Whereupon Wade says, 'So am I.' Chummy goes down and me and Wade only end up drinking sherry with the Magistrate and the Silk over lunch."

One of Lavender's longer stories. Oh, god. He hasn't finished.

"That Wade friggin' Oliver does okay in court. I won't have him in the car with me, but I'd have him representing me in court. What is he doing in this Job?"

I don't dare answer. Answering would be like pulling the string out of a talking doll.

Like Lavender says, I don't believe it. In fact, I don't believe any of it. In fairness, Wade does seem comfortable in court. Lavender makes a good point. Wade would be a fine lawyer. He's certainly useless as a cop.

I grab my hat and high-viz jacket and climb out. "Will you be okay on your own?"

He gives me the finger as he drives off.

I join Wade but, before I can say hello, he steps out into the road to stop an offending driver.

Within a few minutes, he's back with me, scribbling some notes on the back of the ticket he's issued.

"It's good to be back," but Wade steps out into the road to stop another driver for the same no-right-turn.

I watch as Wade deals with the motorist. Right words. Right order. Nothing missed. By the book.

The driver is dismissed and Wade joins me again, writing his notes quickly and precisely. Robotic, I think as I open my mouth to speak but, again, he steps out and stops the next motorist.

The driver starts remonstrating as another car careers around the turning. As Wade explains that he can only deal with one at a time, I walk over and stand opposite the junction so that the motorists can see me before they make their turn.

Right indicators go out, frustrated drivers turn left and Wade's source of work dries up.

"What's this, a lesson in prevention better than cure?" he says on joining me.

"No. More about better things to do with your time."

He darts out again as another motorist goes against the no-right-turn sign, despite our visibility.

I watch as the driver gets out and joins Wade who delivers the same familiar words and, as he issues the ticket, I find myself approaching them.

"Goodbye," says Wade.

The driver moves back towards his car but stops when he sees me leaning against his door. Out the corner of my eye, I see Wade has looked up. "Where did you put your mobile?" I say to the driver.

"What mobile?" He's trying to intimidate me.

I wait.

I keep my eyes on him as Wade finally notices that something's going on.

"I ain't got no mobile," he says.

By now, Wade's come over. I keep my eyes on the driver and move towards him, closing the distance. "This officer's going to search your car, and when he's finished, he's going to search you. The reason why is because…"

"It's not mine. It's my girlfriend's."

From intimidating to feeble in two-and-three-quarter seconds. Jeez. Men are such bloody wimps. "And her name is?" I ask as Wade hands me the mobile he's retrieved from under the driver's seat.

"Look, there ain't nothing wrong with that. I just thought if you saw me with it, you'd do me."

"Don't worry, we won't forget." I flick through the names menu. "Now, tell me about your girlfriend."

* * *

"Police work isn't difficult," I say after Wade's prisoner is charged and bailed. "Just got to keep your antennae up."

"I hadn't even noticed he was on a telephone."

"We all need a helping hand occasionally. Accept it graciously."

"Okay. Thanks."

"You're such a div."

Lavender's got himself another operator and they're now tied up.

Beverley calls. "Doctor Slattery can see you on Thursday at 3pm. Any good?" I tell her I'll be there.

"Come on," I say to Wade, "let's catch another."

Good intentions and everything but there's a queue of outstanding calls and we're both assigned reporting crimes, accidents, disputes, disturbances and god knows what for the rest of the shift.

* * *

After we're given the off, we all meet in the Half Nelson. Any excuse for a piss up and my return to duty is good enough.

Lavender's recounting his story of the day.

"Stopped this BM for running a red light. The driver had an AtoZ open on his steering wheel. His reply to caution: 'Sorry, officer, I didn't see the red light because I was reading my book.' I didn't stick him on because I was laughing so friggin' much. You couldn't make it up."

He undoubtedly did make it up.

Surprisingly, Lavender's the first to leave, passing Cantrell on her way in.

She does her customary buying everybody a drink and turns to me. "We didn't get to your return-to-work interview. You're looking good. Straight in with a burglar and that thief for Wade."

"He's a div."

"The thief or Wade?"

"I doubt the thief's had Wade's schooling."

Cantrell goes quiet, not because she has nothing to say, but because she has nothing she wants to say.

This may be a question but I can't resist. "Help the figures?"

She doesn't react.

I let it go but it does irritate me that I'm relied on to keep the team's figures up.

Wade's not arrived yet. "Anyway, where is he?"

"Sorting out some paperwork. It's all I can trust him with unsupervised." Cantrell puts her hand on my shoulder saying, "Good you're back and, yes, I asked Lavender to take you to the scene of the tanker incident. I hope he wasn't too blunt."

"I deserved it. I've been so wrapped up in my own misery. I'm ashamed."

"Yes. You may consider putting up with one of Lavender's more lengthy stories your punishment."

"Sherry with a Magistrate and a Silk?"

"Complete bollocks. He wasn't a Silk but he was a barrister and, under cross-examination, Wade turned him inside out. I'm sure that's where Wade will end up but if we can give him a flavour of what it's like on this side of the fence, it must be a good thing."

"I see what you mean."

"I'll be posting you and Wade together more often. I want him to really experience what it's like to throw everything behind nothing more than a hunch. If anyone can show him that, you can."

"You can post us together all the time. I'm immune to gossip."

"There are other factors to be considered. Good you're back. Start warming up your impersonation skills. Kathy's here."

As Cantrell moves across to join another group, Kathy comes over. "What did Sargie want?"

"Nothing really. We didn't get to the return-to-work interview."

A raucous outburst of laughter drowns everything.

"Nice little arrest with Wade. You looking after him?" Kathy has to raise her voice.

"He needs a hand."

"Leave him to the skippers."

"You looked after me."

"You weren't a complete wanker."

I let it go and she starts chinking her glass with her keys. Everybody falls quiet. The barman turns the music off.

"Hey. Hey. Listen up. Fantastic day. Charlie's back with us."

Everybody cheers as I go bright red.

"Charlie, the officer who risked her life to save a boy, the officer who's brought credit, not just on our little team, but The Met. Not just The Met, but forces and constabularies nationally. Her bravery and fortitude are second to none."

"Fortitude? That's a long word for this time of the evening," one of the guys heckling from the back.

Kathy's not cowed. "Charlie, the darling of the tabloids, the focus of every photographer's lens, my best friend and I'm so proud of her."

"Hear hear. Yeah yeah. Whoop whoop whoop." Such a din and the locals are joining in.

Kathy stands with her hands held aloft.

Everybody goes quiet.

"We've missed Charlie's impersonations. We know she reserves them for smaller groups but it's only fitting. Come on, Charlie. You owe us."

Everyone cheers. What can I do? There's no ducking out of this. "Okay. Okay." It goes quiet.

I heave in a deep breath, scratch the side of my belly and someone yells, "Lavender."

"In one," I say and step back to the safety of the bar.

"Whoop whoop whoop."

Kathy grabs my arm and drags me back to the middle.

"Okay, okay." Everybody quietens. "Okay. Ummm. Well," I drop my voice as low as I can and hoist my belt, "You know there's been a spate of thefts of musical instruments? Well, Wade friggin' Oliver stops this bloke with a double bass. 'Whose double bass is that?' Wade asks. 'It's mine, innit,' comes the reply. 'Prove it,' says Wade. 'How the hell do I do that?' Reasonable question if you ask me but smart-arse Wade friggin' Oliver had the answer. 'If it's your double bass,' Wade goes on, 'you'd be able to play it.' Wade only makes chummy get his double bass out in the middle of the High Street. Well, by Wade's reckoning, the double bass couldn't of been nicked. By the time the audition's over, chummy's collected about eight-and-a-half quid."

Screaming and cheering goes through the roof. Kathy's holding up her hands. The cheering dies. "You think it's all over."

"If that had been me," I give the side of my belly another scratch, "I'd have nicked chummy for friggin' busking."

The cheers and hollering go up again but in amongst it, I hear words like, "Talk of the devil," and, "Captured." Everybody's looking past me.

I turn.

And there's Wade.

CHAPTER FIFTEEN

I've had a glass too many and Wade's driving me home. Rumours will be rife.

Halfway home, Wade says, "Not a double bass, a cello. I did stop him but it was clearly his. He was on his way to perform the Elgar concerto at the Festival Hall so we were discussing that. He disagreed with something I said and got his cello out to demonstrate."

It's a while before I answer. "I prefer Lavender's version."

Wade shrugs.

Another thing I like about Wade, he doesn't get riled and he doesn't give a damn what anybody thinks of him. Two things. He applauded my Lavender impersonation loudest of all.

I feel I should say something more positive. "Don't tell me you play the cello."

"I don't play cello. Come on, there are more important matters than Lavender's exaggerated stories. What if the detectives come knocking?"

"I'll say it wasn't me."

"Should you announce your memory issues?"

"I want to have a conversation with Doctor Slattery, at least one I remember. I'm nervous. It's more than just forgetting. There's something sinister happening on the far side of my memory."

"What makes you say that?"

"I've had this sort of thing before. Early teens but they were harmless. It was dealt with."

"What sort of thing?"

"Books appearing. Paintings. Homework I hadn't done handed in." I shrug. "This is different."

"Have you another appointment with Doctor Slattery?"

"Thursday, 3pm."

"Want me to attend?"

"Didn't do much good last time."

"You surprised me. We could establish rules."

"No, Wade. I think it best I just tackle this on my own."

"I'm here should you reconsider."

We've pulled up outside my flat.

I put my hand on his arm. "I know you are and it's lovely." I roll my head to my right and look at him.

He looks at me but quickly looks away.

"Would you like to come in for coffee?"

What have I just said?

Wade looks straight ahead and says, "I'll say no, Charlie." He turns and faces me, "I would, however, like to take you for dinner."

"A date?" I can't describe the relief I feel.

"Call me a stickler for convention."

"Where would you take me?"

"The Athenaeum."

"Not a ten-pin-bowling alley?"

"A restaurant on Piccadilly, with a live pianist."

"Better than a dead one."

135

"He plays music too."

"Set it up. I can't wait." I step out, tap on the roof and he drives off.

I can't believe what I said. Even more, I can't believe how he responded. I head inside but, before I get to my front door…

* * *

…I'm in the writing room at Walworth Nick with Kathy Bond and Albert Lavender.

We're writing notes. I flick to the front. Tue 12/1/21 1525 Cadiz St. This is madness. I'm in full uniform. High-viz jacket, belt and clobber, radio, keys to a panda. This is an arrest. Jonny Frakes. Arrested on warrant. Arresting officer? Kathy Bond. How am I involved? Flick through the pages. Lavender was driving. Kathy was operator. They saw Frakes in Cadiz Street. Knowing he's wanted on warrant they stopped him. He pulled a knife. Kathy yelled for assistance. I turned up.

Kathy, sitting opposite, is looking at me.

"Charlie, what's the friggin' problem?" Lavender, sitting next to me, is eyes down for the notes.

"Nothing. Nothing."

"Right. Well, keep up. You put the wrist lock on, right hand, yes?"

"Well. Yes."

"Kathy took the knife off him."

"Okay."

"Well write it down. What's gotten into you?"

"Too much shagging." That's Kathy.

"What?"

"You're distracted. Thinking about Wade?"

I'm piecing this arrest together. "He gave me a lift home."

"Gave you more than a friggin' lift."

"No."

"I don't care. We should of finished these notes by now."

I've got the picture. "What were you doing while Kathy and I were taking the knife off him?"

"Unscrewing his left friggin' ankle."

I finish the notes, virtually at Lavender's dictation, and excuse myself.

Lavender shouts after me. "Pull yourself together, Charlie, you're behaving like a friggin' arsehole."

Kathy's shushing him. Whatever. I'm out to the yard, into my panda and driving. Where's Wade. Don't want to use my radio. I phone him. Shouldn't be on the mobile while driving but sod it.

"Wade. Where are you?"

"Old Kent Road. Dun Cow."

"Wait there."

I'm with him a few minutes later.

"I've just lost sixteen hours."

He's calculating. "From when I dropped you off."

"Yes. Have you seen me since then?"

"Only on parade. You were posted to the panda. I was posted on foot. Haven't seen you since. Heard you respond to Kathy's shout for assistance. I was too far away."

"What was I like?"

"That woman who impersonates you."

"This isn't funny."

"I'm not being funny. You were the you on the train when we were travelling to see Doctor Slattery."

"You make it sound like I'm two different people."

His eyes shift sideways and back. He then looks down. Christ. He does think I'm two different people.

I turn and walk away but stop. There are school children running by. I feel I've just made a breakthrough. Stop. Can't think about that now. I walk back to him. "Lavender and Kathy think we slept together last night."

"We didn't."

"No messing now."

"Charlie. We didn't. I gave you a lift home. We're doing dinner. Athenaeum. Piccadilly. Remember?"

"I remember that. I got out the car and you drove off."

"Yes."

"Headed indoors."

"What happened when you got indoors?"

"Never made it. Before I got there, I'm in the writing room sixteen hours later writing notes for the Jonny Frakes arrest with Lavender and Kathy."

"You remember nothing about the arrest?"

"No."

"He had a knife. Kathy called for urgent assistance. Everybody was on way and then you cancelled all units except the van."

I know all this. I've just been doing the arrest notes. "Wade. I need you to do something for me. We've got to get you an excuse for returning to the Nick."

"I dine at six."

Wade *dines*. Everyone else *scoffs*. "Not soon enough."

Tuesday. Late afternoon. There's not much going on. Of course. School kicking out time. There'll be loads of kids loitering and drug dealers will be waiting to pounce.

Tackling this kind of situation in uniform with no intel is a bad idea but what else have I got?

"Come on." I lock the panda and stride towards the nearest school. It's not far. Loads of kids hanging about. A group of friends bantering – no good. A group, different ages, more interesting, they're friends – no good. A boy with his mum, looks like his mum – no good. Some girls teasing some boys – no good. No, wait. The girls are focussing on just one of the boys. He's loving it. One of the girls puts something in her pocket. Had he given it to her? Maybe fags. He's so distracted he hasn't seen us. No. There's more to this than bloody fags. We're forty yards away.

"Wade. The white male leaning against the railings. Trousers too short. Red socks."

"Got him."

"He's at it. When he sees us, he'll do a runner. Get ready."

Thirty yards. We couldn't be more visible. I speed up. One of the girls looks directly at me. Twenty yards. The rest of the group look round. Fifteen yards. I'm lucky, his view is obstructed by his mates, he has to lean forward to see round them. Ten yards and our eyes meet. His expression says it all and I break into a sprint. The group scatters. He stumbles over his bag as he sets off. If he'd got going, I'd never have reached him but I have him.

"What were you giving those girls?"

"Nuffin. Nuffin. I wasn't givin' 'em nuffin."

"I saw you. You gave her something. What was it?"

"I didn't give her nuffin. Leave me alone."

The other kids of that group, realising we're not after them, have come shuffling back, mobiles out, filming.

Indicating Wade, I say, "This officer's going to search you. How old are you?"

"Thirteen."

"Stop crying. Your mates are filming this. You don't want to be seen crying on YouTube."

While Wade rifles through the bag, I crowd the lad, watching his eyes, aware of his hands, ready to pounce if he pulls a knife or does a runner.

Wade's moved onto the boy's pockets and out comes a plastic Ziplock bag filled with six or seven smaller ones. Inside each of the smaller bags is what looks like a precisely measured amount of herbal cannabis.

I call for the van as Wade arrests him.

* * *

Procedurally, juveniles are a nightmare but Wade's ploughing through the admin. Cantrell's custody sergeant and has him focussing on finding appropriate adults. As there's evidence of dealing, a detective has been assigned.

The important thing is, I've got Wade into the Nick for a valid reason.

Fortunately, the writing room's empty when we finish our notes. "Right, Wade. I need you to find out exactly

140

what I've been doing since I came on duty. What calls I've dealt with. What reports I've written. Where I've been. Who I've spoken to. What reports I need to write."

"You can look all that up, no problem."

"Big problem. It'll look weird." I poke him in the chest. "This is called covering my back. I got you in here with a direct crime arrest. You've now got to do loads of checks. I need you to get those computers dancing your tune, read fast and read accurately. None of the Lavender bollocks," I scratch the side of my belly, "'sometime this after-friggin'-noon,' or Kathy Bond," I raise my arms and shimmy my breasts, "'too much detail, darling.'"

He smiles.

"It's not funny, I need precision. The stakes are high."

Wade nods and leaves. I think I've got the message across. Now, all I'm left with are feelings. There's something wrong. Not only is there something wrong, but there's something going on, on the far side of my memory, and it's sinister.

* * *

I leave Wade with the detective. I've been given a list of assignments.

One of my calls takes me up the Elephant. Halfway there, I approach a street-dweller sitting on the pavement outside Samantha's Café. His shoulder-length hair is grey, his beard patchy, clothing streaked and stained. His shoes are odd, one of them held on with a rubber band and he has no socks. Draped across his knees is a greeny-yellow sleeping bag, his possessions bulking out the bottom of it. He holds a battered cardboard cup with the few coins he's bummed and he looks up as I crouch in front of him, his eyes misty.

"How's it going, Fergus?"

"Charlie?"

"Yeah, it's me. How are you?"

"Cold."

"Come on."

He's slow but he follows me into the café, dragging his sleeping bag along behind.

"We'll be closing soon." That's the girl behind the counter.

I point Fergus to a table and approach her, bypassing the small queue. A few people are scattered around the tables. "I know what time it is," I slap a tenner onto the counter, "and you're going to put a hot meal in front of him."

"We don't want…"

I raise my hand. "Hot meal, hot drink, for him."

The girl behind the counter doesn't know what to say. An older woman comes out from the kitchen. She's hassled and fraught but stops in her tracks on seeing me.

"Samantha, isn't it?"

She nods.

"There are several things I could be talking to you about but, on this occasion, it's hot meal, hot drink, for him."

She nods.

"I'll be back in a minute. His name's Fergus."

There's a charity shop not far down the road. Ten

minutes later I'm back in the café. Fergus is tucking into a piping hot lasagne. Next to that, apple pie and custard and next to that, a mug of tea. Samantha's even put a portable heater next to him.

I lay the things I got from the charity shop on the table. "Any use for these?"

Fergus looks at the items, his eyes watery. "Bless you, Charlie." He wraps the scarf round his neck, fits the woolly hat onto his head and squeezes into the gloves, all while eating. He looks at me with a glimmer of a smile. "Not right to put socks on while eating." He takes another mouthful of lasagne. "Don't want you thinking I'm ungrateful."

I squeeze his shoulder. "I would never think that of you."

He leans over to me and whispers, "What have you got on her?" He's talking about Samantha.

I lean in, maintaining the conspiracy. "Nothing."

"But you said…"

I put my finger to my lips. "Everybody in this neighbourhood has something they don't want ol' Bill to know about. She doesn't know that I don't know what it is."

Fergus grins and tucks back into his lasagne.

I squeeze his shoulder again and stand. I look over at Samantha and nod. She knows she's been had over, but her shrug says *what the hell*.

I leave the café. There's a traffic warden standing by my panda. It might be a marked police car but it's on double yellows. "You going to give me a ticket?"

"If I did, you'd give it to your superintendent and he'd pay it from my wages."

143

"It's terrible. Us coppers just park anywhere."

"You're not setting a good example."

"I'll try harder."

She walks away laughing, "Good to see you back, Charlie."

I have calls to deal with.

* * *

The address Wade found for me is an unremarkable house in Brockley. This is my third visit. Maybe this time, bolstered by the uniform, I can get to that front door and ring the bell. Lights are on. My last call brought me over this way. "Come on, Charlie, if you're going to do it, do it. Otherwise," I bang the steering wheel with both hands. "Otherwise what?" I'm out the car, bowler on and marching towards the front door and... stop short of pressing the doorbell.

"Come on, Charlie, ring the bloody bell." Christ, if Cantrell knew I was here, she'd throw a fit. There are voices from inside, a child and a man. Sounds like bedtime.

I press the bell.

"Who's that?" the child says.

"Only one way to find out," the man says.

The door opens and the man's standing there, the boy right behind him.

I don't know what to say.

"Can I help you, officer?"

Words won't come.

"Officer?"

I take off my bowler and, with that, he recognises me. With his recognition, the words come. "Simon Drake?"

He nods.

"I'm Charlie Quinlan."

He nods again. The boy is gawping at me.

"There will come a time when we meet formally but there will be senior officers, politicians, reporters, photographers. I just wanted to say. I just wanted to," I'm faltering. The boy holding onto Simon's leg looks so… tears are coming. Looks so like him. "I just wanted to say, I'm sorry. For Madeleine and Billy. I'm sorry." I can't disguise it. I can't hold on any longer. I've lost it. My chin's wobbling. I can't trust myself to talk. I'm crying.

Simon puts a hand on my shoulder. "Thank you for coming. Would you like to come in?"

I shake my head. "I just wanted to say I tried but it wasn't enough. Sorry."

His hand is still on my shoulder and his face is kind.

I try to smile but it won't happen. I can't look at him. I can't look at the boy. I back away from them. "I'm sorry, I probably shouldn't have come."

"I'm glad you did. Thank you."

I nod, not knowing where to look. As I walk away, I hear the boy's voice. "Who was that, daddy?"

And the father's reply. "The lady who tried to save mummy and Billy. A very brave lady."

I'm across the street to my car. Without looking up, I get in, start the engine and let the door swing shut as I pull away wondering whether I went there for them or me.

Bloody silly idea. I have calls to deal with.

* * *

With my calls completed, I'm ready for the off.

Wade's finished with his juvenile who's been bailed pending a decision on prosecution.

Everybody thinks something's going on between Wade and me. Let them. Was I egging him on last night? I meant nothing by it, but I should have thought it through better. Fortunately, Wade thought it through.

Cantrell's busy handing over prisoners and, while we're all waiting for the off, Lavender entertains us with a story.

"Shouldn't speak ill of the dead, but…"

We're given the off, thank god.

"Ashes to ashes," says Wade.

"Friggin' smart-arse," says Lavender.

In the locker room, there's one of the Night Duty officers changing, hurriedly.

"Fergus is back."

"The witness?"

"The very one."

"Okay. If I see him, I'll arrange a bed. Drunk and incapable?"

"Indigestion, more like."

She laughs. "Good to see you back, Charlie. Must rush," and she scampers out.

Heading home, I realise the significance of what Wade said and divert to the Phoenix. He's reading his mobile as I walk in.

"Wade," I say as I sit down, "I feel guilty about inviting you in for a coffee last night and all that kind of invitation entails."

"You'd attract less adverse attention if you choose Kathy as an antidote to your loneliness."

"That's not fair."

"You're right because solitude isn't your problem."

Is he angry with me?

"You must see that psychiatrist."

He's annoyed. I'm not used to this kind of annoyed, calm whilst annoyed.

"Tell him everything. To manage it, you must know what it is."

"I'll be medically retired."

"I doubt that."

"How can I do this job if I'm fading in and out?"

"That's what needs managing. To do that, you need to know what the problem is. You're seeing the psychiatrist in two days, on Thursday afternoon." He hands me two sheets of paper. "Here's what you asked for." He stands up, swinging his coat over his shoulders. "I know you're putting yourself out to help me, and I'm happy to put myself out to help you. I'm sorry, but I don't think what you're asking me to do is helpful."

The sheets of paper are covered in his meticulous handwriting giving a detailed list of everything I'd done that day. By the time I look up, he's gone.

That feeling I had, that all I needed was to get back to work and the nonsense would stop; well I've got back to work and it's got worse.

CHAPTER SIXTEEN

Wednesday morning. Nothing missed. I leave the punchbag swinging, towel down and check my fridge diary. I'm getting sloppy.

10 TOG

10th January – TOGETHER.

Could have updated this on Monday before work. I was getting dressings changed. "No excuse, Charlie." I sort through the remaining magnetic letters and numerals but don't know what to say. I lost time between Wade dropping me off on Monday evening and writing notes with Kathy and Lavender on Tuesday afternoon. I should have left something last night. Too tired. Couldn't be bothered. What's the point?

Maybe Wade's right and I should record this more conventionally. I could be under surveillance and people could have been in here. "Come on, Charlie. That's so unlikely." Anyway, must get up-to-date.

Thinking about Wade, brings back the spat we had yesterday evening in The Phoenix and he's probably right about that too. Things aren't working out as expected and maybe it's time to change?

My mobile rings. Number withheld. "Hi, it's Charlie."

"John French. DS. Homicide. I interviewed you last week."

Here we go. "Hi."

"We'd like another chat about the Daventry murder. This morning?"

"Will I be arrested?"

"No. Under caution, same as before."

"Any point in asking what you want to talk about?"

"No."

"Walworth Nick?"

"If that's good for you."

"Yes. Can I have someone with me?"

"Anyone you want."

"What time."

"Ten-thirty?"

"See you then."

I hang up and call Cantrell. Voicemail. I don't leave a message. Wade's upset with me. I don't want to drag in any of the others, not even Kathy or Lavender. I'll go alone. Probably look better from the detectives' perspective. Yes. I'll go alone.

I look up at my fridge. Bugger the fridge.

* * *

DS French and DI Reeve are waiting for me.

"No company?"

The answer to Reeve's question is obvious.

French does the formalities and, we're off.

"The Crimestoppers caller. Called Thursday, 31st December, 4:33am. We played you the recording, you couldn't identify the voice and we gave you a copy. Anyone sprung to mind?"

"No."

"We've had it analysed, digitally, and compared with records we have. No match."

Here it comes.

"Except yours."

Despite expecting it, I'm still shocked. Weird how French delivered it, nonchalantly, like he doesn't believe it himself. Reeve watches.

French goes quiet, his way of saying, 'What do you say about that?'

"You're saying I called Crimestoppers and informed on myself."

"We're saying the voice that called Crimestoppers is a digital match for yours."

With that, I feel safe. The research Wade and I did, found the right answer. Digital voice identification is circumstantial evidence at best. They have no corroboration. On receiving this Lab-report, they'd have had a case review, called in lawyers and seen where they stood. If they felt they had anything, I'd now be arrested.

I'm still sitting here. They're still looking at me.

"Someone impersonating you?" That's Reeve.

French can't hide his irritation.

Reeve has just shown he doesn't get it. Or has he? I'm not comfortable. Reeve's scrutiny of me has increased. French's irritation is staged. I remember Cantrell's description of him, *top notch*.

"Last time we spoke," this is French, "you couldn't remember what you were doing for over an hour at the Elephant & Castle. Anything come back to you?"

I know exactly what I did. Do they know that Wade has accessed the CCTV? I'm suddenly very concerned for Wade and cross with myself for not insisting he tell me how he got those images. I must answer. "I've put it out of my mind. Whether I killed someone I don't know when I was somewhere else, is not a high priority for me." I'm angry. I should stop. "Why someone would tell Crimestoppers that a copper who's been paraded across national and international media is the killer, is also not a priority for me." I can't help myself. It's been boiling up inside for too long. "Over the past month, I've been through hell. I have a life to get back on track. You have a murder to investigate. I want to help. I'm duty-bound to help." I'm looking at French. "Is there anything else I can do to help *you* investigate *your* murder?"

The interview ended soon after that.

* * *

I jog over to Wyndham Road and up to the roof of Kevan House.

I sit cross-legged on my spot, rest my wrists on my knees, close my eyes and let my body go numb. There's a bell chiming, instantly recognisable as Big Ben.

I collect my thoughts.

"Hi, Joel. Much happening on your manor? I've been questioned about a murder. Twice. Can you believe that? Someone's been murdered and then someone else phones Crimestoppers saying I'm the killer. The detectives must follow it up. I haven't been arrested, just questioned under caution. Bit scary but something's not right. They're suspicious. Anyway, on the bright side. I've returned to work. Trouble is, my memory's still playing tricks on me. If I were those detectives, I'd be suspicious. Take care, Joel. Love you."

* * *

My mobile rings. Cantrell.

"It's Charlie."

"Missed your call."

On my way up the Elephant, I've stopped in Samantha's Café intending to thank her for looking after Fergus but she's not here. I'm on my second coffee.

"I was interviewed again."

"Homicide."

"Yes."

"Under arrest."

"No."

"Under caution."

"Yes."

"Charlie, I'm not in the mood for twenty-questions."

She wasn't asking questions. "I'm in Samantha's Café."

"Okay."

She knows I must be guarded about what I say so she must now ask me questions.

"They raised Crimestoppers."

"Yes."

"They've found a digital match between the caller's voice and yours."

"Yes."

"If that's all they have, you've nothing to worry about."

There's something disquieting about how she says that.

She moves on. "Facing them on your own was probs a good thing."

"Yes." How did she know I was on my own?

"You're supposed to be on a day-off. Be sure to book on duty."

"Would I get paid?"

"We'll cross-charge. Homicide can afford your overtime. Remind me and I'll sort it when we're back on Friday."

With that, she hangs up.

The way Cantrell spoke has spooked me. I swirl my remaining coffee. She seems one step ahead of the detectives.

Lavender once said Cantrell can appear knowledgeable when she isn't. He wasn't swearing.

Brings me back to my problem. How can I remember something years old with crystal clarity but can't remember anything between 11.30pm on Monday and 4pm on Tuesday?

Coffee finished, I leave a few coins in their empty tips saucer and Samantha comes in.

"Hello," she says, looking around.

"I've come to say thank you for looking after Fergus yesterday."

"That's okay," she says, not meaning it.

"Great. See you again."

"Charlie. You've done that before, bought Fergus a meal."

She deserves an explanation. "Fergus witnessed a stabbing. Gang-related. Without his evidence, the case would have collapsed. He was reluctant, so I struck up a relationship with him and gave him the confidence to come forward. He did, only to receive loads of threats. Got protection. Stood up in court. Gave his evidence. Coped well with cross-examination. All the defendants were convicted. Some lengthy sentences. Fergus was commended by the judge."

Samantha's wide-eyed. In fact, the café has gone quiet.

"Yeah," I say. "Fergus has a special place in my heart."

Samantha put a hand on my arm. "I didn't know that, Charlie. I'll be sure to keep an eye out for him in future."

"I'd appreciate that. Thank you."

I leave and head up the Elephant. The street market's in full swing. I check out the CCTV I winked at and retrace my steps.

How did Wade get the CCTV footage?

The detectives didn't mention it. If they're aware a copy's been taken, they'd have found out who took it. Wade would have been grilled. Me too. They'd be prying into the relationship between us and questioning everybody on the team. No, the detectives don't know Wade has that footage.

Wade wouldn't let me keep it. How did he get it?

I decide not to approach the Elephant security and walk home along Thurlow Street and Southampton Way.

* * *

The far side of my memory.

This is how I've come to think of it. A place I don't know, a place I can't access but a place to which I go and, when I'm there, I do things.

When I'm there, I take with me this side of my memory, evidenced by my visits to Doctor Slattery. I've set up two appointments with him on this side and gone to see him on the far side.

There's a bench set back off the pavement opposite a funeral parlour. The wind whips up damp mulchy leaves. It's peaceful here and, although it's bitterly cold, I stop.

This side of my memory, I make plans that carry through to the far side.

The far side, I take action and leave messages.

I extract the sheets of paper Wade wrote for me, listing what I'd been doing the day before. The time I turned my radio on; the time I booked out the car; the calls I dealt with; times of assignment; times of arrival; times I gave results; the time of Kathy's urgent assistance shout; the time Frakes was booked into custody; the time Cantrell authorised detention and much, much more. Wade did all this work while sorting out that juvenile. It's frightening how much of a trail is left. I know it's all there but to see it listed is eye-opening. DS French would have done this kind of trawl. He probably knows more about me than I do.

Wade and I crossed paths at parade. He acknowledged me but little more. Compiling that list was a lot of work for him. I don't think he objects to doing the work, he's objecting to *having* to do it.

Probably explains why he was short with me at the Phoenix last night.

The cold's getting to my hands. I wrap them in my scarf. Another gust of wind lifts another flight of leaves.

"Do not follow."

That voice doesn't surprise me now. It's the same voice as the one that said *Trust* and *Together*.

I recognise it and accept it. It could be a sound stirred up by the swirling wind but it isn't. It's too clear, too definite and, another thing, that sliding sensation came with the words. I'd put it down to standing up too fast but, this time, I haven't stood up and I still got those same weird sensations. The dizziness came with the words.

I have a piece of evidence that would move Homicide's investigation into the Daventry murder forward significantly.

That voice I heard is the voice that called Crimestoppers.

CHAPTER SEVENTEEN

I've lost more time.

I was on Southampton Way outside the funeral parlour. It was mid-afternoon. Now it's ten in the evening and I'm looking at a message left on my fridge.

13 PETROL MC RD

MC, not Mary Cantrell, the station code for Camberwell so, Camberwell Road.

This isn't fazing me anymore. Last entry was:

10 TOG

The two previous entries were crap too.

I remember updating the fridge, giving up on it more like, when I got the call from DS French. I attended the interview, checked in with Joel, went to Samantha's Café, went up the Elephant and, walking home, stopped opposite the funeral parlour on Southampton Way.

Okay, so I've lost seven hours and during that time I'm left a message from the far side of my memory telling me I went to the service station on Camberwell Road for petrol.

I check and my car's petrol tank is full. The receipt, pay at pump £34.16 13/01/21 16:33, is in my wallet. The Camberwell Road service station is well covered by CCTV.

I jump into my car and head over to see Wade. Hope he's in.

* * *

He is.

"I've lost more time. A message was left. I filled my car at the Camberwell Road service station at 16:33."

Wade takes my coat.

"This is like the Elephant cash-machine. I need that CCTV."

"I'll see what I can do."

"I need it now."

He looks away.

"You didn't get that Elephant CCTV footage through normal channels and you left no trace. Do it again."

He doesn't move.

"Please."

"What's happened, Charlie?"

"I need to see that CCTV."

"It's risky."

"I need to see what happened. How busy it was. Whether I went into the shop."

"Last time, you trusted your intuition and you were spot on. You've determined that I'm hacking into the CCTV systems but it's not without risk. What's happened?"

This is where I involve Wade. At this point he moves from concerned friend to accomplice. If he's got any sense, he'll arrest me and contact French.

"I've corroborating evidence for the digital voice match." There. I've done it. He's in. Will he arrest me?

He says, "Go on."

"I hear a voice. Sounds like the Crimestoppers

caller."

His eyes flick to the side and back. "Audible corroboration for the digital match."

I nod.

"The corroboration being an imaginary voice." He lets go my hand.

Is he going to arrest me? This *is* murder.

"Sounds like I could arrest you."

He could.

He continues, "For what? Exactly?"

"Well, anything from interfering with a murder investigation, suspicion of murder, aiding and abetting…"

He holds up his hand. "Aiding and abetting? What? Murder? Let's work it through. I drag you into the custody suite at Streatham Nick, tell the custody sergeant you're involved in the Daventry murder currently being investigated by Homicide. New evidence has come to light that you're hearing a voice in your head that sounds like the Crimestoppers caller who says that hero cop Charlie Quinlan did it while she was five miles away drawing money out of a cash-machine. How do I know that? Well, she told me. They wouldn't just switch you across to the Mental Health Act, I'd be sectioned too."

He has a point.

"Look, Charlie," he takes hold of my hand again. "If I was with you when you heard this voice, could I have recorded it?"

"I don't know."

"Would I have heard it?"

"I don't know. It sounds real to me."

"A voice you hear in your head could not have made a phone call."

"Something's there, Wade, on the far side of my memory, doing stuff and leaving messages."

"Charlie, I've read everything I can find about these episodes you're experiencing and I keep coming back to dissociative fugue. There's Dissociative Identity Disorder but that's a way of coping with prolonged and sustained childhood trauma. You need to speak with that psychiatrist and you need to speak with him on this side of your memory."

Do I tell him about Travis Hendry's sadism? "Will you go for me? Tomorrow, 3pm?" Travis Hendry's off limits.

"What? How can I do that?"

"Because I won't be there."

"What do you mean?"

"The service station on Camberwell Road. Same MO as the cash-machine at the Elephant. Someone else has been killed. There'll be another call to Crimestoppers. That caller will be the same as the last caller. She'll implicate me and, with that, the detectives will have enough. They won't invite me in for a helpful chat. I'll be arrested."

"There isn't a case."

"It's enough for an arrest. That DI Reeve raised impersonation. He doesn't know me. DS French showed irritation but I'm sure it was an act. They're suspicious and searching for a way in."

Wade's attentive.

"The first time they interviewed me, they had a team of detectives at their disposal. That team must have been re-assigned. Reeve and French are suspicious and, although I haven't allayed their suspicions, they can't convince their seniors to move resources onto their line of investigation."

Wade's keeping up.

"Whoever's in charge of the squad has spread whatever resource there is over several leads. With another murder, same weird circumstances, same name popping up, my name, and I won't just have the attentions of a DS and a rubber-heeler in purple-tinted specs, I'll get the Full Monty. You must see Doctor Slattery for me."

He squeezes my hand. "You're serious."

I squeeze his hand back. "It's inevitable, Wade. I don't know any of this but I feel it. You said earlier I should trust my intuition because the hacking's too risky. I don't know what it is. It's not certainty, or fact, it's there as a feeling. Maybe it's leaking from the far side of my memory."

"Charlie. This is, I can't think of the word."

"Don't try."

"How will I know if you've been nicked? They might hold you incommunicado."

"Heaven forbid I talk to myself."

"This isn't funny."

"No, but it's real. Please. Do this for me. Go see Doctor Slattery. If I'm there, great. If not, well, enough said." I prise my hand from his and retrieve my coat. As I zip it up, he stands in front of me. "Do this for me?"

"I'll do it for you."

I step forward and push my forehead into his chest.

"Promise."

I feel his arms encircle me and I close my eyes.

"I promise," he says.

I feel his warmth. "I'm scared, Wade."

He holds me tighter.

Enough. I push him away. I don't know where to look. I sniff. I can't speak. I'm through his door and heading towards my car. I feel I'll never see him again.

CHAPTER EIGHTEEN

Driving home, waiting at a junction, I could turn either way.

Turning right would take me south, away from my inevitable arrest.

The driver behind toots. I turn left.

Next junction. The temptation to run is strong. What would I be running from? The detectives? The murder? The alibi? The Crimestoppers call? Myself?

Running is pointless. My car would soon be on the ANPR database and there'd be a *ping* every time I pass a camera. My credit and debit cards would give me away.

The driver behind is gesticulating. I raise my hand and head home.

Where would I be running to?

I haven't killed anyone. Looks like I'm involved though. The detectives think I am. How and to what extent? I won't find out by running. They'll be waiting outside my flat. Oh, god. Run, run, away, away. Come on, Charlie. You can live off the grid. No, not a chance. What am I thinking? I've done nothing wrong.

Another junction.

I push my forehead onto the steering wheel. Head home. It's going to be bad. Kathy said I'm not facing up. Don't think she meant this kind of facing up.

They're probably already behind me. They'll want to search my place. It's easier for them if they arrest me there. There's nothing in my flat I don't want them to see. Yes there is. SHIT.

As I turn into my road, I plug my mobile's earbuds into my ears.

Hope they're not waiting for me in my stairwell. As I pull into my parking area, there's movement. Car doors opening. That'll be them. They're not in my stairwell, thank god.

I'm out and walking fast. Head down, sorting my keys, no looking up. Made it to my front door. First lock, open. Second lock, open. There's movement in the stairwell. Third lock, open. "Charlie Quinlan?" A voice, female. I'm in. I swing my front door shut but it's been jammed. Kitchen, scramble the magnetic letters and open the fridge door.

I'm holding a carton of juice and a woman is in my hall. Did she see me scrambling the letters? "What the hell." I try to sound indignant.

"Charlie Quinlan?" Her voice is not threatening.

I pull the earbuds from my ears.

"Charlie Quinlan?" she says again.

I put the carton back and close the fridge door. TOG has survived but, importantly, PETROL MC RD has gone. There's a PSY and another one, sort of.

Making a play of fiddling with my mobile, I say, "That's me. I'm Charlie Quinlan."

DS John French appears next to her. "This time, Charlie, I'm arresting you for the murder of Peter Daventry, Primrose Hill, Wednesday 30th December."

He cautions me. I say nothing. "And," he's continuing, "for the murder of Vincent Pope, Wembley, today." He cautions me again and takes hold of my arm. I say nothing, again. Two more men have come in. Neither of them is DI Reeve. I'm brought through to the living room.

French indicates the woman who first spoke to me, "This officer's going to search you. Then we'll search your flat and your car. You know the score."

I nod. The two men have boxes and bags.

I hold out my arms and the female detective searches me. She then opens my shoulder bag. After a brief look inside, she kneels and spreads a large exhibits bag on the floor, upends my bag and spreads out the contents. Nothing eye-catching. They'll go through it thoroughly back at the Nick. She bags it all and seals it except for my keys which she places in a separate bag and doesn't seal.

One of the male detectives starts near my telly while the other starts by photographing the magnetic letters on the fridge and those that have dropped on the floor.

The guy in the kitchen is emptying my fridge. He even finds my sieve and empties the carton of juice through it, finding nothing but juicy bits. Fridge, drawers and cupboards, everything out and everything back. Even the oven, washing machine and dishwasher. Nothing sparks his interest.

French has positioned me where I can see both the detective in the kitchen and the detective searching my living room. French stands beside me and the female detective stands at the front door. She shuffles the shoes on my shoe rack.

I've done what these detectives are doing many times. Although I keep an eye on them, I turn my thoughts inward. Driving here from Wade's, I was panicking. Now, I'm calm. I've seen this before, particularly after pursuits. It's not like resignation, more that the circumstances have moved from complete chaos to orderliness. The problems haven't gone away but the madness is over. Back in my car, I was tempted to do a runner and I decided against because I wasn't in control. Now, I'm being controlled and something's changed inside. Not only have I been arrested but the far side of my memory has been arrested too.

"Something amusing you?" DS French is watching me.

I shake my head.

The detective in the living room, having finished before the detective in the kitchen, waits patiently before we all move to the bedrooms. French positions me where I can see both bedrooms and the bathroom. The male detectives take a bedroom each. The female detective takes the bathroom. The detective in my spare bedroom is not only quick but also manages to say nothing. The one in my main bedroom boxes up my computer stuff and anything digital. The one in my bathroom is removing the bath panel.

Finally, before leaving, they handcuff me. They're kind, cuffing me to the front. The female detective uses the keys from the unsealed exhibits bag and locks the door.

Out to my car and she unlocks it. They search it but nothing interests them. She locks the car and seals all the keys in the exhibits bag. She gives me a knowing little smile. I give her a knowing little smile back.

Neighbours are looking and I don't care.

I've been arrested for murder, two counts, and the chaos has stopped.

* * *

I don't think they can take me to Walworth. I couldn't stand being where everyone knows me. Handcuffs. Banged up in a cell. Would coming clean about my memory problems have changed anything?

Thank god. It's not Walworth, we're heading north.

I'm in the back of one of their cars with the female detective. French is driving. The other two are in the car behind.

I try to relax but can't. I settle back into the seat, rest my head against the window and people-watch. We're passing Big Ben, it's well past midnight. A woman, head down, walks fast away from a man while he watches. Two lads, one looks like he's helping the other throw up. I shift back to my own predicament. I tried to find out what's going on but failed. I focussed on myself. Should I have focussed on Peter Daventry?

We're heading through the West End.

All I know of Peter Daventry is what Wade found out from his journalist friend. Never heard of Vincent Pope.

I focus on the procedures. They didn't need to arrest me now, they could have waited till morning. They're wasting time. Whatever. I can't second-guess them.

Do they know I went to see Wade?

They'll be focussing everything they've got onto determining the relationship between Daventry and Pope.

I've lost track of where we are. Somewhere up north of The City.

French said Vincent Pope was killed today but no specific time. Bet it was around four-thirty. 16:33 was the time on the receipt from the Camberwell Road service station. They have that receipt. How soon after 16:33 was Vincent Pope's body discovered? Any call to Crimestoppers by my mystery caller must have been before 10pm when I found myself displaced from Southampton Way and in my kitchen looking at my fridge with the message:

13 PETROL MC RD

What will I do?

"Play the game."

Ah. There she is, my mystery caller. The detective next to me hasn't reacted. French hasn't reacted. It really is in my head.

We're here, Islington Police Station, and the chaos is resuming.

CHAPTER NINETEEN

The Islington custody sergeant is tall and slim and, judging by his pasty skin, looks like he's never left the custody suite. He's looking at his screen, probably a custody record.

The wall clock says 01:23.

Eventually the custody sergeant looks at DS French, a kind of, *can't you see I'm busy?* type look. The look we get from Cantrell on bringing arrests into her. French, pretending to be unimpressed by the custody sergeant's demeanour, explains why he's arrested me while the custody sergeant pretends to be unimpressed too.

"30th December, Peter Daventry died, Primrose Hill, suspicious circumstances, followed by an anonymous call to Crimestoppers naming Charlie Quinlan the killer. Today, Vincent Pope died, Wembley, in suspicious circumstances. His death was followed by a call to Crimestoppers naming Charlie Quinlan the killer. This is Charlie Quinlan."

The custody sergeant says nothing.

French continues. "Both calls were made before news of the deaths reached the public domain and the caller's voice and Charlie's are a digital match. I've arrested her to investigate her involvement in the two deaths."

The custody sergeant sighs.

French continues. "Charlie Quinlan is a serving police officer. Walworth."

The custody sergeant looks at me. "I'm authorising your detention so these officers can interview you. Search her, please." The clock says 01:29. He turns to French and says condescendingly, "You won't be interviewing her until after nine."

"I understand that," French says condescendingly back.

A Designated Detention Officer, Deirdre according to her name badge, searches me, piling what little stuff I have left on the counter while the custody sergeant calls the solicitor I requested and a doctor. My dressings present a risk.

Fifteen minutes go by during which nothing happens. Quiet night.

Then an elderly gent with a briefcase and a stethoscope sticking out of his pocket comes in. The custody sergeant points at me and says, "Fitness to detain and fitness for interview. The dressings on her hands cover burns." He points at the DDO. "She'll stay with you until we know there's nothing concealed in those dressings."

The clock says 02:03 as I go with the doctor and DDO into the surgeon's room. The doctor says only those words necessary to do what he has to do.

When the doctor's finished wrapping my hands up. like a mummy, the DDO takes me out and ushers me down the cell corridor. It's 02:17. Everybody's so polite. Arrested coppers are treated like royalty though the smells can't, I'm sure, be associated with a royal palace – an intermingling of sweat, puke, piss and shit.

Then there are the sounds. I've heard the despair sound many times but never been on the receiving end of it. I'm reminded of Lavender's *Introduction to Custody Suites* lecture from when I was first posted after initial training. "Cell doors are friggin' serious. Best not to get your fingers caught in them. As for the wicket," he said sliding the little head-height hatch in the door back and forth, "everybody catches their fingers in them at least once. When it happens to you, don't whinge about it. It's written in the DDO's job description. DDO? Designated Detention Officer, or gaoler for short. Somebody achieved ACPO rank for coming up with that TLA. ACPO? Association of Chief Police Officers. TLA? Three Letter Acronym. Friggin' 'ell, keep up. Where was I? Oh, yeah. Prisoners spit so, when you open the wicket, stand to the side. We have every kind of hepatitis going – A, B, C. Ummm. D. Yep, E and we might even have a bit of hepatitis friggin' F. So stand to the side when you open the wicket. Prisoners spit." One of the more memorable health and safety training sessions. Lavender hadn't stopped there. "Now we come to the cell door. I don't know how heavy it is, I suppose I should of looked it up, but I couldn't be arsed. Anyway, it's friggin' serious. You can tell because of the three sounds it makes. First is despair, the sound it makes when it shuts. Second is hope, the sound it makes when it opens. Third is frustration, the sound it makes when it's doing nothing at all and whoever's inside is kicking the friggin' shit out of it."

Now, I've experienced the despair sound for real. I curl up as small as I can manage as far from the door as possible.

I cover my ears and squeeze my eyes tight. My mummy-dressings don't baffle the sound of my breath and heart. Thinking of Lavender has made me tearful. I wish he was here. He wouldn't be able to help but just having someone I know who's on my side would mean so much. Doesn't need to be Lavender, could be Kathy or any of them. Wade. He's come to mean a lot to me. He'll be seeing Doctor Slattery tomorrow at 3pm as I won't be released in time.

Come on. Breathe. In for four, out for six.

They won't come for me until morning. I'll be visited hourly by the DDO. I've got anywhere between six and eight hours to wait.

"Sleep now."

There she is, the voice in my head that sounds so familiar. The voice of the Crimestoppers caller.

"Sleep now."

Again. Not a spoken voice. A voice that's so me but not me. The voice that brings on a dizziness, even though I'm sitting, curled up, not moving. I'm going mad. The tanker incident has broken me. I'm fragments splashing and tinkling on an echoing surface that's neither up nor down. My eyes see water and my ears hear sand. Waves crashing in a still underlit cavern. My heart booms and my breathing rasps.

I'm up and punching the alarm. Minutes pass. I press the alarm again.

Footsteps in the cell corridor. My wicket slides back. It's my DDO. "Charlie. You, better than anyone, know the score in here. Why have you called?"

She's nice, patient, fortyish. Dark hair tied back. She's experienced. "Deirdre…"

"Please, call me Dee."

It's quiet except for the frustrated banging of a cell door along the corridor.

"Dee, I don't want any favours but I do want company. Do you have any female prisoners?"

Dee looks sideways, back down the corridor towards the charge room. She looks back to me. "We do, but there's no justification for doubling up."

"What if we both consent?"

Dee looks sideways again. The custody sergeant's probably there giving Dee her answers. She looks back. "It's a no, Charlie. If circumstances change then maybe."

"What's Islington like on a Thursday night?"

"We need another fifteen prisoners before we can even consider doubling up. It's cold tonight. The streets are dead."

"Will you sit with me?"

"You know I can't."

I bow my head and turn away. A floating bowling ball hovers.

"Charlie." Dee beckons me over. I step up to the wicket. She whispers conspiratorially. "That other female prisoner. Mad."

She moves back. I resist the temptation to grab the wicket as she shuts it. The bowling ball plummets, never landing.

* * *

"Sleep now."

"Seems like you're the only companion I'll get." It's

about three. The duty solicitor will turn up around nine.

"Sleep now."

"Okay. Okay." That dizziness feels more like sliding. The bench has a mattress, a blanket and a pillow. At the other end of the bench is the toilet. I go for a pee. The loo-roll's nearly finished. I lie back on the mattress. I'm growing numb to the frustrated banging of a cell door down the corridor. I can hear snoring from a neighbouring cell. I must sleep. My safety's not in question so why am I frightened?

I lie on my back looking at the ceiling. It's warm. I close my eyes.

I don't need to think about my morning meetings, conversations and interviews. What I will need to be is, alert. I must sleep. I control my breathing – in for four, out for six.

I still have all my clothing. They don't see a need to connect me to the scene. Indeed, they didn't take any samples.

Stop thinking about it. Sleep now.

I relax. I feel my body flattening down onto the mattress, let my hands turn palm upwards, let my feet roll outwards. Poor Wade. I've dragged him into all this but, fairness to him, he's showing remarkable aptitude.

Just as I feel myself drifting, I think I must be falling asleep and I'm awake again. Wade will cope. I let the thoughts go and I drift. I think of the floating bowling ball.

CHAPTER TWENTY

"Charlie. Rise and shine."

Deirdre's face is framed in the wicket which grates shut and the door swings outwards.

"You slept well."

Charlie would answer with a sarcastic *and you I trust* but not me. "I did, thank you. Is the solicitor here?"

"He's seeing someone else. You're next. Ten, fifteen minutes. You have time for a wash. Follow me." She looks at me in that *something is wrong* kind of way but dismisses it, putting it down to being dog-tired as she should have gone off duty by now.

The washroom is at the end of the cell corridor. I remove the dressings from my hands and strip right down while the basin fills with lukewarm water. I splash it over my face and body, taking the soap I am offered and, after more splashing, take the towel, dry myself and dress.

I hand the towel back to Deirdre in exchange for a toothbrush. She is still looking strangely at me. After brushing my teeth, I smile at her. "You should have gone home by now?"

"My relief's gone sick. They're organising cover."

Judging by the way she is relaxing, I think that worked but maybe just a little more. "You must be knackered."

"I am. There's time for breakfast before you see the solicitor."

"Whatever comes to hand." She has dismissed any weird feelings she had, associating them with tiredness. "Charge room or cell?"

Deirdre is finishing off clearing up the wash area. "We're still sorting out the morning court run so, cell, if you don't mind."

If I don't mind?

"Shouldn't be too long," she says, handing me cereal and closing the door as quietly as possible with a resounding slam.

Shouldn't be too long. One of Charlie's frequently used phrases. I sit on the bench and eat my cereal thinking about meeting the solicitor. I am not sure how to handle that, to be honest. Probably best to leave him to do his bit while I act scared and concerned.

Then I'll be interviewed by Humpty and Dumpty and they already have as much as I want them to have. Charlie is so much better than me at that because she can think more quickly on her feet but she does tend to get sarcastic and gobby. It is finely balanced. Right now, I need to be in control.

Deirdre is true to her word. "The solicitor's ready for you," she says, opening my cell door.

A new custody sergeant is in the charge room and the wall clock shows 08:48.

The door bangs open and in come the two detectives, Humpty and Dumpty.

"Seen your brief yet?" Humpty of Homicide.

Dumpty of DPS is watching me through his purple-tinted spectacles.

"Follow me." Deirdre.

In the interview room is a balding man in a suit who introduces himself, handing me a business card which I put in my back pocket. We sit.

"Okay. You've been arrested regarding two deaths and you've been…"

"I know."

"…in detention now for…"

"I know what they arrested me for and when. They will interview me and then release me on bail pending further enquiries. Then I will be suspended. It is inevitable."

"But…"

I lean back, pull the door open and shout, "Ready." Not sure I succeeded at sounding scared and concerned.

* * *

I am curious why Dumpty, the DPS DI, is assisting Humpty, the Homicide DS, as it would usually be a DC. Cantrell rates Dumpty highly but he has contributed little.

We arrange ourselves so the solicitor is next to me and Humpty and Dumpty opposite. They are using audio and video and Humpty is going through the pre-interview procedure, rigmarole more like.

They think they are talking to Charlie and I must ensure they continue thinking that. Dumpty's comment about impersonation was too close for comfort. Now I really must impersonate Charlie. Contractions are her thing.

"On Wednesday 30th December, Peter Daventry died on Primrose Hill. What do you know about that?"

Easy one. "Nothing."

"Do you know anyone called Peter Daventry?"

"No." Charlie would have added *told you that last time*. No. She might have said that last time but now? Under arrest? She would be more disciplined. Humpty and Dumpty would understand that.

"We have relevant CCTV images. Would you like to amend your previous answer?"

"No."

"We believe the CCTV images include you."

Difficult not to respond but, something I have picked up from Charlie is to only respond to questions.

"Why would those CCTV images include you?"

And if they do ask a question, keep the answers short, though Charlie slips sometimes. "They don't."

"Why do you say that?"

"Because," I lean forward, "I've never been to Primrose Hill."

"What were your movements that Wednesday?"

What would Charlie say? *I've explained all this in previous interviews.* No. Not under arrest. "I've nothing to add to what I've said previously."

"All in good time." Humpty.

Interesting. Humpty's comment is out of sequence. Deliberate? An attempt to disorientate me? Maybe they have not wasted eight hours of custody time. They think that Charlie, being quite gobby, has difficulty holding back when annoyed, so stressing her with a night in a cell means she would be more likely to slip and give them something they so desperately need. Trouble is, they are not talking to Charlie, they are talking to me.

"Thursday, 31st December, about 4.30am, where were you and what were you doing?"

I shake my head in fake ignorance. "Probably at home, asleep."

"At that time, a telephone call was made to Crimestoppers. What do you know about that?"

"Only what you've told me."

"Yesterday, Vincent Pope was found dead at his home. What do you know about that?"

"Nothing."

"Do you know anyone called Vincent Pope?"

"No."

"Where were you and what were you doing?"

"When?"

"Yesterday afternoon and evening."

So, they do not have an exact time of death. "Went for a drive."

"Where?"

"Dulwich Park. Took a walk and had coffee in the café. Stopped for petrol on the way home and, later on, went to see a friend. On returning home, you were there."

"Did you make any phone calls?"

"No."

"So you didn't phone your friend to see if she was in before you left."

She? They do not know about Wade.

"You didn't make any phone calls."

More non-questions but I must be careful about not

saying anything as it could be taken for agreeing with them. The word has slipped my mind but I will stay quiet for the moment and wait for a question.

"Detective Sergeant French, have you a question for my client? Wouldn't want you thinking she's acquiescing."

Ah, my solicitor has not fallen asleep though I would not blame him if he had. Anyway, acquiescence is the word and the solicitor has dealt with it.

Humpty shows no emotion. He is very good.

"Did you make any phone calls yesterday?"

Fishing. "No."

"Did you make any phone calls other than from your phone?"

Boring. "No."

"I'm playing a recording of a telephone call made to Crimestoppers yesterday at eighteen-forty-seven. Exhibit JF7." He takes out and manipulates a small device. Not so slap-dash.

"You're through to Crimestoppers. How can I help?

"Murder this afternoon. Wembley. Charlie Quinlan."

"How do you…"

The line goes dead and the recording stops.

Humpty re-sets the device. "Do you recognise the caller?"

"No."

"You seem very sure."

I know exactly who the caller is and, despite Humpty's lack of question, it is worth reasserting my last answer. "I don't recognise the caller."

"Your voice is the same as the caller's voice. What do you say about that?"

"I didn't call Crimestoppers so it can't be my voice."

He waits, using the silence to provoke me into explaining why the voice sounds different to mine. He will be waiting a long time.

"Does sound like you." Humpty is back to making observations. "Bit of an Irish twang in there, don't you think?"

"If you say so."

"The first call, about the Primrose Hill death, was more South London."

No need to speak.

"Both calls were made by the same person."

So, they are going digital but, again, no need to speak.

"And the person who made those calls has the same voice as you."

Another observation so this must be the only evidence they have. My plan is working.

"All three voices, Daventry's caller, Pope's caller and your voice, are a digital match."

Humpty is running out of things to say and I cannot see exactly where Dumpty's eyes are behind those purple-tinted spectacles. I look up slightly and stare at his receding hairline and, wow, that did it. He has looked away.

"Detective Sergeant French, what exactly are you accusing my client of?" Solicitor.

Humpty doesn't answer.

Charlie is stirring so I better put an end to this. I grate my chair backwards, fold my arms and stare down at the floor where a stain, probably blood, has never been successfully cleaned.

The interview ends and I am escorted back to my cell.

* * *

That's nice.

Comfortable. Warm.

No it's not. I'm in a police cell. Suddenly wide awake. How can this be happening?

The wicket slides open. I sit up. The door opens. It's a new sergeant. They'll be wanting to get me ready for the solicitor and interview.

"Follow me," the sergeant says.

I go with him and stand at his counter. The clock says 11:32. That's late. The door bangs open and DI Reeve comes in but, instead of being followed by DS French, he's followed by a superintendent in uniform.

"Charlie Quinlan," the custody sergeant is presenting me with bail forms, "I'm releasing you on police bail…"

What? They haven't interviewed me yet.

The sergeant's still talking, a three-week bail date. February. A DDO empties a plastic bag with my property over the counter.

The sergeant's finished and is holding out a pen for me to sign.

"Where's my mobile?"

"We're keeping that."

"My computer stuff?"

"We're keeping that too."

"And you're letting me go."

"What I said."

Something's very wrong. They haven't interviewed me. I haven't seen a solicitor. Or have I?

Oh, god.

I search my pockets and find a business card. A solicitor. I've lost more time and the time I've lost has been a meeting with the solicitor. What else?

I show the business card to the custody sergeant. "Is the solicitor still here?"

"Nah. Left after your interview."

So, I've been interviewed.

Oh, god.

The custody sergeant's finished with me.

"Over here," DI Reeve says. I follow him into an interview room and I'm followed in by the superintendent whereupon I'm duly suspended, warrant card taken and told I can't meet with any of my colleagues. This was inevitable but I still feel like I've been punched in the guts.

Within minutes, I'm ushered out of Islington Police Station, a civilian.

CHAPTER TWENTY-ONE

I can make my three-o'clocker with Doctor Slattery but I don't know how to contact Wade to cancel him. All my contact information's on my mobile.

I'm in a coffee shop wondering whether I should curb my spending. Might lose my job. Least of my worries. Latte, extra shot.

Sitting with that latte, I feel the impact of what's happened to me. Arrested for murder. Interviewed. Bailed. Suspended. I don't know how to contact Kathy or Lavender. Not even Cantrell. I could phone Walworth Nick from a telephone kiosk but, god, how does one of those work?

Which is worse? Arrest for murder or losing time?

An elderly gent sits opposite me. He holds a book but stares into space. His eyes speak a lifetime but his face is flat.

The couple near him are pretending not to look at me. Not surprising. How can I see Doctor Slattery looking and smelling like this?

I must get home to smarten up but Harley Street's only a couple of miles down the road. It's gone one and I haven't got time to get home and back.

He'll have to put up with me as I am.

Latte finished, I go to the toilet but my attempts to

smarten up are futile. All I see is this mess of a person in the mirror.

I remember nothing of the interview. I don't know who interviewed me though I can guess. Nor do I know what was said.

I get another latte and a panini and sit back where I was.

The couple have gone and the elderly gent is extracting himself from his seat. He's up but he can't negotiate the tables and chairs. His right leg is stuck and he's looking down and concentrating. I move to help but his leg comes free and, as he limps away, he nods at me, his eyes appreciative, his expression flat. He leaves and I watch his rolling gait receding along the pavement. Tears are in my eyes and I grab a napkin. It was his face, his expression. He didn't show any stress, annoyance or frustration. He has a problem. He doesn't let it upset him, he just figures out how to deal with it and moves on.

That's what I must do. I've got a problem. I won't be able to figure it out if I let it upset me. That gent's problem is physical and mine's mental. The first part of figuring it out is understanding the problem. Doctor Slattery can help me do that but I can't meet him. The far side of my memory has taken over for every appointment with Doctor Slattery. I must break that.

I leave the coffee shop and head west. Kings Cross is half-a-mile. I run. Running calms me. The faster I run, the calmer I feel. In less than ten minutes, I reach W H Smiths on the concourse at Kings Cross. There's a post box just outside. Paper. Envelopes. Stamps. One thing I do remember is Doctor Slattery's Harley Street address. His business card has been pinned to my bedroom wall for long enough. Pen in my bag. The run has settled me, breathing steady, expression blank.

> Dr Slattery,
> I haven't met you on this side of my memory.
> HELP.
> Charlie Quinlan
> 14 Jan 21 13:43

I write the address on the envelope. Affix a stamp but, as I'm walking towards the post box, my legs go. I feel myself falling but not just to the ground.

A woman comes over, "Are you okay?"

"Please post this. Please."

"Oh, don't worry about that. You've had a nasty fall."

"No, post this. Please." I'm pushing the letter into her hand.

"Dear. Dear." She's kneeling on the ground next to me, her arm around my shoulders.

A man has stopped. "Do we need an ambulance?"

* * *

"No. No ambulance. This has happened before. I have an appointment with my doctor this afternoon but thank you for your concern. I am fine, really." I take the letter back from the woman.

"Are you sure? You were in quite a state, my dear." Woman

"I feel fine. Honestly." I look at the post box and down at the letter. That was close.

"So, we don't need an ambulance." Man.

"No, no. I am so sorry for disrupting your day and causing alarm."

The man leaves.

"You've made a remarkable recovery." Woman.

"Sometimes I surprise myself. I do have a condition and I will raise this episode with my doctor." I swing my bag over my shoulder and, with a little smile for the kind woman, I walk away.

It has gone two. I want to get to Harley Street before Wade so I walk fast.

If Charlie had got that letter into the post box, everything would have been ruined.

* * *

"I know I am early but may I wait?"

"Of course, Charlie." Beverley is sweet but predictable.

No one is waiting and there is no sign of Wade.

I sit on a leather sofa and flick through a magazine. At two-forty, a smart man comes down the stairs from the direction of Doctor Slattery's room and walks straight out. Maybe he was the patient before me.

At two-forty-five, the buzzer goes, the door clicks open and in comes Wade.

"I've come to sit with Charlie," Wade.

"Of course," Beverley.

Wade sits next to me and takes my hand.

I look down and back up.

He lets go and shifts along to the other end of the sofa. I doubt my appearance is repelling him so he must recognise that something is wrong, different, weird even. Has he figured it out?

"They kept my mobile," I say. "I could not cancel you, so sorry to have caused you a wasted journey."

"I'm happy to stay."

"No need for you to stay."

"Well, you know, just in case."

How am I going to say this without Beverley hearing? "Wade, without my mobile I…" Lucky break, Beverley's desk phone rings and she answers. I lower my voice. "On arriving home last night, I was arrested. Another murder. Wembley. Another incriminating call to Crimestoppers. They have found a digital match between the Crimestoppers callers and me. My mobile and computer has been retained in police possession. I was interviewed, released on police bail pending further enquiries with a three-week bail date and suspended."

"Why don't you tell me all about it over dinner. I've booked the Athenaeum for this evening."

"Wade. If you meet a person on bail, you must file a report."

"I know. You can tell me you're on bail after dinner."

"Charlie." Beverley is smiling at me and pointing up the stairs.

I acknowledge her. "I am hungry," I say to Wade. "Prince Regent pub, Marylebone High Street. Meet you there around four. We can then go to the restaurant." With that, I run up the stairs for Charlie's three-o'clocker with Doctor Slattery.

* * *

"Hello Doctor. Are you happy?" I take my seat.

"Yes, thank you, Charlie. You?"

"No. There are three things making me unhappy. One, I am not getting any…" I stop. Wade has distracted me. Doctor Slattery has spoken with Charlie on the phone a couple of times. I have imitated Charlie during earlier appointments and I must maintain that. Doctor Slattery is smart and I do not want his suspicions aroused. I must talk like Charlie. I find a tissue in my bag and blow my nose. "Excuse me. Where was I? Oh, yeah. Three reasons. One, I'm not benefitting from our sessions. Two, I'm not happy about coming here. Three, I'm not happy the Job's wasting money on this."

"Very methodical."

"Sorry. Four reasons. Four, I'm not happy with your smartarse observations on everything I say. Next, you'll be commenting on everything I don't say." This would be so much easier if I could be myself but I need to extract us from this cycle of appointments. Currently, Charlie is driving the appointments. If she had succeeded in posting that letter, Doctor Slattery would be driving them and that would be disastrous. I cannot afford to have him growing suspicious.

"You're very angry."

"There you go again."

"Would you prefer if I asked a question?"

"You just have. It would be better than me trying to second-guess what you want me to say." Yes. Sharp, but not so blatantly rude.

Doctor Slattery looks at me. Unlike Dumpty, his all-encompassing scrutiny is not intrusive. He is about forty, wearing a dull grey suit with purple socks. From purple-tinted spectacles to purple socks.

We sit in Alice in Wonderland chairs. One side of the room is bookshelves crammed with books. A coffee table is off-set leaving nothing between us, no barriers. Do people really fall for this? Last time there was coffee. This time, no coffee.

Behind him is his desk. Behind that, his window and outside, a leafless tree.

"Here's a question, what's upset you today?"

What can I say? Arrested for murder? Mobile and computers retained? Slept in a stinking cell? Interviewed by detectives? Turning up for this appointment in dirty clothes looking a mess? "The way I'm talking to you. That's upsetting me."

"You're being quite aggressive. Don't worry on my account but I would like to know what's rattled you."

Great. I have brought it back down. I can be more myself. "I have thoughts I can't get out of my head. The main one is *why I'm coming?*"

"Why do you think you're coming?"

"I think it's what everyone expects. Big traumatic incident. Painful injuries. Horrific memories. Everybody thinks I should be a mess. I'm getting into a mess about not being a mess."

"You said you were going to resume work on Monday. I wrote a letter to your CMO supporting that. Did you resume?"

"Yes. Late Turn, afternoon shift, and thank you for your support."

"How did it go?"

"Fine. Sergeant Cantrell, I think you know her…"

"Spoken with her on the phone, never met her."

Wow. He interrupted me so, good, more conversational which, I think, is what I want. Means I am less of a concern for him? No. Doctor Slattery is smart and he knows exactly what he has done. He is lulling me into a false sense of security so I must not let my guard slip, not for a second. Difficult enough having to talk like Charlie and I cannot afford for him to find out what is really going on. "She posted me out with Albert Lavender…"

"Your colleague who dragged you away from the burning car?"

Interrupted again. Good or bad? Not sure. Must stop thinking about that and concentrate on what I say and how I say it. This is hard. Doctor Slattery is far more of a threat than Humpty and Dumpty. "Yes, that's right. Without warning, he took me back to the scene. He stayed with me as I walked around. I think they were checking whether I was fit for duty."

"Bit in-at-the-deep-end but I understand what your sergeant was trying to achieve. How did it go?"

"I actually surprised myself. I was okay. I had the whole incident come back to me in every detail but I coped. I didn't have a break-down or anything. I'm sorry, I don't know the right words."

"That's okay."

"Then Lavender had a word and, without swearing, said they all suffered that night and I was the one getting attention."

"Probably took a lot of courage for him to say that."

"Yeah, made me sit up and think." Probably best to stop here. He understands what I am saying and labouring the point would make him think something else is hidden beneath. I think of Sergeant Cantrell's *you get a mention – again* comment but bringing that up would be labouring the point.

Doctor Slattery has gone quiet. Thinking. Assessing.

There's something else that I think would be a good idea to raise. The more I can give him to suggest I'm being proactive the better. "There's something else. I went round to see Simon Drake. I wanted to say I was sorry but I couldn't speak. I couldn't get the words out and then they came out in a torrent and I'm left feeling guilty that perhaps it was a bad idea."

"Simon Drake is the father of the boy you dragged from the car and husband to the woman who died in the front seat."

I nod, trying to look feeble and putting in a lot of effort to well up. Charlie would have no difficulty.

"How did he react?"

I shake my head like I am finding this hard. "He thanked me for coming." I think about shuddering and wringing my hands but if anybody can see through an act like that, Doctor Slattery can. No, I will be myself for this. "The thing I wasn't expecting was Billy's brother hanging onto his dad's leg. Such a strong likeness."

"How do you feel now that you've done that?"

"Immediately afterwards, I felt terrible, but now, I'm pleased I did it."

"I think it was a good thing to do and particularly brave. You can be proud of yourself."

I try to look embarrassed. If he moves on, then I should be in the clear.

He opens his mouth to speak and closes it again.

I wait.

He sits forward, adjusts his jacket, and sits back.

I wait.

"When we spoke on the phone a couple of times, you were concerned about your memory. You said it was playing tricks on you."

"Yes, it has been," I say, hiding my relief that he has moved on. No time to relax though. Must keep up the Charlie impersonation. "It seems to have all cleared up now. Maybe lack of routine. Days merging. Disorientating me. I even started a diary to help keep track. Hindsight's a wonderful thing, but now I'm back at work, everything has slotted back into place."

His silence is nerve-wracking, so much more compelling than Humpty and Dumpty's. He remains unconvinced.

"I'm sorry I was a bit off with you earlier. Please forgive me."

Again, his lack of response is unnerving me. Doctor Slattery's silence has substance.

I move forward on my chair. "I feel a bit of a fraud. I don't want to waste any more of your time." I stand up and walk towards the door.

Still no movement or word from him.

As I open the door, he says, "Feel free to call me, Charlie. Any time."

* * *

Wade will be waiting for me in the Prince Regent. Only a five-minute walk.

On the way, I reconstruct my conversation with Doctor Slattery, particularly when he went quiet at the end. I was explaining away what Charlie said to him about memory loss and he was giving no indication on whether I was being successful. When he said, 'Feel free to call me, Charlie. Any time,' was that him discharging me? The Met's CMO must have received a report from him and considered it regarding my return to work. He said he had been supportive. There had also been those questionnaires – I think he called them inventories. Have I been able to conceal our condition from Doctor Slattery? Will that be an end to it? Recounting the visit to the scene with Lavender I think went down well and, in particular, Lavender's bollocking about selfishness. Also mentioning the meeting with Simon Drake. The biggest problem is Charlie contacting Doctor Slattery. I must stop that. Another big question is whether the Job will tell Doctor Slattery about my arrest and suspension. Can he be told? It's personal information, not medically related. I do not think the Job can tell him. My suspension moves things away from the medical angle and gives me the chance to bring Charlie on board. It will be difficult, but I think Charlie will come round.

Someone else I must bring round is Wade and he has figured things out. However, having fallen for Charlie, Wade might be my greatest asset.

The Prince Regent is virtually empty when I get there around half-three, though it will be crammed in an hour once the offices turn out. Wade is at a table facing the door with a pint and a paper. He half stands as I walk in. "No need to stand on my account."

"Drink?"

"White wine."

"Any wine in particular?"

"You probably know what I would like better than me."

"Won't be long," he says, heading for the bar.

"Wade."

He turns.

"Can we eat here?"

He looks me up and down, nods and turns. What does Charlie see in him?

"Wade."

As he turns back, his hair falls over his face.

"Burger and chips."

He sweeps his hair behind his ear and heads to the bar. Charlie finds his hair sweeping charming but I find it intensely irritating.

I shake my head and spin his Evening Standard around, flip to the beginning and work through. No mention of a death in Wembley.

Sudden thought. In my bag is the letter Charlie wrote to Doctor Slattery. I turn it over in my hands. Should I destroy it? Seems little point as she can easily write another and maybe get it into the post before I could intervene. Charlie could ruin everything. I must bring her in as soon as possible. I will see Ush tonight and get things moving on that.

Wade arrives with two drinks and I slip the letter away.

I must lighten up with him. "Evening Standard? No longer superficial?"

"Not mine. How was it?"

"Being banged up is bad. Made me shout at Doctor Slattery. I have been rude to you and you are putting yourself out so much for me."

Wade sips his beer, not taking his eyes off me and leans forward, "Shouted at Doctor Slattery?"

He has it. "Well, not really, though I was pretty curt with him."

"Which side of your memory were you on?"

Confirmed. The way he said that, he knows. All the more reason for bringing Charlie up to speed soonest but, I have a lot to dump on Charlie. Having Wade there, someone she knows and trusts, would help.

What am I thinking? There will be people there she knows and trusts.

No, for the moment I think Wade is best kept at arm's length.

Most important though is deterring Charlie from contacting Doctor Slattery.

CHAPTER TWENTY-TWO

Snuggly. Cosy. The duvet's heavy.

I sit up. This isn't my room. Dark. Not my room.

Out of bed. Groping around. Hanging fabric, must be curtains. Pulling them back lets in some light. At last, a switch. Light. Stark. This isn't my room.

I'm alone.

Double bed, bedside table, lamp, clock, 03:37. An envelope. Chest of drawers, cupboard.

I out the light and go to the window. I'm about three floors up. Streetlamps stand in their pools of light.

Trees. Cars. Post box. Nowhere I recognise.

Post box. The last thing I was doing. Kings Cross. I'd written a letter to Doctor Slattery and was going to post it. Envelope, bedside table.

I switch on the bed-side lamp. It's there, addressed to Doctor Slattery. My handwriting. Stamp. Unopened.

Turn it over, turn it back, open the envelope. Just the letter I wrote – the letter I know I wrote.

Is this where I live on the far side of my memory?

I open the door, carefully, slowly. No creaking hinges, no rubbing along the carpet. Poke my head out. The light from the room only goes so far. There's a door opposite. Open. Bathroom. In. Door locked. Light on. An ordinary bathroom, bit like mine at home. I gaze at myself in the mirror, expecting to see someone else.

Nope. It's me. I'm even pulling down my cheeks to check... check what? My eyes? Jeez.

Come on, Charlie. No use sitting here.

I unlock the door and edge out.

"Don't be alarmed. You're safe."

A woman's voice. There's a figure at the end of the short corridor. She switches on a light behind her and moves away. Something about that voice reassures me. I follow.

In the living room, sitting in an armchair, is a beautiful woman. A beautiful woman I know. "Ursula?"

When she was ten, she was cute. Now, fifteen years later, she's striking. Her blonde hair curls around her shoulders. She's wearing a white dressing gown. Her eyes are dark, a perfect contrast to her fairness.

"Everyone else calls me Ush. You insisted on calling me by my full name."

"Ursula?" I'm still not sure I believe this but I feel safe. It's definitely her, my best friend from the children's home.

"And you're Charlie." She points to the matching armchair. "Why don't you sit?"

I'm with my best friend who I haven't seen for fifteen years and yet, somehow, I feel disappointed. Ursula's clearly non-plussed. I sit in the other armchair realising I'm wearing pyjamas with a heavy floral pattern.

Ursula, my best friend. She hates her name and it was me who came up with Ush. She loved that. Everybody called her Ush but then she started calling me Lottie. I retaliated by calling her Ursula. Childish, yeah, but I was only eight.

"Would you prefer me to call you Ush?"

"Ursula's fine."

She's being so nasty. Her body language exudes distaste.

Wait a minute. I've woken up somewhere I never came. I've withdrawn money from a cash-machine I never went to. I've kept my appointments with Doctor Slattery but never met him. I found myself writing notes for an arrest I was never at. I lose time, whole days.

"Ursula?"

She looks at me, flatly.

"Who got into that bed?"

"Lottie."

I take a breath. "And who got out of it?"

"You, Charlie."

In some way, I feel relieved. I don't know why. This is disturbing. Maybe it's relief at getting some confirmation. Wade was talking about this. What did he call it? Dissociative Fugue? What is disturbing is Ursula's attitude. She really dislikes me.

"How did…" It sounds daft but I don't know how to say this. "How did I come here?"

"You didn't. Lottie came here."

She's so matter-of-fact. "Ursula. Please. Help me."

Ursula's face softens. She twirls a strand of her hair round her finger. "Lottie asked me to bring you up to speed. She will explain in detail. We don't know how you might take it."

"Take what?" I think I know.

"It's not Dissociative Fugue. It's Dissociative Identity

Disorder. You and Lottie share the same body."

Thinking something is one thing. Hearing it is quite another.

* * *

I've installed myself in Ursula's bathroom avoiding the mirror.

Dissociative Identity Disorder?

Is this what they call multiple personalities?

Oh, god. How? How can I have someone else inside me? I don't feel it. How can I not be aware of it?

A voice. Ursula's talking. Can't make out what she's saying. A phone call? Who can she be calling at this time?

No point in hiding in here. I dart across to the bedroom where I slept, woke. Can't find my clothes.

"I've washed your clothes and hung them on the airer. Lottie showered before bed." Ursula is at the door holding a robe. "Here, put this on. Come out and sit with me. Let's talk. We have a lot to catch up on."

Feeling like a scolded child, I follow her back to the living room, swinging the robe around my shoulders. There's a pot of coffee. She pours.

"How long was I in the bathroom?"

She pushes a mug of coffee towards me. "About half-an-hour."

"I'm sorry."

"No need, I have an ensuite off my bedroom."

I'm doing my prevarication act. Whatever Ursula's going to tell me, it's not going to be good.

"Do you remember Zach?"

I nod. One of the boys at the children's home.

"I've just been talking with him," she continues. "He's on his way over. Do you remember any of the others?"

I'll be seeing Zach again. "Rob and Eileen of course. There were many but we were a gang. Gang of five. You, Eileen, Rob, Zach and me. Oh, god. And Zach's coming round."

"Not just Zach. Rob and Eileen too. They'll be here soon."

"All five of us will be back together?" I'm excited but concerned at the same time. This isn't a normal reunion. There's something below the surface, something sinister.

"Yes, Charlie, all five of us and, of course, Lottie."

"Lottie's here?"

"Charlie. Have no doubt. Today's going to be difficult for you. It's difficult enough for us. We have a lot to tell you. It's not pleasant but we will all be here for you."

* * *

I'm in for a difficult time? Since the tanker incident, it's been nothing but difficult. Like I thought earlier, maybe getting some answers, no matter how disturbing, will help.

Ursula disappears to her room. She emerges dressed and offering me clothes. "You'll be more comfortable in these."

Tracksuit, trainers, baseball cap, layers for the cold and anorak for the rain. Running gear. All new. I dress and Ursula takes the robe and pyjamas.

I want to know about Lottie, this condition and how I can know nothing about something so intimate, but Ursula's made it clear that she won't answer those kinds of questions until the others arrive. "Ursula, what happened to you after I left the children's home?"

She folds her legs up under her, nursing her mug of coffee. "The home was closed. Travis Hendry. Remember him?"

I nod, "Warden."

"One of the wardens. He was dismissed. The home's been closed down. I moved to another. Eileen got fosters, like you. Rob and Zach, another home."

Why was the home closed down? Why was Travis Hendry dismissed? Questions I want answers to but silence is my best bet. Let her talk.

"My new home was lovely in comparison but I wasn't there for long before getting fosters. Then it was school. I worked as hard as I could and, after A levels, I went to uni. Then I joined the Civil Service. Been there for the last three years."

"Where in the Civil Service?"

"Benefits Agency."

I don't know what to say.

"How's Elly?"

She knows?

"I kept her all that time." Ursula speaks so nonchalantly about something that's caused me so much stress. "Lottie wanted me to send her to you," she smiles though it's more a smile of one-upmanship, "like a message. Is she safe?"

I'm being played but what the hell can I do about it? "Yes, she's on my desk."

There's banging outside.

"That'll be Zach." Ursula opens the front door.

Not just Zach. It's all three of them. I recognise them immediately, despite the years and the cycling gear. Eileen's hanging back.

Zach approaches me. "Charlie?"

I get up. "I don't know what to say."

"Don't say anything." That's Rob. He pushes past Zach, wraps his arms around me. Rob and I were very close but his hug is, sort of, half-hearted. How did our friendships lapse?

Rob and Zach are still so alike. We used to joke about it, accusing them of being brothers, twins even. They're not much taller than me.

They're all smiles but no warmth.

They move aside, very slightly.

Eileen. Standing back. She always did. Even as kids, Eileen and I were outshone by Ursula but, there's something odd about Eileen, like she's trying to be someone she isn't. Her hair is styled and coloured like Ursula's, like she's trying to impersonate Ursula but I remember her as being so strongminded. Has Ursula really got such a pull over them?

Eileen comes and wraps her arms around me. "It's good to see you, Charlie."

"You too," I say. A funny feeling rises in my stomach. Like the others, Eileen's hug is a pretence. She's as nervous as me. They all are.

"We're here to tell you about Lottie and how you developed Dissociative Identity Disorder."

Ursula's turned away. Rob and Zach are troubled too. Eileen continues. "You better take a seat."

I sit back in the armchair I got up from. What are they going to tell me? They're all behaving so strangely. They're all nervous. Ursula said it would be difficult. Okay, I can handle difficult.

Eileen looks at the others. "I think we all better take a seat."

CHAPTER TWENTY-THREE

Ursula tucks her legs up under her. Zach and Rob sit on the sofa.

Eileen sets a dining chair with its back towards me and sits, leaning on the high back and resting her chin on her arms. Ursula, Rob and Zach seem to be waiting for her to lead.

I feel like I've been naughty.

"Charlie," Eileen says.

I force a smile while wringing my baseball cap.

Eileen continues. "Between ages eight and ten, we were sexually abused."

Sexually abused. Oh, god. Ursula, Rob and Zach are as uncomfortable as me. Only Eileen seems able to hold her composure.

Eileen continues. "Travis Hendry, the warden, gave access to paedophiles. The five of us were the ones selected."

I feel strangely remote. I must be remote. How can I not know?

"We were visited, on average, once a month."

Rob is cradling his cycling helmet, not looking at me. Zach looks away when I make eye-contact. Ursula is twiddling her hair looking down at her feet. Eileen's concealing something. Once a month. On average.

AVERAGE?

Eileen is focussing on me. "We had our ways of dealing with it," she looks down, "or not dealing with it." She recovers and looks back at me, her eyes more intense. "Your way was to…"

She's stopped.

This is more difficult for them than for me. I have no memory of what she's saying but it must be bringing everything back in stark clarity for them.

"Look," Eileen's found her voice again, "I'm no shrink, counsellor, whatever. Your way of dealing with it was through Lottie. Lottie briefed me."

So it's Lottie who's been seeing Doctor Slattery. It was Lottie who made my trainers muddy, withdrew cash at the Elephant & Castle, filled the car with petrol on Camberwell Road and left cryptic messages for me, messages from the far side of my memory. Lottie hasn't just briefed Eileen, she's briefed them all. Why didn't Lottie come clean with Doctor Slattery? Why aren't I hearing all this from him? Eileen, Ursula, Rob and Zach seem more traumatised by this than I am.

I don't even know what my feelings are. I've been subjected to sexual abuse and have no recollection whatsoever. My feelings. Eileen's giving me a bit of time. My feelings. I feel incomplete. A whole part of my life is missing but, more importantly, what about Eileen, Ursula, Rob and Zach who experienced it, lived it?

And Lottie? Who is she? What is she? Who am I? What am I?

In amongst all this, my antennae are up and buzzing. A lot is not being said. Eileen's *average* can go two ways and, amongst all this revelation, what's not being said is disturbing me most.

Think. Think. Take stock.

I woke up in Ursula's home. Lottie brought me here. Ursula tells me about my condition. She's then on the phone to the other three who come right round. At 5am? They must have been expecting this. And why cycle?

When they arrive, Eileen tells me about sexual abuse I was subjected to in my last two years at the children's home. Eileen's holding back. They're all holding back. What they're holding back on must be Peter Daventry and Vincent Pope. I want to ask but, if I do, I may as well make allegations of murder.

They're working to a plan. Let them finish. This is hurting them more than it's hurting me. They've been through it. I haven't.

This is not the time for an investigative interview of four murder suspects. It's also not the time to ask inane questions about what everyone's been doing for the last fifteen years.

No. My grudge is not with them. It's with Lottie. It's Lottie, I need to speak to.

There's been a long silence. No one wants to fill it. I take it upon myself. "How do I speak with Lottie?"

Their relief is palpable. Ursula laughs. Rob and Zach have relaxed.

Only Eileen maintains her intense scrutiny of me, bit like Reeve. "Lottie said she would speak to you."

"How?"

"I don't know. She didn't say. She did ask us to give you a message. You're in Ilford. You'll undoubtedly want to go home. She'll speak with you there. She asked that you stay under the radar and that you would know what that means. It's eleven miles."

The running gear.

I stand. I want to stay but I need to get out of here.

Ursula hands me a little backpack. "I've put your purse and keys in there."

I nod my thanks and move to the door. Halfway through, I turn. I can't think of anything sensible to say, let the door swing to and head down the stairs.

* * *

Ilford. Northeast London. No clue and no mobile. A man is getting into a car. I soon lose sight of him but I've seen which turning he took. Another car drives past and I follow for as long as I can. I'm soon on a main road and I run with the traffic queue, passing the first car I followed.

After thirty minutes, there are signs for Tower Bridge.

Lottie. Who is she? What is she? Who am I? What am I?

I won't get any answers until, until what? Until I speak with myself?

I was sexually abused. Kathy's always saying it's not natural I'm a virgin in my mid-twenties. Explains stuff though.

Explains memories of spotty boys with poking tongues and pawing hands under rumpled clothes on living room sofas. Squeezing out and away saying, *I'm sorry, I'm sorry*, with no clue what I was saying *sorry* for. It always started so well but always went so wrong.

Nights out with Kathy involved her teasing men while I scowled at them and sometimes ended *physically*, though not the sort of physically she envisaged. I remember one of those times when Kathy overdid it and I had to get physical with a guy who wasn't taking Kathy's *no* for an answer. I twisted his threatening hand into a wristlock, forcing him down to the ground. His three mates were quite taken aback. Fortunately, Kathy hailed a cab before they overcame their disbelief and we legged it.

I've crossed Tower Bridge, the streets are familiar and I turn my mind back to the prospect of meeting myself. How will that happen? The voice I've been hearing. The words *trust, together, do not follow, play the game, sleep now.* Was that Lottie communicating with me from the far side of my memory?

A little bit of the Old Kent Road and into the back streets for the run down to Camberwell.

How can I be sharing my body with someone and not know about it? How can I live like that? Not fair. Why me?

Home. The eleven miles from Ilford has taken just over ninety minutes.

Straight into the shower.

Quick wash and out. Towelling down, I catch sight of myself in the mirror.

I lean on the basin. This is bollocks. How will this work? Someone else inside me? "So, come on then. Talk to me." Like I thought. Complete and utter bollocks.

"You did the right thing."

I look up. "Lottie?"

"Yes."

There's that sliding feeling. "Lottie?"

"Sorry, but I had to keep you away from Doctor Slattery."

I rush round the flat, my head spinning.

"No. You are not alone. You never have been. You never will be."

That voice is so clear. "Why haven't you said anything before?"

I hear nothing. The dizziness is subsiding.

"Lottie?"

There's nothing.

"Lottie?"

The silence is oppressive.

"Lottie!"

I'm screaming.

"Lottie. Lottie. Lottie!"

Nothing.

I hide under my duvet. Maybe she'll come and make everything better. Maybe she'll make everything worse. Experience suggests the latter.

* * *

"Lottie, please. Talk to me."

This is harder than I thought it would be. Charlie is so strong – mentally strong.

"Come on. I know you're there."

She does not know how and in which direction to focus her effort. These revelations have unbalanced her emotionally so, although she finds it possible, she finds it hard.

We are, back in front of the mirror. Makes sense I suppose.

"Lottie, we've got to talk. We've got to work out a way forward."

A way forward? She means her way forward. Stop, stop. What am I thinking? I must be gentle with her. She is so distressed and therefore easy to displace but knocking her back would be counterproductive. "Before we find a way forward, let me explain your situation."

That would be the first time she has knowingly seen me. She has just seen herself talk without saying anything. Her face is now a mask of confusion and fear. "What do you want?"

How she is managing this is impressive. "A life." She has just heard and seen me speak. "You think you are talking to the far side of your memory. You are not. You are talking to me. Not you. Me."

"Can you read my thoughts?"

This is good. I was never really sure I could make room for her and, at the same time, stay with her. "No, reading each other's thoughts is not possible. We can communicate without vocalising. For now, let us just talk. It is easier."

"Trust. Together. Do not follow. Play the game. Sleep now."

Charlie is one smart cookie. "It probably sounded to you like those words were spoken but they were not. It is complicated. For now, just talk."

Staying here, together, is hard. I find it hard, even with my years of practice. Her strength explains why coming out has never really been there for me.

"Why haven't you spoken to me before?"

"Not possible but, when you get emotional, the barrier between us becomes leaky and I can be more than just an observer." Letting her fire question after question at me will be unproductive. I must tell her everything, very quickly. Eileen told her about the sexual abuse though she concealed the imbalance. I was *selected* so much more than the others. It all started years before the sexual abuse. "Charlie, listen. You were abused in the children's home, physically and mentally. I was your response to an escalation of that abuse. You know nothing of the sexual abuse because, by the time that started, your response to the threat, me, was fully formed."

I must stop now, see how she is reacting. It seems like Charlie is taking it in her stride. She seems calm. Bit more. "Because you were unaware of the sexual abuse, we were concerned about how you would react. As an intelligence officer in The Service, Eileen is used to briefing seniors. Briefing you fell to her. She volunteered in all honesty. The others, Ush, Zachery and Robert, wanted to be there for you, to offer support. Thank you so much for not grilling them about Daventry and Pope."

Charlie is holding back on a million questions and she will have her day of reckoning but not yet, not yet.

"Charlie. To protect himself from any comeback from the paedophiles, Travis secretly filmed them. As far as I know, he has never used the videos but he lost five."

Got her. Anything likely to be evidential gets her.

"Travis did not actually lose them. I stole them. Each video features a different paedophile abusing each of us."

Now that is a big piece of information for Charlie so I must let her digest it.

"Lottie." Look at that, coming back already. "Where are those videos?"

As I thought. Straight to the evidence. "Safe. Zachery has them."

"Who knows about them?"

"Only the five of us."

"What about Travis? Does he know they're missing?"

"I believe he is unaware of the theft."

Charlie pauses. When she speaks, her voice has that tone saying there is no satisfactory answer you can give. "What have you done, Lottie?"

Okay. This is it. "Charlie, we spent the last fifteen years trying to identify those five paedophiles. Google. Facebook. IT comes easy to Zachery. We made no progress. Facial identification has been improving, but long-winded trawling is the only way. Hours and hours of work. Nothing. At the first opportunity we took jobs that we thought might help, that would open up new databases."

I stop, not wanting to talk for so long.

Charlie says, "Ursula, Benefits Agency?"

"Yes. Ush got a position there, Zachery got a position in Revenue and Customs, Robert in the Serious Fraud Office and Eileen in the Security Service."

CHAPTER TWENTY-FOUR

I don't know. I don't know what to know. How should I act? Shouldn't I be running down the street screaming? Part of me wants to push Lottie away. Part of me wants to embrace her. Everything she's said explains the weird events and lost time. Everything Wade found out is making sense. The thing that's got me most, is the videos. Their evidential value could be priceless. I hope Zach has kept the originals and not allowed them to degrade.

All that can wait.

Right now, I've got to understand this DID. Dissociative Identity Disorder.

Lottie has stopped me seeing Doctor Slattery, deliberately.

Yes, the evidence can wait but, for now, a warning shot. "Lottie. Very soon, I will ask you to explain the link between us and Peter Daventry and Vincent Pope." I can't see any kind of response. She's not taking over and saying anything. Taking over? How does that work? Do I have to move aside or does she push me aside? I am getting feelings though. She said a lot in a short time and it came with feelings of relief. "But first, why didn't you let me see Doctor Slattery?"

"Five people know about our condition. We do not want that to increase."

Lottie was ready for that. "Okay but what about treatment?"

"This condition is very rare. Little is known about it and Doctor Slattery would be all over us. No way would you keep your position as a police officer and we would become a specimen in a jar."

There's a hell of a lot she's not saying. "Okay. Not sure I agree with you but that argument can wait. What I need to know right now is how this thing works."

* * *

I knew Charlie was capable of this but seeing her in action is, frankly, humbling. To think of what she has had to endure since the tanker incident and, just as she thought that was ending, she is hit with all this.

How it works. Our inner world. Something she would never get from Doctor Slattery. "Think theatre. Dressing rooms, wings, stage and, of course, the spot. To take control, you must take the *spot*. When we were being abused, I was on the *spot*. When we were hauling the boy from the burning car, you were on the *spot*."

"So, who's on the *spot* now?"

Look at Charlie, so quick. "We both are, sort of."

"I can't deal with *sort of*."

"Let me finish. On the *stage*, I can see, hear, feel, smell and taste everything as you do. In the *wings*, everything is muffled. In the *dressing room*, nothing, sleep."

"Where are we now?"

"Are you finding it hard?"

215

"Incredibly hard. When I'm talking it's okay but when you're talking, I feel like I'm sliding down a slope scrabbling for a handhold. Then, when I'm talking, like now, I feel steady again."

"Charlie, believe me, I know how it feels. Having spent fifteen years where you are now, on the *stage*, I have learnt how to hold there."

"Why didn't you say?"

"To be able to talk, I must take the *spot*. For you to be able to hear me, you must hold the *stage*. Your acceptance is helping you hold the *stage*."

"A mental strength."

She has it.

* * *

"You get it, Charlie. You will be better at this than me."

So, this is DID. Dissociative Identity Disorder. A constant competition for the *spot*. I'm steady. Lottie's moved aside. She's on the *stage*. I can feel her there. "Lottie, do you see what I see?"

"When I'm on the *stage*, yes."

I'm sliding but I get back up there. "Hear what I hear?"

"Yes, all the senses."

I hold on. "The burns?"

"Taking pain is why I exist. I imagine our experience of pain differs."

I push back to the *spot*. "Like punching the buttons of a cash-machine."

"You get it."

"Tell me about the scars my salamander tattoo hides?"

Lottie pauses. "A moment of weakness."

Good god. What must it have been like for her? "So I ran away from the abuse leaving you to face it. How did you cope?"

There's another pause and I'm scrabbling to stay with her.

"Charlie, I coped by numbing myself to it. Cutting helped me break through the numbness. To be honest, it was also a way to send you a message."

I clamber back. "Send me a message? Message received loud and clear. I just didn't know what it meant."

"You hid it well. Had it been found out, the abuse might have stopped. A few years later, you covered it up with that salamander tattoo."

Oh, god. "I didn't know."

"Charlie, I know you did not know."

I must stop. This is hurting us both. Lottie knows I won't let her get away with Daventry and Pope but, for now, I must stop. I'm tired. It's not the eleven-mile run from Ilford, it's the scrabbling around on the slippery slope. Of utmost importance, right now, is getting to grips with this condition. Everything else can wait.

"Lottie, how do you hold on?"

"Not easy to describe. Holding on is more a mental thing than a physical thing."

I get back. "It's been fifteen years. Why haven't I known you? Why haven't we had this conversation before?"

"I wanted to, Charlie, believe me but you were too strong, mentally. And in that strength is your weakness. When you get overwhelmed, you crash, catastrophically."

* * *

Before I reveal everything, Charlie must be better at handling this. Unlike me, she has someone to help her. Me.

"Charlie. I could only take the *spot* when you suffered emotional upheaval."

I move aside and allow her a breather on the *spot*. She says nothing.

I move back in. "You often talk about your antennae. Everybody has them but yours are more sensitive than most. At the children's home, when the abuse started escalating, you went into emotional meltdown. The sexual abuse was yet to start but you foresaw it. I was your way of running from it."

I move aside. Charlie gratefully takes the *spot* and, again, says nothing.

I move in again. "And so, I was formed. Bit too *cause and effect* for Doctor Slattery. My purpose was to protect you from the sexual abuse."

I move aside and Charlie clambers back, very tired. We must take a break.

"You took the sexual abuse for me?"

"I was hardly a volunteer."

"What happened when we moved away from the home? When the abuse ended?"

"You regained your emotional stability and I was locked out."

* * *

"What do you mean? Locked out?"

"Consigned to the *stage, wings, dressing room*. Like you now, I had terrible difficulty staying on the *stage*. It took ages but I learnt how to hold there. It is only on the *stage* where everything is clear."

I like Lottie. She speaks so gently. She said before that the *dressing room* is where she sleeps. That's how this slipping and sliding feels. Tiredness.

"Lottie, what's life like for you?"

She's taken the *spot*. I feel the sliding. She's taking her time, but that's okay. I'll hold on.

"Frustrating," she says at length.

"Can you tell me about it?"

"I will but not now. Daventry and Pope. You need to know. I need to tell you."

She's changed the subject. I'll go with her, I need to know about this. "Bad?"

"From your perspective, yes. Peter Daventry was in one of those videos Travis Hendry took. The video shows him abusing Zachery. Identifying him from those pictures was hard, but we got there. They landed all those jobs getting close to extensive databases and sophisticated software but, in the end, we found him on LinkedIn."

She's moved away to give me a breather. She didn't need to. I know what's coming.

She's back. "They found where he lived, figured out his movements, confronted him and Zachery killed him."

I was right.

Lottie comes back. "Ush assisted him, Robert laid an alibi for him and Eileen laid an alibi for Ush."

I keep quiet. I think Lottie knows what I'd ask.

"You want to know why I laid an alibi for you and stitched you up to Crimestoppers."

I was right.

"I had to keep you off balance. You were recovering after the tanker incident and I was finding it harder and harder to take the *spot*. Being pushed back down was not an option for me."

"So you stitched me up for murder."

"Insufficient evidence and the case against you will be dropped followed by reinstatement."

"That's not the point." I'm shouting.

"It is, Charlie, exactly the point. Now you know about me, now you accept me, we can move forward."

"What do you mean? Move forward?" I'm still shouting.

"Vincent Pope…"

She's ignoring me.

"…identified from the video of him abusing Ush. Killed by Ush and assisted by Robert. Eileen laid Ush's alibi and Zachery laid Robert's. I did the same for you at the service station on Camberwell Road and followed it up with a Crimestoppers call. It had the desired effect. Got you suspended."

CHAPTER TWENTY-FIVE

"Charlie, you have taken on a lot. Four old friends, sexual abuse, DID. Add to that, your alter, me, with your four friends, are involved in murder. Your world has been turned upside-down. You need time alone. I will be in the *dressing room*."

"Lottie, wait."

She's gone.

I'm sitting on the edge of my bath looking at my reflection. Lottie has moved away. I feel alone.

Actually, this is one of the few times I've felt truly alone. There's a vacancy around me. I've always been so critical of people's stress over paranoia. It's been part of my life. I've always had Lottie looking over my shoulder.

Sitting around in my bathroom will achieve nothing. I'm hungry but, before sorting that out, I steady my punchbag and left foot – front kick, side kick, round kick, heel kick, BANG, BANG, BANG, BANG. Right foot – front kick, side kick, round kick, heel kick, BANG, BANG, BANG, BANG. Right foot, again. Left foot, again.

I steady the punchbag.

Fists.

Left hand – jab. Right hand – jab. No. My hands aren't ready for this. Bugger it. Left hand – jab. Right hand –

jab. Again. Again. I stop. My hands are bleeding, the pain nothing.

Through to the bathroom and hands under warm running water, soothing.

The storm in my head is calming.

I suffer Dissociative Identity Disorder because I was sexually abused as a child.

My alter, Lottie, took the abuse so I didn't have to.

Lottie got video of the abuse.

Ursula, Eileen, Rob and Zach have been looking for those paedos ever since. They've even taken jobs to help in that search. They've found two of them.

After the tanker incident, my alter can take the *spot*.

Then the killings start.

I dry my hands. They're okay.

Through to the living room. Notepad. Pen.

Why did the killings wait for Lottie?

Why did Lottie want me to stay under the radar?

Lottie said there are five who know about us.

I thought the fifth was me.

Who's the fifth?

It's mid-morning. Into my running gear. There's a little phone shop on Denmark Hill. Half an hour later, I have a cheap mobile and five pay-as-you-go SIMs.

I type a message:

Ashes? Lunch?

Lucky I've memorised Wade's number.
[SEND]

* * *

On the way home, I pop to Morrisons. There's a police car outside. Lavender's standing by his door. Kathy's bringing out a prisoner.

They've spotted me.

We shouldn't meet but, sod it.

"Hi, Kathy."

Kathy's guiding her prisoner into the back of the car. "Charlie. We can't meet."

"I've got enough paperwork." Lavender's not swearing.

He gets in. Kathy's into the back with her prisoner. They're not looking at me and they're away.

I walk into Morrisons with tears in my eyes.

* * *

"You're upset."

I've met Wade in the Phoenix. No cycling gear so he's driven. Christ. Where do I start?

"You settle down, I'll get you a drink."

The pub's not crowded but there's enough of a hubbub to make it hard for anyone to overhear. Kathy dissed me. Lavender too. What do they think of me? If things had been the other way around, I'd have been straight over. Hugs. Checking out how they were, what

I could do for them. Their prisoner wasn't a problem. What's happened?

If I'd been them, I'd have been getting everything I could about the murders. They'd have found people on the edge of the investigation, found out what was going on, even if not the exact detail. So, what have they found out? Whatever it is, it's bad enough for them not to want to know me.

Specialist squads are always getting these kinds of approaches. No. Kathy and Lavender have been fed a line.

Wade places a glass of wine in front of me and sits.

I still can't speak. What Kathy and Lavender have been told is enough to break friendships. Cantrell would see through this but she'll give nothing away. All I have is Wade.

"Charlie, rumours are rife. Will you tell me what's really going on?"

Should I tell Wade? Let's just take it slowly. "It's Dissociative Identity Disorder." Taking it slowly? Jeez. "I found out this morning. Not from Doctor Slattery. From my alter, Lottie."

"I found out from her too."

I don't know what to say. Perhaps saying nothing is best but I can't help myself. "How? When? How did you find out?"

"Yesterday. I went to Doctor Slattery's like we agreed. You were already there. I sat down with you, took your hand and it wasn't you."

"How can you be so sure?"

"You're Charlie. You say her name's Lottie, makes sense I suppose. She didn't introduce herself."

"Did you go with her to see Doctor Slattery?"

"No. She didn't want me there. We met afterwards in a pub. She maintained the pretence, but it wasn't you."

"How did you get on with her?"

Wade doesn't respond immediately. He's weighing up possible answers.

"I don't need you to protect me, just be honest with me."

"She's bright. Well read. Knows her mind."

"Are you saying I'm not well read. That I don't know my mind?"

Wade clasps his hands round his beer and looks down. I don't know what I'm feeling. I've never been this way before, never had my mind spinning in out-of-control spirals unable to latch onto anything. I look away from Wade. Tears are forming. There's someone watching from across the bar. She's noticed the mood between Wade and me.

Wade's taken hold of my hands.

"Charlie." Wade's eyes are intense. "I suspect you have a lot to tell but here and now's not right. While we're finishing our drinks, I'll tell you about what's going on at work."

I take a large gulp of wine. I want to finish up and go.

Wade's cottoned on and he chugs down half his beer. "Kathy, Lavender and the others have been sniffing around Homicide trying to find out what's going on with you. Their efforts have been," he shrugs, "blatantly subtle."

What I suspected but I'm only picking up the gist of what Wade's saying. Come on, focus.

"I spoke to DS John French."

I'm now fully focussed.

"He addressed all my questions with answers that reiterated what's written in the press."

Makes sense.

"As I was leaving, he said something he didn't need to say."

I sip my wine.

"He said, 'Charlie's fine.'"

I finish my wine.

"It wasn't so much what he said," Wade hasn't finished, "it was more that he didn't need to say it."

I set my empty glass down on the table. "He was fishing."

"I don't think so. It seemed more like he was trying to tell me something."

Like Wade said, now is not the time and this is not the place.

* * *

This is so frustrating. Frustration has been with me all my life but now the stakes are so high.

Trouble is, I have confined myself to the *wings*. Over the years, Charlie has grown accustomed to me being on *stage* and associated that presence with a feeling of paranoia.

Now, if I move onto the *stage*, Charlie will understand the sensation, think me spying and bang goes the trust. Trust is essential for us to get through this in one piece, well, two pieces.

So, the *wings* it is but, from here, I know Wade is there but I cannot hear what they are saying or see what they are doing, not properly.

They are walking home and I think Wade has been brought up to speed about the DID and I think they were talking about rumours at work. Charlie's upset.

So frustrating.

* * *

As we walk home, I tell Wade about how Kathy and Lavender treated me outside Morrisons.

"They're sticklers for the rules."

"Aren't we all?"

"I don't want to be. You can't be." He holds up his hand.

High five.

Five. Something Lottie said is bugging me. Five. Oh, yes. She said there were only five people who know about my condition, our condition. I thought she meant the five of us – Eileen, Ursula, Rob, Zach and me. Lottie wouldn't have included me. Wade's the fifth. Lottie was telling me Wade knows. Why doesn't she speak plainly?

Did she recruit him?

"Wade. When did you first realise it wasn't me?"

"Immediately."

"That obvious?"

"Is to me. Others might think you're having a bad or good day but I know a little of your history. Lost days, weird events, displacements, far side of memory. Not remembering visits to Doctor Slattery. I was joining dots."

"You didn't tell me."

"Only joined them up yesterday when I met Lottie at Doctor Slattery's."

"Well, you still could have…"

"No, Charlie. The last time I saw you was at my flat. I haven't seen you until now. I've seen the other you, Lottie, but I haven't seen you."

"How much time did you spend with Lottie?"

"About an hour. We had a drink and a burger."

"Did you talk about DID?"

"No. I think she knew I'd figured it out but she didn't confide in me. Our conversation was polite."

I found out about my DID this morning. So Lottie didn't confide in Wade before speaking with me. She made sure I was surrounded by people I know and trust and got them to tell me before announcing herself to me.

She's not bugging me right now. She's giving me space. She's thoughtful, considerate. She's someone I'd like.

While I fill Wade in on everything I've learnt from Ursula, Zach, Rob and Eileen and the more detailed stuff I've learnt from Lottie, including the video clips she stole from Travis, my mind keeps wandering off onto what I don't know about the Daventry and Pope murders.

CHAPTER TWENTY-SIX

No sooner are we indoors, Lottie moves onto the *stage*.

"Tea or coffee? I'm making coffee."

"You talking to me?"

"No. I think you're already acquainted but, Wade, Lottie, Lottie, Wade."

"Pleased you could be here."

"Of course I'm here. How else would you be here?"

"I was talking to Wade."

"I've got wine." Wade shrugs his bag off his back.

"Great."

"On top of the wine in the pub?"

"No stamina."

"I did an eleven-mile run this morning."

"So did I."

"I thought I could tell the difference between you."

"Shut up."

Wade looks at me.

"Sorry."

"Me too."

"What?"

"I think we just said, 'Shut up,' at the same time."

"So we were both on the *spot* at the same time."

"Not possible."

Wade holds up his hands and disappears to the kitchen. There's rummaging, a cork pops and he comes back, two tea-towels over his shoulder, a bottle of wine in one hand and three glasses in the other. "Anyone else joining us?"

He sets the bottle and glasses on the coffee table and arranges two dining chairs opposite the sofa. He places the green tea-towel on the back of one chair and the blue one on the other. "Charlie, when you're talking, please sit on the blue chair and Lottie, when you're talking, please move to the green chair. Will help me keep up with you guys."

"Okay, but you said you could tell the difference between us."

"After what I've just witnessed, I'm not so sure."

"Where did you get this idea of the chairs?"

"I read it somewhere." Wade pours the wine.

I sit on the blue chair. "I'm starting to find this easier."

Lottie moves over to the green chair. "You are such a quick learner."

I move back to the blue chair. "I have a good teacher."

"Excuse me." Wade is waving his hands. "Can we stop with the self-adulation? Dissociative disorders arise through serious childhood trauma."

Lottie moves to the green chair. "I was Charlie's way of coping with hideous sexual abuse she was subjected to between eight and ten."

"You didn't tell me this last night."

"It didn't seem right to tell you before telling Charlie."

"How have you grown up?"

"You mean why am I not still eight years old?"

* * *

Wade has read a lot. "I think it has something to do with being able to experience the outside world. I found a way of getting out. Has Charlie told you about *spot*, *stage*, *wings* and *dressing room*?"

Wade nods. "She told me on the way back from the pub. The fact that you don't know that, means you must have retreated to the *wings* or the *dressing room*."

Remarkable. Wade has his head around this already. "I could only take the *spot* when Charlie was in the *dressing room* and, as the *dressing room* is like sleep, I was concerned about waking her so I could not do very much. When she wakes, she displaces me by default, so when I had the *spot*, I spent my time reading. Smart phone or Kindle. Charlie had to be inventive when Harry and Harriet, the foster parents, asked why she had downloaded so many books, especially some of the titles." I put my hand on his arm. "Our Charlie is very good at talking bollocks."

Wade is all ears and Charlie, on the *stage*, is all ears too.

"Emotional stress weakens Charlie, allowing me to take the *spot* more easily, and I can do more without alerting her. When she was in trouble, at school, late home or something like that, I would have more freedom. I could move around but I was always careful to leave Charlie where she was when I took over."

They're still with me.

I sip my wine. "I was a bit playful, I suppose. Charlie was all running and jumping. I was all reading and drawing. Once, Charlie was reprimanded by her arts teacher for not doing her homework and she ran away," I use my fingers to show quotes around the word *ran*. "Well, there was the *spot*, vacant. I took it and painted the scene for her. The arts teacher was dumbfounded. Charlie, having recovered from her chastisement, recovered the *spot*. She took the praise while all I could do was watch from the *stage*."

"Is that what you've been doing?" Wade sits forward, "Standing on the *stage* observing everything Charlie does?"

"Pretty much. She reads slowly." I must be careful. Charlie is on the *stage* now. "Like everyone, we have our strengths and weaknesses. Do you remember when you were doing those no-right-turns and Charlie joined you? You had already let the motorist go but Charlie intervened and it turned out the motorist had a stolen mobile under his seat. When on the *stage*, I see exactly what Charlie sees. It was as much a surprise to me as it was to you. Charlie calls it her antennae up and buzzing. How come those antennae work for Charlie but not for me?"

Wade is rapt.

"Charlie will follow her hunches because she has confidence in them and I don't know how she does it. Just as she has no idea how I paint an artistic scene. Her attempts involve a line of blue for sky, a line of green for grass and some matchstick people in between."

I have been talking for a while now. Time to let them digest.

* * *

Lottie's lovely. I don't want her in my life and, considering what she's been through, I'm surprised she doesn't despise me. Wade enjoys her company too.

"I want to get a couple of things straight. Sorry, I forgot to move to the blue chair." I get up but sit back down on the same chair. "This is bloody silly. I've already done an eleven-mile run. When I'm talking, I'll wave the blue towel and when Lottie's talking, she'll wave the green. Everyone okay with that?"

Wade has the decency to look embarrassed.

Lottie waves the green towel. "Fine with that but no forgetting whose glass of wine is whose."

I even like her sense of humour. "When I'm on the *stage*, I see everything you're looking at, hear everything you're hearing, smell and taste the wine, feel its coolness. It's hard work staying on the *stage* but, you're right, it's getting easier. Where was I? Oh, yes. Straighten out a couple of things. I haven't forgotten Daventry and Pope but what was happening in the week or so after Joel?"

Lottie waves the green towel. "Does Wade know about Joel?"

"Before I joined," Wade says. "Charlie's never confided in me on that. I understand she's never confided in anyone, not even Kathy."

Lottie delays.

I think she's waiting for me. "I'm not unpacking that incident. I'm asking about what happened afterwards."

"Charlie, if you slip back to the *dressing room*, I will explain that incident to Wade and we can pick up when you re-join us."

"Is this really necessary?"

"I think it is. Besides, you need rest."

I'm suspicious but I get the feeling Lottie's on my side and yes, I'm knackered. "Okay. Will you wake me?"

"Not that simple. Shaking your shoulder doesn't really work but yes, I will wake you."

I'm not convinced. I feel like I shouldn't be leaving. Will I ever get back?

"I understand your concern, Charlie. Trust. Together. Sleep now."

"You'll let me back?"

"How can I not let you back? Wade can tell us apart."

Wade's looking so confused. Do I trust Lottie? I don't know her well enough. Do I trust Wade? Completely. Wade will tell me everything that happens.

"Okay," I say, "I'll do it." I sit there. I haven't been waving the blue towel which probably explains why Wade's having difficulty keeping up. I'm still sitting here. "Ummm. Lottie. This may be a stupid question but, ummm, how do you get to the *dressing room*?"

* * *

Charlie lets herself slide off the *stage*, through the *wings* to the *dressing room*.

"Bless her," I say.

"Won't you wake her?" Wade is whispering.

"You think she is sleeping? She may be, I do not know

234

but, rather than thinking of the *dressing room* as a place, it is easier to think of it as a level and there are levels beyond the *dressing room*. I call them the abyss. The more upset she is, the deeper she sinks. I have touched the *abyss* many times."

Wade is attentive. "Isn't Charlie the host?"

"The word *host* is misused, or misunderstood. You're a singleton. People with DID were singletons but have fragmented into parts, generally referred to as alters. I do not like that term, it suggests individuals. We are parts of one individual. Some parts are concealed behind amnesic barriers. Some are protected by amnesic barriers. I hold memories Charlie cannot access."

"Memories of sexual abuse."

"Correct."

"You have different skills and talents."

"Correct."

"You have a different personality."

"Correct."

"And a different identity."

Wade understands. "Yes."

"Doctor Slattery would attempt integration and help you recover singleton status."

"Yes, but all the King's horses and all the King's men… Who says dissociation is a disorder? Just imagine if Charlie and I could work together."

Wade goes quiet.

It's time for me to go quiet too.

Wade wants to ask a question.

I know what that question is.

He opens his mouth and closes it again.

I do not want him to ask that question. Change the subject. "The jumper incident affected Charlie more than the tanker incident. The jumper, Joel, early twenties, was on the roof of Kevan House. Charlie got up there with him, talked with him for over an hour and even coaxed him back from the edge. She was about to take his hand when he turned, ran and threw himself out into space, his legs running, his arms circling before he dropped out of sight on his journey down twenty floors."

Wade sits forward. "She was developing a relationship with him."

"You have the crux of it. The tanker incident was horrendous but, with Joel, she was getting to know him and I saw, from what he was saying, that he was a sexual abuse victim like me. Charlie sensed the closeness, recognised the shared experience but had no idea where those feelings were coming from. Then, when he threw himself into oblivion, she was bereft. She went into emotional meltdown."

"As coppers, we all have our moments. Charlie seems to have had more than most."

"She was given substantial time off after that. Counselling. That she bounced back so quickly is testament to her mental strength."

"But?"

"Yes. Big *but*. While she was emotionally unstable, I could take the *spot* at will. I used my time to link up with Ush, Eileen, Robert and Zachery. Got them identifying the paedophiles in those films. After the tanker incident, I linked up with them again to implement our plan."

"A plan that involved stitching Charlie up with your murders."

"To be able to take the *spot*, I needed Charlie off balance. I needed her suspended so I have more time."

Wade goes quiet. It is difficult to tell what he is thinking.

"Well, Wade, as a dutiful constable, are you going to arrest me for murder?"

He takes a breath to speak but stops. He stands by the window, hands in pockets, deep in thought. When he turns back, it looks like he has come to a decision.

"Tell me more about Joel."

That was unexpected. "I know nothing about Joel. I do not know how, but she got keys to Kevan House and the maintenance door to the roof. She goes there occasionally and sits. She likes to feel close to him. I make myself scarce. A very intimate moment for Charlie."

"Thank you." He stares back out the window. "What will I do? Whatever I do to you, I'll be doing to Charlie. It seems like she's an innocent party. I want to talk with her."

CHAPTER TWENTY-SEVEN

"Run to Zach's place?" Wade doesn't seem keen.

"Yes."

"In Putney? Long-distance running isn't my forté."

"Five miles isn't long-distance. Drive back to yours first. You can cycle if you want." I thought all the running and cycling was over-the-top but I get it now. Very clever. With just a couple of words of explanation, Wade's got it too. Don't take a mobile. He's got it.

Lottie's told us to go to Zach's. She said I'm *running and jumping* and she's *reading and drawing* and retired to the *dressing room*.

"What will be at Zach's place?"

"Probably the abuse videos."

"What then?"

"I don't know, Wade. I don't know."

Wade and I have had a long chat. Lottie was good for her word and didn't listen in. I told Wade what I think he's letting himself in for. He said I needed someone who believed in me. He said I'm losing Kathy and Lavender. He said I've probably already lost Cantrell. He said the detectives don't believe me. He said the courts wouldn't believe me. The other big test, he said, is the jury. He said jurys are fickle. I'll have to look that word up. He said he has complete faith in me to think of a way through this. Well, that's a load off my mind.

* * *

I'm the last to arrive at Zach's. Well, technically, Lottie is as she only came out onto the *stage* after I'd hugged them all. Eileen, Ursula and Rob are in their cycling gear. Wade arrived just before me and is still breathing heavily. I'm surprised he didn't ride his bike.

Lottie's pushing so I move aside and she hugs Eileen, Ursula, Rob and Zach. Their hugs are heartfelt unlike the straight-armed-head-turned-to-the-side for me.

Now, they're all looking at Wade.

Sticking around on the *stage* is hard but I'm getting better at it. Lottie recognises my effort and moves on quickly.

"Okay. This is Wade, a friend of Charlie's. He might be a copper but he is on our side. I trust him."

"How? How can you trust him?" Eileen is staring him in the eyes.

Wade doesn't back down.

Eventually Eileen turns and looks at me, well, Lottie. "This is a bad idea."

"Wade is out of place in the police. I am more concerned about Charlie because her world has been blown apart. She needs a friend."

Eileen's not convinced.

Zach finds the TV remote. "Shall we get on with recruiting her then?"

"Go for it." Lottie moves aside so I can relax on the *spot*.

Relax?

Zach brings the TV to life. The picture is of a naked young girl. It's me. There's a man in the picture. I close my eyes and my left leg gives way. Rob supports me, guiding me back into a chair.

My body feels strange. That wasn't me but it was me. My eyes are shut tight and all I see is myself but I know I'm not seeing myself, I'm seeing Lottie. I'm vacant and numb.

Lottie has left me on the *spot*. I must take charge. Zach has moved the images on and is showing a still of the man's head and shoulders.

So, this is my abuser, Lottie's abuser, but my body, I mean, our body.

Wade is right by me, Eileen is watching me and Rob still has his arm around me. Ursula is studying her nails and Zach is fiddling with the remote.

I had no doubt this was the sort of thing I was going to be seeing but I don't understand my reaction. How should anyone react? It's not me. It's my body but it's not me. Am I right to feel this way? Am I wrong? Am I a callous bitch?

Lottie's right there. Is she scrutinising me? Is she wanting me to suffer like she did?

More to show myself I'm in control, I stand up, move to the side of the room, turn and face them.

I'm not sure how my voice is going to sound but I must move on. I must test the evidence. It strikes me that this kind of activity is my defence mechanism.

"How did you identify Peter Daventry and Vincent Pope?" My voice has come out more hostile than I would like but I'm pleased I said that solidly, fluently and calmly.

It's Eileen who opens her mouth to speak. I'm wondering whether Eileen is the one who's driving this and the others are just following. No. It's Lottie. She's the driving force behind all this. Peter Daventry and Vincent Pope would still be alive had it not been for the tanker incident. Mustn't forget Lottie.

"We have videos of Peter Daventry abusing Zach and Vincent Pope abusing me, similar to the one you didn't watch." Ursula got in before Eileen and couldn't hold back on her derision. "That's how we identified them."

I walk over to Ursula and bend down so my nose is right in front of hers. "Those videos are over fifteen years old. How did you identify Peter Daventry and Vincent Pope?"

Ursula is flustered and looking to the others. Eileen goes to speak but stops when I hold up my hand. Continuing to stare down Ursula I say, "How do you know the men you killed are the men in the videos?"

* * *

"I killed Peter Daventry." Zach's speaking. "He abused me. I killed him."

I turn from Ursula to Zach. "Okay then, Zach. How do you know the man you killed was the man who abused you?"

"It was him. I know it was him."

I step up to Zach. "Not good enough."

"I killed Vincent Pope." That was Ursula. Without looking away from her nails, she continues. "There's a video in which I'm being abused by Vincent Pope. I killed him." She looks up from her nails. "I feel better now."

I can't believe this. "Why didn't you take your videos to the police? You've done their job and the court's, not to mention the executioner's."

I feel a hand on my shoulder. It's Wade. "Charlie, your voice is raised. We don't know who's within earshot."

I throw myself on the sofa next to Rob. He says, "Charlie, trust us. We know what we're doing."

"How can you say that? What you've got is evidentially bullet-proof. Why haven't you handed it in? It's been over fifteen years. How many children have been defiled by these people in that time? How many lives screwed up?" I'm screaming at them. "Why didn't you hand it over?"

Rob's hand is on my shoulder but I shrink away from him. "What the hell have you done?"

Wade steps in. "Charlie, please, let me?"

"Let you? Let you do what? Question these fucking imbeciles?" I've never been so angry. "All you had to do…"

"Charlie. Let me."

"I don't know what you hope to…"

"Charlie." Wade's holding both my shoulders. "Let me."

I shrug away. Christ. I've been through hell and just as I think I'm getting my life back on track, Lottie turns up and it doesn't stop there. The sheer fucking stupidity.

Wade is talking. Must pay attention. "…is all a bit of a surprise. I can't even begin to imagine what it must have…"

Christ-all-fucking-mighty. All they had to do was take their videos to the police. Instead, they've gone on some mad rampaging vengeance thing. They probably haven't even killed the right fucking people.

Fuck it. Wade's still talking. "...if the other videos are like that one, they're gold dust, evidentially. Why didn't you take them to police?"

Wasn't that what I just fucking said? Jeez.

It's Eileen who speaks. "If we had handed these videos over, what would have happened?"

"They'd have been analysed."

"No. What would have happened to us?"

"You'd have given a statement."

"What do you think that would have been like for us?"

"Well, I don't know but..."

"Absolutely right. You don't know. Let's move on a bit. Let's say the detectives find these five disgusting perverts and convince the CPS to charge them, do you think they'd have pleaded guilty?"

"Probably not."

"Probably not? Don't you mean *definitely* not? They'd have contested the provenance and admissibility of the videos. Then they'd have contested the veracity of them. Then there's the press and the media who'd have been whipped up into a frenzy and our faces and names would have been splurged across every conceivable glossy magazine you can think of, not to mention the dark web, for other bloody perverts to have a wank over."

"Your names and pictures wouldn't have been released. They'd have held it..."

"Not released? You really believe that? Do you think our statements would have been served and accepted or do you think the defence might have wanted to cross-examine us?"

"They'd have obviously wanted to…"

"Too bloody right, they'd have wanted to cross examine us. But hey, that's okay. They'll put us behind a nice screen and a nice social worker will hold our hands. Do you think they'd have had five individual trials or brought them all together into one big trial? We'd have been cross-examined by five different QCs, one after the other." Eileen looks away. She's trembling. When she looks back at Wade, her eyes are wet with tears. "How do you think Ush would have got on with that?"

"Stop it. Stop it." Ursula has buried her face in her arms. Her shoulders are shaking. I hear soft sobs.

Eileen wraps her arms around Ursula and they both cling to one another.

I don't know what to say. I don't even know what to think. Rob and Zach are both as distressed as Ursula and Eileen. Wade's still thinking. Just as well, as I'm not.

"I think," says Wade, "Charlie and I need to go but, before we do, there's a couple of things I need to say." He pauses. "Charlie and I are both police officers but before that, please understand, we're both human. Neither of us can walk away from you. Charlie can't walk away because of Lottie. I can't walk away because I'm Charlie's friend. Right now, we need space – space to think. We'll meet and talk again, without the emotion."

He holds his hand out towards me.

I stand by myself and frump out.

CHAPTER TWENTY-EIGHT

I'm so angry. When the anger bubbles over, I end up putting on a spurt and only realise when Wade's a hundred yards behind. I jog on the spot waiting for him.

"I hate this baseball cap Zach gave me," he says as he catches up.

"Keep it on. You're less identifiable on CCTV." I run on.

I get to his place and he's still way back. Stretches. The anger in me won't subside. "Why me?"

"Not just you, me as well."

"Ah, Lottie. Where have you been all my life?"

"Sarcasm is unbecoming."

"I'll give you unbecoming."

"You seem to be finding it easier hanging on in there."

"It's not hard."

"Not hard, so long as we accommodate one another."

I use the kerb to stretch my calves. "When you embarked on this murder spree, you were accommodating me, were you?"

"You would never have agreed."

"Too bloody right, I wouldn't have agreed." I bend forward and touch my toes with my elbows, nearly. "So you presented me with a *fait accompli*."

* * *

Fait accompli? Yes but what choice did I have? Charlie would not have agreed. So, I am getting our lives back on track. Sure, Charlie did not ask for any of this but neither did I.

Letting Charlie in is necessary but maybe I let her in too quickly. She is not as well read as me, but she is smarter, street smart. She trusts her instincts. I have to think things through.

I know I have dropped Charlie right in it but if anybody can work this out, she can.

"You say, *'Why me? Why me?'* Think of the soldier about to go over the top, the passenger on a hijacked aeroplane, the patient whose condition is terminal."

"They have no choice."

"There are always choices."

"You failed to include me in any choice."

"*Failed to include you?* Maybe that choice would have been avoided had you stood your ground and taken the pain. Instead, you ran away."

"Ran away? Ran away from what?"

"You found Elly."

Charlie is stumped.

I know Ush explained a little but not enough. I am cross. Is explaining fully a good idea?

"You hid her in the cupboard." Charlie is catching up.

"Pots and pans, Charlie. Pots and pans." There, have the whole shebang.

* * *

Silent. Not a sound. Squeezed between pots and pans. The light flickers on working its way in through vents. I hold my breath. Footsteps. Mustn't move. Shadows. I clamp my mouth and eyes tight. Tears escape my eyes but no sound escapes my lips. My right leg trembles. I hold it. Any movement will rattle the pots and pans. The footsteps move away. The light flicks out. I wait. How long? He always finds me. I wait. Maybe not this time. My leg settles. I must wait all night. Only in the morning is it safe. The light flickers on. The cupboard door bangs open. I raise my hands against the glare. A strong hand grabs my arm and I'm pulled out sprawling with clattering pots and pans.

"Get upstairs you little bitch."

* * *

Lottie's angry. I'm sensing embarrassment. "Travis? The warden?"

"Yes. Travis bloody Hendry."

Very angry.

"Sorry, I..." Wade has finally caught up and is breathing heavily, "can't do long distance."

I shift the thought of Travis Hendry from my mind as Wade finds his keys.

"Has Lottie surfaced yet?" he asks as he opens his door.

"Yes, I am here. Where else would I be?" Lottie's so angry she's even sounding off at Wade. He's well capable of dealing with that.

He stops on his way in and looks at me, probably more Lottie than me. "You two been having a chat?"

We're inside and Wade sits, pulling off his trainers.

"We have a lot to catch up."

"One of us more than the other."

Wade's watching. This quick switching must be difficult for him but he seems to be keeping up. At least he's not asking us to wave bloody tea towels around.

"Xavier Viceroy."

"Who's Xavier Viceroy?" Oh, god.

"The next victim."

"What do you mean?" Now, my anger's rising.

"Wait, wait." Wade has stood up. Looks like he's going to try and get between us. That'll be interesting.

I hold up my hands. "I'm okay. Lottie, I think you better explain."

"Xavier Viceroy, identified from the video of Rob's abuser."

I want to jump in but best leave that to Wade.

"Would you explain how you identified him?"

"Long story. Mostly Zachery, Robert and Eileen to be honest, trawling social media sites and then, when finished with school and college, they took jobs which might increase contact with facial recognition systems."

"You can't simply mount your own personal investigation." Wade's recovered from the run. Recovery from Lottie's relaxed description of heinous crimes is not so easy.

Wade's right. Just doing checks on people's criminal records can attract supervisory interest and the *why did you do that search?* question.

"Yes, it has been more difficult than we thought it would be. Eileen, intelligence researcher in The Service, has more freedom in that respect." Lottie looks up to the ceiling. There's an emotion of exasperation but I can't tell whether she's exasperated with Wade, me or both. "I think I've already said this. Our break came through LinkedIn of all places. That's where Zachery found Peter Daventry and Vincent Pope."

"Lottie." There's a bit of condescension creeping into Wade's voice. I should take over but all I'll do is shout and scream at her. "How do you know that the men you killed were the men in the videos?"

Oooh. Lottie didn't like that. "Look," she's keeping her voice level, I can feel her anger but she's keeping a lid on it. "I'm tired. Though Charlie did all the running, it still takes it out of me."

"Do you question them?"

Nothing.

"Simple enough questions, Lottie."

I hold up my hand. "Wade, she's gone."

* * *

"What will we do?" Wade is pacing around.

"You don't have to do anything. If you want out, just say."

"I'm not leaving you."

"That's lovely but you know this will end in tears."

He takes my hand. "Charlie, I can't…"

I prise my hand from his. "My advice to you is to step away. The care they got us to take with no vehicles, no public transport, no mobiles, nothing digital and these baseball caps give easy outers if allegations start flying. At some point, you'll have to act. The most I can ask of you is to delay that as long as possible and give me a chance to come up with a way through this." I move towards his front door.

He blocks me. "Two minds are better than one."

"I already have two minds."

"Not funny."

"I'm involved whether I like it or not." I step forward and push my forehead into his chest. "My prospects aren't good. There's no point in you flushing your life down the toilet."

I feel his arms encircle me and I close my eyes.

"I'm here for you, Charlie."

I feel his warmth for several seconds. "I'm scared, Wade."

He holds me tighter.

Enough. I push away. I don't know where to look. I sniff. I can't speak. I'm through his door and out onto the street, straightening my cap and running hard.

I'm soon across Streatham High Street, heading for Camberwell.

It occurs to me that Lottie doesn't come out when I'm running.

Is it that wrong to accept help from Wade? What are the chances of finding a check made on the PNC? I've done a couple of fishing expeditions and never been caught. Cantrell is meticulous, always asking why we made specific searches but she only supervises one in five. Thing is, her checks are random. DS French will be scrutinising anyone who's done a search on Peter Daventry and Vincent Pope.

So, if Eileen, in MI5, started using facial recognition systems to identify the man in the video by sweeping pictures on social media, that search might not be picked up in a supervisory sense but would be picked up in a subsequent investigation.

I drop down through Tulse Hill. What did Lottie say? 'Though Charlie did all the running, it still takes it out of me.' I decide on a diversion around Brockwell Park. Xavier Viceroy. What the hell kind of name is Xavier Viceroy? Xavier. Not even sure how to spell it.

Pretty identifiable. Won't be many Xavier Viceroys on the system.

Alright. So, they've identified him and let's say they haven't left a trace doing it. Then they've got to locate him. That's easier. Hints on social media. Voters' Register. Any number of public directories. They'd be able to find him. What then? Walk up and stick a knife in? Is that it? Can't be. Zach, Rob, Ursula and Eileen wouldn't be so reckless and, from what I've found out about Lottie, she wouldn't be either. So, what do they do? Follow him? Try and catch him in the act? Too much time. Too much effort. They don't have the resources. How will they verify that Xavier Viceroy is the man in the video? How did they verify that Peter Daventry is the man in the video? Same for Vincent Pope. Not just verify, verify *beyond all reasonable doubt.*

CHAPTER TWENTY-NINE

Lottie emerges as I emerge from the shower. "Anything to say for yourself?"

"More explaining."

What will I do with anything she says? I don't trust her. If she wanted me to trust her, she'd have introduced herself before engaging in murder. "Go on then."

"They will not come forward and include me with them. If you step forward, you'll be on your own, describing how you were sexually abused and why you have no memory of it."

There's stepping forward and there's stepping forward. Mustn't interrupt. Hear her out.

"We decided, as a group, to do this and we establish alibis for one another. Eileen and Ursula have adjusted their appearance, Eileen more than Ursula I might add. Robert and Zachery look alike anyway."

That's true. I'm the odd one out. Neither Ursula nor Eileen could stand in for me. I'm five inches taller and a different shape.

"Another thing, if one of us goes down, we all go down."

Problem there, neither Wade nor I agreed to that.

"Your anger is evident but, Charlie, please understand that we have lives to live. We cannot move on. We have talked it through, considered different options, all the time dreading an approach from Child Exploitation saying they suspect abuse."

Time to speak. "Considered all the options? One of the options was to involve me. How did that discussion go?"

"I wanted to involve you to be honest, but the others were against. They thought you would drag us all kicking and screaming through the judicial process. I told them I would win you round. Would I have done?"

"No."

"There was another option."

This sounds ominous. "To do with our condition?"

"They saw you as a threat and they wanted me to send you down. Charlie, after the tanker incident, you were weak and, after years of being in the shadows, this was my chance. I could have dropped you straight into a nasty public incident or had you wake up in a strange bed with some bloke smoking a cigarette. You would have grown weaker and weaker and, eventually, I would have been able to hold you down. Instead, I gave you karaoke, muddy trainers, Elly."

I don't want to hear this but I can't exactly walk away. "Why didn't you?"

"You never know, it could be that, over the years, I've grown to like you."

Bullshit. "You kept me away from Doctor Slattery."

"Charlie, with so little known about DID, do you think the Job would keep you on as a warranted police officer once they know you have this condition?"

She's right. I'd have been medically retired.

"The way you were reacting to the counsellors in Rehab was ringing alarm bells. Doctor Slattery was happy when you started reacting positively to the counselling and we have been discharged with a favourable report to the Met CMO."

"So you pulled the wool over everyone's eyes."

"Yes, because I think you and I can work this out. I think we can make a go of living a productive life together. We have to set ground rules. Work out how to give each other personal space. We must trust one another and we have a small network of reliable friends who know and understand."

With Lottie saying, "We must trust one another," I realise where we are. She's making a pitch. She's trying to convince me that this is the way forward because, if she fails, she's vulnerable to being pushed under. She's being political, trying to make it sound like she's doing me a favour whilst pushing her own personal agenda. "Coffee?"

"Tea."

"Living a productive life together is going to be a challenge if we can't even agree on what to drink."

"Coffee will be fine."

With the towel wrapped around me, I make tea. While the kettle boils, we're silent, an ominous stand-off. Everything she says sounds laudable. Provided, of course, we avoid the little matter of two murders. "Okay then, Lottie. Couple of things niggling me. First off, why did you stitch me up to Crimestoppers?"

"To keep you off balance."

"You've said that. Now, in the interests of trust and honesty, the real reason would be good."

"Can I get nothing past you?"

"No. I mean yes. For god's sake, you can't get anything past me. Now, come on. Level with me."

"I needed you suspended from duty for two reasons. One, it isolates you from your colleagues and your support network and two, it gives me a bit more time, not having to fit in with your shift pattern."

Thinking about the way Kathy and Lavender dissed me, Lottie's succeeded there. I feel like I'm getting somewhere with Lottie. "That explains why you winked at the CCTV camera up the Elephant. You weren't winking at me. You were winking at the detectives. Goading them."

"Without that, they probably would never have interviewed you so I had to move them past the obvious alibi."

"Dodgy."

"With insufficient evidence to substantiate the allegation, give it two or three weeks, the case will be dropped followed by reinstatement."

Hell of a thing to have on your record. Again, she's hedging the issue. "What were you planning on doing with these *two or three weeks*?"

"Xavier Viceroy, Rob's target, has been located. We are working on the approach but I believe it will be in the next day or two. Eileen's target has been identified but we are yet to locate him. My target is yet to be identified."

Got to hand it to her, Lottie's confiding in me.

"In addition, your target."

"What?"

* * *

"You're joking. Lottie, tell me you're joking." Charlie is cross.

"Deadly serious."

"You guys might need to exact your vengeance so you can move on. I don't."

"You do, Charlie. You do." I got carried away earlier, mentioning the pots and pans but maybe it was for the best. Maybe I should trust to my instincts in the same way that she trusts to hers but how do I broach this subject with her? I suppose, in a way, I already have, but I was angry then. I have been in the position of an observer and, yes, the frustration was hellish but I learnt to accept it and consider it a privilege.

Maybe, in time, Charlie will come to consider it in the same way.

"Charlie, imagine you got to meet Doctor Slattery and told him all your experiences. What do you think would have happened?"

"I have no idea."

"You do, Charlie. You do. Now come on, humour me."

We are back in the bathroom, standing in front of the mirror. Charlie clearly dislikes this as she is distracting herself, drying her hair which is already dry. "Well, I'd have told him about the karaoke and the muddy trainers. Elly. Told him about losing time, loss of memory, finding myself somewhere without knowing how I got there. I wouldn't have told him about the cash-withdrawal at the Elephant."

"What do you think he would have done?"

"I don't know. I'm not a bloody shrink."

"Come on, Charlie. This condition is rare."

"Alright. You said it. We'd become a specimen in a jar."

"Do you want us to be the focus of attention for the psychiatric world? Do you want everybody to know about our condition? With the notoriety you gained after the tanker incident, Britain's hero cop, the press and media would find out. Somebody would let slip, accidentally or deliberately and the only future for us would be a circus act. Roll up. Roll up. Two for the price of one. The woman who impersonates herself."

Charlie has stopped towelling her hair.

She is thinking.

I think I might have got through to her but must let the silence work its magic.

Into the bedroom, slipping on fresh clothes and dumping her running gear into the linen basket, collecting the empty tea mug and out to the kitchen. She makes herself busy, wiping down clean surfaces. Busying herself is something she does when deep in thought. Finished in the kitchen and now she has the hoover out. This will take a while.

* * *

Lottie's been banging on about pots and pans. She hid Elly amongst them. What's the significance of pots and pans?

I put the hoover away and start cleaning the bathroom.

Okay. I would hide to get away from Travis Hendry. One of the places I hid was in a kitchen cupboard with the pots and pans. Travis Hendry was a bully and as childish as we were. He once tore out the last page of a book I was reading and ate it. He'd change the TV channel from a show we were all enjoying to something boring.

Then he got more physical. He would hold a lighted cigarette over my skin, not close enough to cause a burn, but close enough to cause intense pain. He once taped my eyelids up so I couldn't blink. He would slot pieces of tin foil between my teeth. I went to the other wardens but they told me not to be so silly.

One time, one of the other wardens made me point my finger at Travis and say what he'd done. I couldn't.

To get away from Travis, I'd hide.

He'd always find me, I'd get told off and smacked but the smack wasn't the problem.

It did start upsetting me when it turned from childish bullying to something more sinister. Travis became more edgy and more sadistic. He found Rob and Zach somewhere they shouldn't have been and he said he would cane them. He gathered the rest of us, told us what Rob and Zach had done, made them pull down their trousers and pants and bend over. He flexed the cane but didn't strike them, probably thinking about leaving marks. He made Rob and Zach stay there for a whole afternoon and made all us children stay there too. All of us confused and crying.

Rob and Zach were bent over with their little white bums in the air and Travis standing there, flexing his cane.

Was that the time that Lottie formed?

My antennae were buzzing and telling me *get away, get away*. Was that my recognition of the impending abuse? Was Lottie my way of dealing with that? My way of getting away? My escape?

Wade comes to mind.

CHAPTER THIRTY

No matter how hard I try, I can't get past the identification issue. How do they know they've got the right man? Then there's the judge and jury issue. The videos are convincing but they need analysis to ensure they're original and haven't been doctored. Then comes the executioner issue.

Lottie's left me alone, my flat's sparkling, my punchbag's swinging but no answers.

I'm concerned for Wade. He'll help me find those answers but I can't involve him.

Right. Look at this from the other direction. I have the key to solve a murder investigation. So, approach Homicide. DS French. What will he do?

He'll interview me and record what I say. Let's say he goes with the DID? He'll want to speak to Lottie. He'll have me sectioned. Would I give him Zach, Daventry's killer? Ursula, Pope's killer? The roles played by Eileen and Rob?

I can't.

How can I say that? I'm a police officer.

On suspension.

Okay. Would I have them all dragged in?

Why can't I answer that?

Wade.

I send Wade a message. We need to nail down how we use these burners.

It's early evening, and as I'm gearing up for the freezing drizzle, I get a message from Wade. He's on duty. Oh, god. I've been so preoccupied with myself I hadn't noticed that Wade's on a different shift pattern. He must have been moved to another team. He's in trouble.

* * *

I'm lucky. Wade's posted alone down Camberwell. He's on Redcar Street.

I run fast, hopefully get there before he must move or is called away. Redcar Street's short and I find him immediately. I put my finger to my lips and point to his radio. He removes the battery.

"What's the number of your next SIM?"

He rattles it off.

"You were expecting that."

"Yes, what's yours."

I give him a slip of paper.

"You were expecting that." It's dark. I can't read his expression. He takes it, holds it under his torch and drops it into a drain.

"Okay." I'm pretty sure Wade understands this system but I've got to make sure. "One phone call, one message. The message is the phone number of the next SIM, but only the last nine digits. Add two onto each digit."

"The first two digits, always being 07, will give away the cypher key. You are taking this seriously."

Does he think this is overkill? "We're dealing with murder. Get this wrong and we could be facing difficult questions."

"Okay. Two on each number. What if it's a nine?"

Good question. Reassuring. "Nine becomes one."

"Got it. Repeat the number I just gave you."

Now he's testing me. I repeat it to him.

He raises a brow. "Funny he says. I remember things I see. You remember things you hear. Explains why you're so good at remembering conversations."

"We haven't much time. You must get that battery back in your radio. Three issues. One, target ID. Two, reliability of the videos. Three, conviction, sentence and execution."

"You asking me if I'm in?"

"Yes."

"Are you?"

"I don't know."

"Is Lottie listening?"

"Not sure. Assume she is."

"We won't find any answers unless we go along with them."

"Okay. So we're in, but it's conditional." I turn away from him. I didn't mention that a target has been identified for me. I turn back. "Wade, how are you getting on?"

He shrugs. "Been moved to different team. They want me out and they're getting a second opinion."

"Why this sudden development?"

"To do with being late, going sick, not being where I'm supposed to be."

"Sorry."

He waves, a dismissive wave.

I watch as he walks away. A solitary figure.

* * *

Wade needs help to stay in the Job. Cantrell's on his side but there's only so much she can do. He's been switched to a different team. It's a way of getting rid of people like Wade, isolate them and eventually they'll make the decision and jump. This is not the profession for Wade and Wade's well capable of sorting himself out. As for me…

On the way home, I pass a deserted children's playground. I'm soaked, the rain's getting heavier and I'm freezing. If I stay out here too long, I'll end up with a dreadful cold, but this isn't a conversation I want to have at home.

"Lottie, I know you're there. If I get a cold, will you get it too?"

"What do you think?"

"I'll take that as a yes." I carry straight on. "We need to know that the videos and identifications are sound. To be convinced, you must tell us the provenance of the videos and method of identification."

"I can do that."

I've perched on one of the swings. "Sounds like there's a *but* coming."

"A big one. Before we hand you the key to the murder investigation, we have to be convinced of your commitment."

263

In a way, I'm proud of her. Maybe she was listening to Wade and me in Redcar Street. Also, she's had loads of time to think about all this and she's pushing more than me for Wade's involvement. "Thought you'd say that. What have we got to do?"

"Xavier Viceroy will be confronted by Rob around seven-thirty tomorrow evening. Because of this target's circumstances, all four of them will be involved. You and Wade are to lay the alibis. Tomorrow morning, you will get the means to do that." She's got all this planned. "During the day, I will tell you what you need to do. It will involve covering large distances. You might want to think about using bikes."

"Wade will be happy with that but I've never worn Lycra."

I don't hear it but I do feel Lottie chuckle. "Funny," she says, "how wearing high-visibility gear is one of the best ways to avoid identification."

"Wade's on duty tomorrow, Late Turn."

"I know. He will have to go sick. Now, can we get indoors, it is somewhat cold out here."

* * *

This shower is good. Will Charlie come in with us, or no? I really think we can pull this off but I understand her reticence. I think Wade is on our side. It seems Charlie is developing feelings for him, something I was not expecting. Should I discourage it? No. Let it take its course. Wade is not attractive to me but I do like him, particularly the way he thinks.

"If we stay in here any longer, we'll dissolve."

Something Charlie finds difficult is luxuriating. I could stand in this shower all night. Now, a little test for Charlie. "Tomorrow, early, I will need the *spot* and I will need you to be in the *dressing room*."

"How long for?"

Promising response. "Like I said, I will brief you once I have the means for you to lay the alibis."

"Okay."

"Charlie, you will wake up and you will be able to come up. I need you to stay down."

"After today's exertions, I'll sleep like a log."

That was too easy. "Agreed but, if you wake up, you must stay down."

Remarkable. It was only this morning she found out about all this. The fact she is already moving up and down the levels, even if somewhat clumsily, is a good sign of acceptance. I do not need her to stay in the dressing room if she wakes but I do need to know whether I can trust her.

CHAPTER THIRTY-ONE

The alarm I set for five has disturbed a poor night's sleep. Feeling groggy, I scrunch the carpet between my toes.

No sign of Charlie.

I brush my teeth. Still no sign of Charlie. It is unlikely she is asleep so, by staying down in the *dressing room*, she is good for her word.

I find a muesli bar in the biscuit tin. That will have to do.

By quarter-past-five, I am doing something I hate – running. Only down to Peckham Road. I do not understand what enjoyment Charlie gets from this. Running is the pits. Not raining though.

On Peckham Road, I wait for Robert who will be along soon. This is an arterial route into London and, at this time, cars are outnumbered by lorries and vans.

The road goes suddenly quiet. No vehicles. No cyclists. Nothing. The wind blows a can rattling into the gutter. Am I doing the right thing with Charlie? Funny how I feel more confident about Wade. Sticking the knife in would be asking too much of him but, going forward, he will be invaluable. What about Charlie? I need her involvement in this right up to her neck. We need her fighting our corner like her life depends on it.

She is in it right up to her neck and that is something she is coming to terms with, not because she wants to, but because she must.

A cyclist hoves into view.

I believe Charlie will come on board, not through being forced, but because we satisfy her that our identification method withstands the test, the test being *beyond all reasonable doubt*.

The cyclist stops by me and pulls out a small package from his backpack.

I go to take it but he pulls it back.

I know why. "Okay, Robert, reliable as ever."

He smiles and hands me the package. "Hi, Lottie. How are things working out?"

"Good. Charlie and Wade are doing well. Could go either way but, you know me, optimistic to a fault."

"I understand the need to involve Charlie but why Wade? You said because Charlie needs a friend. We're her friends."

"Charlie is unpredictable. Of all her friends, Wade is the one who has a calming influence over her. Funny to think that just over a month ago, Charlie could barely be civil to him. Wade is looking for meaning in his life and I think, in Charlie, he has found it."

Robert nods, the light on his helmet catching me full in the eyes.

I doubt he is convinced but he once said that he trusts me, that he would do anything for me. Not a crush. Those kinds of feelings and emotions have been burnt out of us.

"I don't mind telling you, Lottie, I'm nervous."

"Your turn tonight, Robert. Erasing Xavier Viceroy. You having second thoughts?"

"No. Not second thoughts. Just nervous."

"Eileen, Ush and Zachery will be with you."

"There's so much that can go wrong. Five-hour ride to Oxford. Do the deed. Five hours back. It's a lot."

"Everything is prepared. You have done all you can. You all have."

Robert nods, the light on his helmet again catching me full in my eyes. "I'm meeting Zach and Ush on Putney bridge. We'll link up with Eileen near Heathrow. Then the long haul to Oxford." He shakes his head. "It's tight. A puncture could throw out our timings."

"Stay positive. Charlie and Wade will be watching your backs."

"I'd feel better if you were watching our backs."

"You leave Charlie to me. By the end of today, you will be free, like Ush and Zachery."

He nods. "Free." He clips into his pedals and, within seconds, he is out of sight.

I stand for a while and let my mind go blank. Charlie is there but she stayed down. Good.

* * *

I walk home and, by the time I get indoors, I feel Charlie in the *wings*. "You can come out now."

Charlie comes out onto the *stage*.

"Thanks for staying down."

She moves onto the *spot*. "If I say I'm going to do something, I do it."

In all honesty, I know I can trust Charlie. What concerns me most is her ability to jump three steps ahead leaving me trying to figure out what attracted her attention.

She must feel the same. Over the last month I have jumped many more than three steps ahead. I know she can handle it but is she up for it?

Together, we would be formidable.

"How do you get on in the *wings*?"

"I don't like it. I know something's happening but it's not clear."

"Like being under water?"

"Exactly. Blurred. Distorted. Everything's patchy. Jumpy. I don't know how long things are taking. Sort of disconnected."

"What do you think happened?"

"I know you went for a run. Not very far. You met someone you know. There was a bike. When his light shone in your eyes, our eyes, it was painful. I tried going deeper, but the pain got worse so I came up. I did catch the end of your conversation with Rob. I'm sorry."

"Bright light is more painful the deeper it gets. No need to worry, I understand. Not many would. Listen, I must bring you and Wade up to speed. To save me having to say everything twice, can we go over to Wade's and would you mind doing the running?"

* * *

I've messaged Wade. If he does go sick today, it'll be curtains for him and his *escape*.

I've been running a lot but skimping on limbering up and stretching. It's getting painful. I do a proper warm-up.

Running over to Wade's, I'm wondering what Lottie wants to say. A briefing on alibi-laying no doubt. This lifestyle does have its positive side – good for fitness.

Wade is up by the time I'm there.

"We getting our orders?" he asks as he lets me in.

"Not before coffee."

He starts work on his coffee-bar contraption while waiting for Lottie to surface. I extract the little parcel Rob gave Lottie and unwrap it. Four debit cards and four pieces of paper. The debit cards belong to Ursula, Rob, Zach and Eileen. The pieces of paper show what are obviously PINs identified by initials U, R, Z and E. Along with the initials and PINs are their addresses.

Jeez.

I'm exasperated but I don't really know why. The lack of security? The simplicity? My involvement? Wade's involvement? Probably a combination.

"You okay, Charlie?" Wade hands me a mug of coffee. Smells good. It's then I notice he has a blue sports support round his wrist.

"No, I'm not okay." I take a slug of coffee. "What's wrong with your arm?"

"You mentioned sick leave in that text message. Soon after I left you on Redcar Street, I walked straight into a theft-from-vehicle. You'd be proud of me. I did a Lavender."

"Oh. Go on then."

Wade grins, hoists his belt and says, "I comes round the corner and, would you believe it, there's this Vauxhall complete with smashed window, door open and two friggin' legs sticking out." He scratches the side of his belly. "So I goes over and chummy's lying across the front passenger seat with his head under the dashboard. I wait till he's extracted the car radio and I leans on the car door, trapping his legs. Should of seen his face as I said, 'Is this your friggin' motor?'"

"Nice one." His imitation of Lavender is appalling.

"I haven't finished yet." He scratches his side. "Chummy had a lookout. Not a good lookout. More a kind of, after-the-fact lookout. Turned into a scuffle. I've hurt a finger because he assaulted my fist with his friggin' chin."

"So you've been placed sick?"

"Went to hospital and everything."

"Hospital?"

"Yeah. Had to escort my two prisoners. I don't know how, but chummy had contracted a broken leg from the car door and the lookout was sparko on the pavement."

"So, you're back in everyone's good books. How's your hand?"

"Nothing wrong with it. Spoke to the A&E doctor saying I needed some time off and he gave me this support," he waves his hand, "and a sick note for a week. The skipper told me, when I resume, I'm to fuck off back to Mary Contrary's team."

"Reeeesult," I say. "Remember, Wade. You're not out of the woods yet."

Good to hear Wade sounding upbeat about the Job. It's now time to sound upbeat about something that could land us in prison for a couple of decades. "Come on then, Lottie. Curtain call."

There's no noise, just sounds of grunting and groaning, then footsteps, a china cup knocked onto a tiled floor and whoosh of water over dry sand.

"Hello, Wade."

"Lottie."

"Right. Xavier Viceroy lives in Oxford. The hit will be at seven-thirty this evening. All four of them will be there." Considering what she's saying, Lottie talks so easily. "Despite height discrepancies, your jobs are to lay their alibis. Set up their alibis near their homes. You have their PINs in case contactless fails or is unavailable. You must do two each and the distances involved are large but make purchases as close to seven-thirty as you can. Debrief will be at Eileen's."

"That's the wrong way round. Don't you mean Ursula's or, better still, Rob's." Wade's got something there.

"It will be a long day for them. You want to make them ride all the way across London?"

"Where's the sense in laying an alibi for Eileen if she could lay it herself?"

"We debrief at Eileen's."

"Lottie. Oxford to Harrow takes about an hour by car."

"Just get those alibis laid and we debrief at Eileen's."

"Charlie's not an experienced cyclist. You're asking too much of her."

"Wade."

"The ride from Ursula's to Eileen's is more than two hours."

"Wade."

"What?"

"She's gone."

"This is crazy. We just need to reverse the order. Why make it difficult, if not impossible?"

"Lottie's thinking about them, not us and I'm kind-a with her on that."

"For Eileen's alibi to work, you must lay it before eight-thirty."

"In that case I'll get there before eight-thirty."

"Sheer stupidity."

"Wade. They're testing us. It's ninety minutes by car from Oxford to Ursula's. I can pinch some time at that end. We'll make it work."

"How will it work if you end up under a bus?"

"Wade. I'll manage."

"Lottie's expecting you to keep the lid on it while they continue their murderous campaign."

I take his hand. "I said before, you can step away."

"No. I'm not stepping away."

I've never seen him so determined. Actually, he's annoyed. "What's bugging you? I mean really bugging you?"

Wade twists out of my grip and returns to his coffee machine. When he comes back with two fresh mugs, his face is set. "You know, Charlie. What's upsetting me most, is that I actually agree with what they're doing. Hear me out. Giving evidence in court is no place for people who have suffered like they have. So, who's going to test the evidence?"

"We must."

"How can we? They haven't come clean about their identification process."

"Fine words, Wade, but what do we do?"

"We draw our line."

"What about these alibis?"

"We lay the alibis, then draw our line. Our line will depend on their identification process."

"Okay." This isn't very different to the conversation we had yesterday.

"How are you?"

He's done it again, changed direction. I'm thankful in all fairness but it still irritates me. "Why do you ask?"

"In less than a couple of months, your life's been derailed. I can't believe you're being so sanguine."

"Sanguine? What does that mean?"

"Accepting."

"I have two options. Breakdown and cry or carry on. I've chosen the second. Now stop this. After laying these alibis, we'll grill them about their identification method."

"An innocent man might be killed."

"Wade. What can we do about that?"

Wade goes quiet.

"Now. The alibis. I must do Ursula and Eileen, in that order. Ilford to Harrow is twenty-four miles and my bike's not the best. You have Rob and Zach, Lewisham to Putney, eleven miles. Then you've got to make your way up to Eileen's. We better get going."

Wade starts smiling. He disappears and returns with a bag of clothing, including a cycle helmet. "I've bought you a decent bike."

* * *

I'm nervous. I've never really ridden a bike in traffic.

Wade shows me how to change a tyre. Then he holds

the bike while I practise clipping in and out of the pedals. I have my arm around his shoulders. Our faces are close. I look away. "Now go up and down the street," he says, hurriedly. "Stop every few yards. Get used to those pedals."

We work out routes and timings, figure out where we'll make the purchases and squeeze into all the gear. A lot of layers. "You'll be grateful for those padded pants," he says.

By late morning, I'm heading north for Ursula's place. Plenty of time. The rush will be Ilford to Harrow, a two-hour ride. It's a ninety-minute drive from Oxford to Ilford so I'll make Ursula's purchase as soon after six as I can. That'll give me two-and-a half hours to get to Harrow and make Eileen's purchase. It's cold but thank god it's not raining. The lorries worry me. Wade said to avoid skulking in the gutter. When I started, I did a lot of skulking but, on realising I'm generally faster than the traffic, I'm out in the middle. This bike is a joy to ride and my confidence is growing.

Wade has to get from Rob's place in Lewisham to Zach's place in Putney, a one-hour ride, and then make his way up to Eileen's in Harrow.

I stop at a coffee shop and relax. People are looking at me funny. Why wouldn't they? I've kept my helmet and goggles on.

CHAPTER THIRTY-TWO

18:15. I've been outside the convenience store for ten minutes pretending to search my pockets. I need to get in there. I'm right outside, in high-viz with flashing lights. Nothing quite like hiding in plain sight.

As expected, from our rudimentary research, this convenience store doesn't seem to have CCTV. There are no signs advertising CCTV. There's no evidence of cameras but I can't really tell. I can't see any local authority cameras on this street. If there are, I hope they're high up.

It's still busy.

18:25. I'm eating into my travelling time to Harrow. Still busy.

18:30.

Not good. Still busy. Not good. There's a queue at the counter. Bit longer. I secure my bike to a lamp post and start rummaging through the little saddle bag.

18:40. I won't be able to make Harrow in time. Can't delay any longer. Must go now.

Thank god. The queue at the counter has died down.

I make a play of finding my purse and I'm into the store. Refrigerated displays. Tuna wrap. Up to the counter. Ursula's debit card. Contactless. It works. I'm out and unlocking my bike.

Now the long slog over to Harrow.

I wish I had satnav. I've memorised the route but every junction and every turn fills me with anxiety. Is this the turn? No. Next one. Is this it?

I'm ten minutes behind schedule.

It's dark, car lights are blinding and my goggles, being shaded, makes picking out street names hard. A couple of times I'm looking so hard for a street name, I miss what's right in front of me. Both times, pedestrians stepping off the kerb.

I'm all right, still going.

At Stratford, I make a right past the Olympic Park. Another thing, I know south London like the back of my hand. North London is just a load of place names. Wade helped me memorise the route. Must skirt round Stoke Newington. Through Holloway. Chalk Farm. This is near where Peter Daventry was killed. Soon I'll be passing Wembley, where Vincent Pope was killed.

Getting better with the gears. Hills aren't such a problem. This bike is superb.

At last, Harrow.

20:35. I find the Tesco Express Wade and I identified. It's busy. If I go in there, I'll be standing close to other people. Same as for Ursula, my height will work against Eileen. This is no good. The crowd's not showing any sign of letting up. I've made up a bit of time but not enough. I'm already late. Must find somewhere else. Just fifty yards down the road is a Spa. Again, crowded. No good. There's a petrol station opposite. Possible. This isn't working.

20:40. There's a cash-machine. The temptation is strong. No. Too many cameras and there'll even be one in the cash-machine itself. No good. A pub. No. I would have to spend too long in there. Come on. Come on. A coffee shop. Looks closed. No. Hang on, someone's in there.

20:50. Got to be it. Lamp post. Secure bike. In. Takeaway latte. Debit card works. Out.

20:53. How do you ride a bike while carrying a latte?

As I stop outside Eileen's, Lottie pops up.

"Late."

I know I was late – by twenty-three minutes. Will it make a difference? Eileen's in Oxford. Seven-thirty is the critical time. They were uncomfortable with an hour. One hour and twenty-three minutes. Have I let everyone down? "You saw the problems I was having."

"No need to worry. Tell you what. Cycling is easier than running."

"I suppose it is if you don't have to do it." Shouldn't have said that. Lottie's pissed off with me but still trying to make me feel better.

"You can lock the bike up over there and Eileen has a key-safe holding a key for her flat."

I'm in no mood for feeling either better or worse. "Tell you what, Lottie. You do it."

* * *

I like Eileen's place. Nothing overstated. Clean and organised. It's like my flat but her furniture is more coordinated. It's obvious hers has been decorated and furnished in one shot. Very calm.

Her spare bedroom has a bed.

IF I WERE ME

I peel off my layers. I would have preferred running but it would have taken me three hours to run from Ilford to Harrow.

I'm starting to wonder if Lottie's lazy. She locked up the bike, found the key but then buggered off. Maybe losing so much time and then being sarcastic has pissed her off. Like Wade was saying, by being so late, Eileen's alibi has been rendered useless.

I sit with my tuna wrap and coffee. Doesn't last long. I'm sure Eileen won't mind if I have a shower.

Her shower's a walk-in one. Very nice.

As I'm turning the shower off, Lottie materialises.

"Bit longer."

I turn the shower back on and stand there like a lemon. A few minutes go by.

"Thanks."

"You feeling better now?"

"You know as well as me, that was a test. The delays will not be a problem. I always have trusted you but you can now be confident the others will trust you as well."

Am I supposed to feel flattered?

I wipe down the shower and then start towelling myself down with the hand towel. Eileen might take exception to me using the bath towel. Then it dawns on me. It's me doing everything.

"Tell you what, Lottie. Thanks for the vote of confidence. Right. I got us here. I got us fed. I got us showered. You do something. I'll be in the *dressing room*. Give me a shout when Wade turns up."

* * *

There goes our Charlie.

So confident but never tries to prove herself. Fiercely independent but having it dented. She is concerned about involving Wade because she wants to avoid becoming dependent on him. She is realising that she is dependent on me but then I am dependent on her, though I have had many years to get used to that.

She will find a way through this. I have complete faith in her.

A knock at the door, probably Wade.

"That's a handy bike shed," he says as I let him in. He looks at me. "Is Charlie here?"

He takes off his helmet.

"Or do I have the pleasure of your company this evening?"

I try, but fail, to hide a grin. Wade is so accepting but, in the right context, he misses little. "Charlie asked me to call her when you turned up. Before I do, may we chat?"

Wade looks at me suspiciously, at least, his version of suspiciously. "Yes. Go on."

"I had not even spoken. How did you know it was me?"

"You look different. Your features are the same, obviously, but your expressions single you out. You have a more controlled look about you whereas Charlie is more, I don't know, wild. Also, the way you speak and your posture. Your poise as well. Mostly, though, it's mannerisms."

Expressions. Mannerisms. I have never considered them. There is something I need to ask him. "Why are you doing this?"

"Fair question. You and your friends seem intent on dropping Charlie in trouble. She's a victim in all this and I'm doing what I can to help her."

In most conversations, particularly with the likes of Albert Lavender and Kathy Bond, Wade is ridiculed. In this kind of conversation, Wade needs treating with respect. He is already half a dozen exchanges ahead. I choose my words carefully. "The word *victim* has many meanings."

"True. The five of you are victims of exploitation by Travis Hendry and horrendous sexual assault by Peter Daventry, Vincent Pope and Xavier Viceroy though I'm yet to be convinced by your identification process. Daventry, Pope and Viceroy are the victims of murder."

"Deserved."

"I don't think we do capital punishment in this country."

He has this conversation all mapped out. Best to jump to the end. "Born that way. Mentally ill. Cycle of abuse. Choice."

"You know that those proposed causes of paedophilia need a million words of context."

He recognises I have circumvented an entire discussion. Jump again. "This evening, you laid two alibis to facilitate a murder which makes you complicit."

"Who says I've been laying alibis?"

Very clever. Wade has so much to offer. "Charlie is stirring. You want to be spending time with her."

"That would be nice. Please understand, I'm happy to spend time with you and with you both."

He really accepts us as two separate identities. So as

not to let him get away too easily, a parting shot, well, broadside more like. "Of all those millions of words laying context round the causes of paedophilia, are any of them devoted to the therapeutic effect of killing one's abuser?"

* * *

"What were you talking about?"

"*Hi, Charlie.*" Wade's all friendly.

"Don't *Hi, Charlie* me. What were you talking about?"

"The therapeutic effect of murdering one's abuser."

That's the bit I heard. "Heavy."

"How did you get on?"

He's changed the subject. May as well go with it. "Ilford, six-forty. Harrow, eight-fifty."

"Eileen's alibi is compromised."

"I know. Things didn't work out. How did you get on?"

"Lewisham, nineteen-hundred. Putney, twenty-hundred."

"CCTV?"

"None, as far as I could tell. You?"

"I assumed there was. I made sure each venue was as empty as possible to avoid height comparisons. The delays made me late. Can we find out what CCTV coverage there is without showing out?"

"Checking could be more damaging than leaving images of ourselves. Our faces were covered, we wore several layers distorting our body shapes, cameras invariably look down so that will help mask height differences and camera images are generally grainy."

Wade's right.

My thoughts move on to reliability. If Ursula's hoiked in and questioned by someone like DS John French, how long will it be before my name pops into the conversation? Zach, Rob and Eileen are probably stronger but I think Ursula would crack. That reminds me of something Lottie said. "Wade. I don't know if you know, they have a pact among themselves. Lottie said, 'If one of us goes down, we all go down.'"

"Very Three Musketeers."

"Three what?"

Wade leans forward and takes hold of both my shoulders. He bends down so his face is right in front of mine. "So no half-measures. In or out. You're in, you have no choice. I do have a choice. I'm in because I can't walk away from you and, after what I did today, my decision's confirmed."

He moves one of his hands and cups my cheek.

I nuzzle his hand.

His face is right there.

No one has ever been so kind and understanding towards me but these circumstances are all wrong.

Over the past month, and particularly the past couple of days, everything's changed. I no longer know who I am. All the feelings of being watched and feelings of paranoia have sprung out, jack-in-the-box-like, and I need time, time to find myself. Lottie, Eileen, Ursula, Zach and Rob aren't allowing me that time. I'm vulnerable. All I have to ground myself is Wade.

I turn my face away, hating myself.

"Is Lottie there?" Wade asks.

I shake my head not daring to speak. In truth, I can't tell whether she's there.

I pull away from Wade and move over to the window. It's black outside. I see Wade's reflection and then feel his hands on my shoulders.

"Come on," he says, "come on."

I turn and push my face into his chest. The tears I didn't want him to see are soaking his shirt.

I push him back, keeping my face turned down.

"Tell you what, Charlie," he says, "it's been a difficult day. I've been here for a while now and haven't been offered a drink. Shall we rummage?"

"You go ahead," I manage. "When are we expecting the others?"

"Early hours."

"I'm sorry, Wade, I umm, I'll take the spare bedroom. You take the sofa. There's a throw you can use as a blanket. I'm sorry. I'm sorry."

I'm through to the spare bedroom and shut the door.

CHAPTER THIRTY-THREE

I can't sleep. Don't even have Lottie for company. Am I destined to spend my life alone, pushing away anyone who comes close?

Or is it that I have Lottie? She's close and I can't push her away.

I don't know what to think. I'm adrift, being drawn into a whirlpool and there's nothing I can do. My life has been ripped away. From tanker incident to the DID revelation. From DID to complicity in murder. With all that came a closeness with someone, a closeness I've never experienced before. It's a closeness I wasn't expecting and it's a closeness I want but, when my life's in such a state, how can I?

I heave myself onto my side and puff up the pillow. No good.

The clock shows 23:16.

So, since the tanker incident… Oh, god. I can't go through this again. I turn onto my front. How are they verifying the identification of… Stop it, stop it.

I'm exhausted but my brain's spinning. I must relax. Come on, relax. I wish I could be with Wade. Not possible. What would Lottie think? Do I even need to involve Lottie? Of course I do and the circumstances aren't right, too much at stake, call it bad timing.

No, I mustn't make this any more complicated.

The next thing to happen is a debrief from Eileen, Ursula, Zach and Rob about their trip to Oxford. Did Rob get to exact his vengeance?

* * *

There are noises. The clock says 04:37. Must be the gang. The funny taste in my mouth means I've been asleep.

They're all in the living room, talking quietly.

Wade is calling through from the kitchen, kettle in hand.

Zach says he's busting for a pee and disappears towards the bathroom. Ursula says she's never doing that again and throws herself into an armchair. Rob's very quiet. Eileen is peeling off layers, unembarrassed.

"I used your spare bedroom, hope that's okay?"

"Should have used my bed. Wade needn't have slept on the sofa."

Wade comes in with hot drinks as Zach returns.

We settle. The central heating hums.

No one speaks. Rob looks uncomfortable. Maybe things didn't go to plan.

I want to ask but I'm not sure it's my place. Wade's finding it awkward too.

Are they waiting for Lottie? Maybe that's my way in. "I haven't heard from Lottie since yesterday evening."

"Wasted trip." Ursula's knackered.

"He wasn't there?"

Zach blows out his cheeks. "He was there alright.

Xavier Viceroy's not the man in the video."

I'm stunned. Of all the things I was expecting, I wasn't expecting that. Even Wade is looking lost for words but my thoughts shift to Rob. He's sat on the floor leaning back against some bookshelves. I kneel by him. He won't look at me. I take his hand. He doesn't speak.

"We've got to start over, Rob." That's Ursula. She's knelt by him too and taken his other hand. "I know you're disappointed. Xavier Viceroy was the wrong guy. We found that out and let him go."

"Rob," this is Zach, "we always knew a non-verification is a possibility. In fact, a likelihood. It's happened twice to me and once to Ush. We know how you feel. Your opportunity will come. We'll get there. We'll make that identification and it'll stick."

"I thought I was going to be free." Rob is staring at his hands, one held by me, the other held by Ursula.

"It's okay, Rob. We will find him." Ursula pulls Rob into a tight hug.

Rob lets go my hand and clings to Ursula. "I thought I was going to be free."

Eileen, wrapped in a white robe, is neither talking nor looking at Rob. She's turned away, her face a mask of anguish. What does Zach mean by it happening before? Twice to him and once to Ursula?

Lottie's not even here. Wait a minute. She is there, in the *wings*. I'm feeling for Rob and, with my emotions running high, I hadn't noticed her. I allow her onto the *spot*.

"Did things go according to plan or no?"

Zach holds out his hands. "It wasn't him."

Lottie takes a deep breath. "Come on guys. Our targeting works perfectly. I know you are disappointed, Robert, but an innocent man is still alive because of our targeting process. We must keep on keeping on. We were very lucky with Peter Daventry and Vincent Pope. Achieving two verifications from the first six identifications, what were the chances of that? Since then we have bolstered our verification process. Our targeting is sound."

Lottie knows both Wade and I are listening. Is this an act?

"I understand." Rob pushes away from Ursula. "I understand," Rob continues, "but it still hurts. I thought I'd be free."

Lottie turns to Eileen. "How quickly did you decide it wasn't him?"

"Immediately." Eileen still won't look up.

Lottie fixes on Zach.

"Immediate," Zach says.

"Ush, what do you say?"

"Immediate," Ursula says.

"Robert. You were there. What did you make of the test?"

"I don't know. I had the knife ready when they gave the thumbs-up.

Lottie called it targeting. Whatever it is, it works. An innocent man has not been killed and it sounds like it's happened on three other occasions. What did Zach say? Twice to him and once to Ursula? What did Lottie say? *Two verifications from six identifications?*

I need to know their process, from end to end, but

they've been skirting around it. This is an act and I'm tired of it.

The interesting thing though, is that Lottie is clearly in charge. Maybe time to challenge that.

I move onto the *spot*. Lottie's annoyed but she accommodates me. "Lottie. Wade and I have cottoned on that you have a system. You're clearly not ready to share it with us. Everybody's dog tired. Except you. Five of us still have long journeys home."

Lottie moves back but Wade speaks. "We need to know two things. First, your targeting process clearly involves two steps – identification and verification. We understand the identification step. We need to understand your verification step. Second, we need to know how you all communicate with one another. I'm in, but if I don't start getting some trust from you guys, count me out."

Wade has seen deeper into all this than I have and Lottie is rattled. Eileen fires a look across to Ursula. Zach has stood up. Rob is still dwelling over his dashed hopes.

Surprisingly, it's Ursula who speaks. "Charlie, we need to talk things through. Weird question but would you leave us, go to the *dressing room* or whatever. You must promise you won't listen in."

I nod.

"And, Wade," Ursula continues, "would you give us half an hour. Go for a walk or something."

Wade heads for the door. "I'll be back in half an hour."

* * *

"Why aren't we telling them?" Zachery.

Charlie has gone and I am left, not just on the *spot* but, on the spot. This whole plan works because of Charlie and Wade. I could not have done what Charlie did last evening. Without Wade, Zachery and Robert would be at greater risk. Charlie has no choice. Wade is the loose cannon. "Are we comfortable with Wade?"

"The alibis he set for Zach and Rob are sound." Eileen.

Zachery is checking the receipt Wade gave him. "I know the shop. It's good."

Robert is still in the doldrums. Ush reaches into Robert's pocket and pulls out the receipt. "Mannin Convenience Store. Do you know it, Rob?"

"Yes," Robert is still brooding, "near my place, it's good."

Ush hands the receipt back to Robert and says, "Wade's fallen for Charlie."

"That's obvious." Eileen. "How are you with that?" She's looking at me.

"Completely fine."

"Sure about that?" Eileen.

"Why not?"

"How will you feel when, not if, they become intimate?" Ush.

"I can leave them to it."

"Can you?" Eileen.

"Yes." This is annoying me. "Look, are we going to tell them how we do this or not?"

"It's a risk," Zachery, "but there's a lot of risk in what we're doing. Tell them."

"Ush?"

"Happy with Charlie. Not convinced with Wade."

"Eileen?"

"We safe-guarded ourselves by saying the approach would be at seven-thirty when we intended eight all along. The test was whether they would go against you and do it in reverse order. What happened there?"

"Wade wanted to reverse the order. Charlie wanted to follow my instructions. She overestimated her ability. The task was impossible. She did everything she could. She took so many risks getting across London, not being an accomplished cyclist. Incredibly brave. Scared the life out of me several times."

Eileen nods. "It was a tall order. Charlie's good." She plonks herself on a dining chair, the wrong way as usual. "Our concerns about Wade arise because he could have been inserted undercover by police but, if that's the case, they'd have intervened when we approached Xavier Viceroy. Wade's good. Tell them."

"Robert?"

Robert doesn't respond. Ush curls her hand round the back of his neck. "Rob," she says, "we need to know what you think. After what Eileen said, I'm good with Wade."

"Oh. Ummm. Yeah." Robert squirms out from under Ush's hand. "Yeah, yeah. Tell them."

"Okay. When Wade gets back." How could I have missed that argument Eileen presented?

"We haven't finished yet." Eileen. "Lottie. Do we let Wade in?"

What is this? Are they really asking me? "Of course. Charlie and I have things to work out. I am confident we can do that."

"I'm good with Charlie but she seems uncomfortable." Eileen.

"To be expected. Over the past month she's had her life ripped from under her."

"Completely agree it's to be expected." Eileen talks so smoothly and confidently. "Makes her unpredictable and therefore a liability. She's not undercover, same argument as for Wade, but she is struggling with the ethics and morality of all this."

It dawns on me. They are not seeing Wade as the loose cannon. They see Charlie as the loose cannon. Which means they consider me the loose cannon.

For the remaining twenty minutes, we sit in silence, total silence.

* * *

I come up onto the *spot* and there's a strange atmosphere. Lottie's all too willing to move aside. Wade arrives shortly after.

Eileen's straight in. "Despite our jobs, we've made the identifications via social media. We recognise that an identification in this way is suspect, so we've devised a verification process. We confront the target with the video of the abuse. Their reaction verifies the identification," Eileen looks at Rob, "or not."

"So your verification's based on a funny feeling." I couldn't help saying that.

Wade comes in. "Charlie, Eileen hasn't finished."

"We decided there would be a significant difference

between someone who doesn't recognise themselves in the video and someone who does. With that in mind, we approached random people and showed them a video. We got a reaction. Frequently unpleasant but we learnt how people react to this stuff."

"You've been showing this stuff to the general public?" I'm incredulous.

"Charlie. Let Eileen finish." How can Wade be so calm?

Eileen continues. "We made four identifications of Zach's abuser. The first two, when shown the video, reacted in a way that made it clear it wasn't them. The third was Peter Daventry. His reaction was indisputable. Ush, please describe that reaction."

Ursula clears her throat. "The reactions of innocent people are a range of disgust and offence. The reaction of Peter Daventry was guilt, caught. The difference was so stark. I gave Zach the thumbs-down. He stuck the knife in."

"You're murdering someone on a hunch." I can't keep my voice down. I'm yelling.

As Wade stares at me, raising his finger to his lips, Eileen continues. "We obviously didn't need to approach the fourth. Two identifications for Ush's abuser. We did Vincent Pope second. The first we approached was let go. Rob verified Vincent Pope and Ush stuck the knife in."

Rob nodded. "Clear as day."

"This isn't proof." Again, my voice is raised.

"With both the Daventry and Pope killings, we worked out that the verification from the one holding the knife is unreliable. Probably because of having to psych up for the act. As you two have come on board," she means Wade and me, "we can increase numbers doing the verification, from one to three."

I can't believe I'm hearing this. "Well, I'm sorry. What you've just described, is complete and utter bollocks."

Lottie bounds onto the *spot*. "You do it, Charlie. That guy with the stolen mobile phone under the driver's seat. The boy with the drugs in his pocket."

I push back. "There's a big difference between stopping on suspicion and killing on suspicion." I stand up. I'm not sticking around listening to this fucking bullshit a minute longer. "Sorry guys, gotta go." I'm out the door.

* * *

"Suspend your disbelief."

Wade's caught up as I'm unlocking my bike.

"Don't defend them. If they end up in court, they're going down. Murder."

"That's my point Charlie. Not just them. You too."

"All the more reason for not carrying on."

"If dissuading them from continuing is the objective, then telling them their carefully thought out and tested plan is complete and utter bollocks is, I would suggest, not the best approach."

...is, I would suggest, not the best approach. Who talks like this? Even in my rampaging mind, I find time to wonder, for the umpteenth time, what Wade's doing in the Job.

294

"I found a coffee shop earlier. It'll be open by now." He's unlocking his bike from the stand.

"No." How can we have the conversation we need somewhere so public? "I'm going home. I must talk to Lottie."

"The gang's together now."

"I'm going home." I swing up onto my bike but the gears are wrong. I stand up on the pedals.

Wade is soon next to me. "Sorry, coffee shop's a bad idea. We'll head for Vauxhall Bridge and then we can choose, your place or mine, or we can split up if you want time on your own."

"Time on my own? Wouldn't that be nice." We're cycling side-by-side. It's Sunday morning. Traffic's light. It's mostly downhill. I drop back, happy to sit in behind Wade. It's bitterly cold but not raining or windy.

I can't help but work through the inevitable cross-examination. "Pray tell the court how you knew it was him?" "He looked guilty when we showed him the video." "He looked guilty? Do you not think that any reasonable person might look shocked?" "Reasonable people look shocked. Guilty people look guilty." "Please, for the benefit of the court, describe a shocked response?" "Jaw drops open, questioning gape, disgust, turning to anger as they find their voice." "And a guilty response?" "Jaw drops open, questioning gape, disgust, turning to anger as they find their voice." For fuck's sake.

Lottie's obviously calling the shots. Without her, the others wouldn't be going ahead. Stopping Lottie is my only option. How? Dob her in? I end up in prison having done nothing wrong. Persuade her to stop? Listening to Ursula and Zach and contrasting their confidence with

Rob and Eileen, persuasion won't work. Force her down into the *abyss*? She says I'm mentally stronger than her, but she has years of experience traversing the levels. Force an appointment with Doctor Slattery having got Wade to clue him up? Like Lottie says, specimen in a jar, could be worse than prison. Remove her from the equation? Kill Lottie?

Shit. Wade's stopping. I squeeze the brakes, but too hard. My front wheel skids. Can't correct. I slide straight into the back of Wade. I'm toppling, or is it flying? I tuck my shoulder as I land and roll a couple of times. My knee bangs on the road and I come to a stop.

My cheek's on a yellow line. There's no pain but I know it's coming and there it is, my left shoulder, my right knee. I dig deep not to scream out. I feel hands on me. There are other people. I hear someone say, "Should I call an ambulance?" I hear someone else say, "Is he alright?" I'm a girl for god's sake. Then I'm thinking Wade, what's happened to Wade? Then I hear him. He sounds calm. The pain in my shoulder is wearing off but my knee is bad.

"I think she's unconscious. I'll call an ambulance."

Then Wade says, "Could we hang fire on that? We weren't going fast. I wouldn't want to waste their time for a couple of scrapes and bumps."

More voices have joined in, all concerned, all eager to help.

Then it hits me. Ambulance. No. Can't have emergency services involved. We'd be identified. I must move. I must make them realise I'm okay. What did Wade say? A couple of scrapes and bumps?

I sit up. The pain in my right knee is unbearable. I rub it. God knows what I've done to it. My shoulder hurts, probably road rash. My elbow too. Don't care about my elbow. I must stand up. Wade is kneeling, looking intensely into my eyes. There are others holding mobiles. The word ambulance comes out again. I must say something to stop the 999 call. "Hey. So that's what it's like to fly." I swing my good arm around Wade's shoulders and he helps me up. I can take the pain. I just need my right knee to take my weight.

I'm hopping on my left leg, Wade helping me balance. "How's the bike?" I ask, easing my weight onto my right leg.

"I'll check in a minute."

"I'm okay," I say with a smile on my face and agonising explosions in my right knee. I can't maintain this. I won't be able to get away from these witnesses.

"You need an ambulance. I'll call one now."

"No, there is no need. I am absolutely fine."

That's Lottie.

"Bashed my knee. Hurts, but it will be okay. Look." I'm flexing my knee, bending my heel up behind my bum and straightening it out in front. I'm taking steps now, backwards and forwards, every movement excruciating. Now I'm standing on my right leg, my left heel pulled up onto my right thigh and I'm lifting my arms up above my head. Yoga. As Lottie holds Tree Pose, she says, "I am really in no need of any medical treatment. Please don't waste their time."

My right knee is erupting, volcanic, white hot but Lottie's holding the pose. Voices start fading as Wade's presenting my bike and I slip-slide off the *stage*, away from the pain, through flooding corridors to the *wings* and onto the summit of a hot-air balloon that is the *dressing room*.

CHAPTER THIRTY-FOUR

"Robert, would you examine my right knee?"

I rode away from the over-helpful witnesses but I needed to stop using my knee. As we rounded a corner, I stopped and told Wade. I have no idea how he did it, but, with his strength and balance, he kept me going back up the hill to Eileen's.

I ease myself down onto the sofa and Eileen pulls over a footstool.

Robert feels my knee with both hands, probing the joint with his fingers. He shakes his head. "I need to remove your leggings."

I lift my bottom and wriggle out of my padded shorts and leggings.

"What happened?"

"Ran into the back of Wade. Turfed off, broke out of the clips and rolled over a couple of times banging my knee. Hurt my shoulder and elbow too."

Robert starts poking my knee again. My bare legs stretch away from me. My right knee is developing a bruise on its outside edge.

He lifts my knee and pushes my heel back towards my bum. He straightens my leg again, all the time watching my face.

Robert looks down at my knee, then back up at me.

"Lottie. I need Charlie."

I nod.

* * *

I don't feel like I'm being woken. I wasn't really asleep. It's dream-like but I decide my thoughts and where they're going. It's a safe place, a soft place.

I'm being called down a spiral staircase from a mountain top. I don't want to go. It'll be pain. I want to stay here. Not fair.

I'm at Eileen's. Rob has his hands on my right knee, moving it up and down. "Stop." I'm yelling. "Stop."

"Charlie, I need you to tell me how it feels."

"Stop. Stop messing with it." I try sitting forward but Ursula has her arm around my shoulder. She's not comforting me, she's holding me still and I'm wriggling and squirming to get away. Zach lends his weight to help Ursula. My legs are bare, looking waxy. Rob has his hand on my shin, asking me to push. I can do it, but it hurts. I begin to relax. Ursula releases me. Rob now has a hand behind my calf asking me to pull. I can do it. Zach moves away. There's stinging on my shoulder, Eileen is dabbing the grazes there but it's nothing compared to my knee. I turn back. "Rob, please stop."

"I have, Charlie. You have full range of movement and you can take some strain. Your ligaments seem okay. Bit of bruising. How does it feel compared to when it happened?"

"Different. Not better. Different."

Rob's watching me. His hands are firm and soft. "By keeping it moving, Lottie's done you a lot of favours. You don't want it stiffening up. Keep it moving but try not to put it under strain. Now, what about your elbow?" He takes my arm and bends it every which way.

"My elbow's fine," but it's not.

"Bruising," says Rob. "Like your knee, keep it moving."

Ursula and Zach move away. Eileen finishes dabbing my shoulder. "You can stay here, Charlie. We're all staying. We need sleep."

I don't want to stay here. I shuffle forward to the edge of the sofa and, with Wade's help, stand up. I gain my balance and tentatively shift my weight onto my right leg. It's okay. I hobble backwards and forwards. I smile. "It's okay. Rob, you must have magic hands."

"Don't overdo it, Charlie. There's a lot of trauma. Remember, keep it moving but avoid strain. Cycling's quite good for that. Power on with your left leg. Just let your right leg go round."

"Thanks, Rob." I turn to Ursula, Zach and Eileen. "Thank you."

They nod and smile, except Eileen. "Were you recognised?" she asks.

Good point. The others have seen the significance too. "No."

"How can you be so sure? You've had a lot of publicity recently."

"They didn't even recognise that I'm a girl."

Eileen's not happy. The others are looking to her for guidance. I really don't need this.

Wade joins in. "I was thinking about that. She had her helmet on. Her goggles. She wasn't recognised."

Lottie's pushing. I let her onto the *spot*. "They had their phones out. No one was taking pictures. I am confident Charlie was not recognised."

The others have accepted what Lottie said but Eileen's still thinking. "It's a risk. It will need managing."

"I agree. Like Zachery said, we can add that risk to all the others." Lottie moves off the *spot* and I retake it.

I'm with Eileen, definitely something to consider, but all I can think about right now is my right bloody knee.

My confidence is returning. My knee's alright. Painful, but strong. As my confidence grows, I start putting it through its paces. Squatting up and down. I stand on it, Yoga, Tree Pose. That's good. I try squatting on my right leg only. No, too much.

"Rob, you seem to know what you're doing."

He smiles, embarrassed, the way he smiled when he was a little boy. "I'm a paramedic."

"I thought you were Serious Fraud."

"I am. Once our project is over, I'll be returning to the ambulances."

"Project? Is that how you think of this? A project?"

Wade's moved into the corner. I continue flexing my knee as he says, "Project. A start, an objective and an end. Interesting way to describe the murder of five people."

"They're not people. They're paedos."

* * *

Cycling home. Wade leads and I tuck in behind. We don't talk, even when we come up alongside one another at red lights. He watches me as we set off, sees that I'm not struggling and resumes his position in front.

I'm grateful for the silence because something's happened. The dynamic between the gang and me has changed. I feel closer to them.

I'm concentrating like mad on Wade's back wheel but my head is filled with memories. Travis Hendry would play his games but the five of us would never get upset like many of the others. I remember the time I was told to wait in Travis's office. I was on my own and I read everything on his walls. So many certificates. I don't remember exactly but they were degrees or diplomas in childcare or something.

The time when all five of us were caught in the park long after we should have been back heralded a change. Things started getting uncomfortable and Travis seemed to focus on the five of us. It was about then, I started hiding from him, hiding in different cupboards. The pots and pans cupboard in the kitchen was no longer any use as it became the first place he'd look. I was hiding in Zach's bedroom cupboard one time, peeping through the keyhole, when Travis asked Zach if he'd seen me. "I saw her outside in the garden," Zach lied.

We all covered for one another. Ursula would get upset but we'd buoy her up. Eileen was best. One of the other wardens was a fisherman and she stole one of his rolls of fishing line. Travis Hendry was due to talk to all twenty-six of us in the dining room and we were sat waiting. Travis always kept us waiting. One huge table with cutlery, plates and glasses. Eileen jumped up and started feeding this practically invisible fishing wire around glasses and under plates and left the two ends trailing where she sat. Everyone was wondering what she was doing. Travis came in and started ranting. A little way through, another warden came in to speak with Travis. While they were distracted, Eileen ducked under the table, emerging a moment later. When Travis finally finished, he stood up and left the room, dragging all the plates and glasses and cutlery behind him which Eileen had tied to his shoelaces. The crashing and smashing, the screaming as all the children jumped back, the laughing… The laughing didn't last long.

After that, things got nasty. My hiding places stopped being a game with Travis. They became necessary to hide from him while waiting for his mood to change.

Another set of red lights and I pull up alongside Wade.

"After Vauxhall Bridge," he says, "I'm going to head home to Streatham. You okay for the run down to Camberwell?"

I nod. Things have changed.

He continues. "I need to be in on a conversation with you and Lottie but I think you two need to iron some things out first. I'll come round to yours fourish?"

I nod. Things have definitely changed.

At Stockwell, we go our separate ways.

CHAPTER THIRTY-FIVE

The ride from Stockwell to Camberwell takes ten minutes.

I'm soon indoors, peeling off my layers. My leg's sore but working. I flex my elbow and remove the dressing from my shoulder.

I run a bath and lower myself into scolding water filled with bath salts and bubbles. My skin adjusts to the heat and I try to relax. Something's bugging me. Hiding amongst pots and pans, gripping my trembling leg, clamping my mouth, screwing my eyes shut.

Why was I there?

Hiding in Zach's wardrobe, I'd been throwing food in the dining room. Hiding under Ursula's bed, I'd been drawing on the wall with a felt-tip pen. For every time I hid, I remember why. Raiding the fridge because I was hungry, filling the sugar bowls with salt, switching the mustard and custard, adding pepper to the marmite, but the first time I was caught amongst the pots and pans, I don't remember why I was there. More than that. I don't remember anything from before that.

I was six.

Lottie comes out onto the *stage*.

"Question for you, Lottie. After I fell off my bike, there was no way I'd have been able to do Tree Pose on my right leg. How did you do that?"

Lottie comes forward. "Pain is different for me."

I feel immense relief. She doesn't seem to have noticed my mood. "You don't feel pain?"

"I do but I experience it differently to you."

"We share the same body," and I could kill you.

"All I know is that what is agony for you is a minor irritation for me. Remember Nurse Olu?"

She's not recognising the difference between what I'm saying and what I'm thinking. "Of course."

"Remember her commenting on whether you were having a good or bad day?"

I remember something like that.

"When she thought you were having a bad day, you were on the *spot*. When she thought you were having a good day, I was on the *spot*."

Lottie's making me feel useless.

"Charlie. The pain of the abuse was serious. Taking that pain is why I exist. I learnt to deal with it. The burns from the tanker incident were bad but I could manage them. The bang on the knee was nothing."

I rub my knee, lifting it out of the water. My leg is long and skinny, a runner's leg. The bruise on my knee is starting to show. Should I be immersing it in hot water? Shouldn't I be wrapping it in bags of frozen peas? The hot bath is helping in other ways. "I hear you but I don't understand."

"We could see Doctor Slattery. Would you expect an explanation from him?"

"Wouldn't it be worth getting his input?"

"We are a multiple looked at from a singleton's perspective."

"A specimen in a jar?"

"Doctor Slattery would aim to turn us back into a singleton. Put us back in our box. They call it integration."

I'm starting to get it now. What Lottie's saying is that the only people who can manage this condition is us and we're talking easily with one another. If we don't declare the condition, there'd only be five people who'd know about it: Zach, Rob, Eileen, Ursula and Wade. It's not in their interest to announce it. "Okay. We keep this to ourselves."

There's a long pause. When she speaks, Lottie sounds tearful. "Thank you, Charlie."

"That means a lot to you."

Again, a pause before she answers. I can feel she's emotional but I can't tell what about. I can hear her gentle sobbing but it's short-lived. My vision has blurred because of tears that aren't mine. "More than you can ever know. I have spent so many years in the shadows. I want a life."

"If we're going to live together, we must ensure we don't get caught for these killings." I'm amazed that I can talk so easily when the only thought in my head is suicide.

"Only four more to go, Charlie." Lottie's recovered from her emotional release and returned to her smooth convincingness.

"No. The killings stop." She really has not picked up on my thoughts.

"You saw how distraught Robert was. This is a path to freedom for us. Robert even used the word *free*.

Several times. Zachery and Ush have taken that path and compare them with Robert and Eileen."

I lever myself out of the bath and towel down. It's gone three. Wade will arrive at four. I thought my life was being destroyed but what's happened today has reinvigorated me. The way Eileen, Ursula, Zach and Rob, especially Rob, mucked in to sort me out after I fell off my bike. Not just that, the way Lottie took over to deal with the pain of my damaged knee so we could avoid the 999 call, disclosure of who we are, questions of what we were doing, where we'd been and who we'd seen and the uncovering of CCTV images of me in Ilford and the *why were you there?*

Wade, of course, would have the same questions fired at him. "What were you doing in Lewisham and Putney?"

DS John French would have a field day.

What about their identifications and verifications? At best they're offering opinions. Only expert witnesses can offer opinions. We would never be declared experts.

Are they getting it right? Probably.

Does it justify murder?

No.

Why am I even thinking this?

By laying those alibis yesterday, I've made myself complicit. The actions I took, using Ursula's and Eileen's debit cards amount to offences in themselves.

Lottie and I must draw lines. We will need our own personal space. I'm beginning to understand why Lottie did what she did. She needed to establish herself. If she hadn't done all those things, karaoke, muddy trainers, grassing me up to Crimestoppers, I'd have got back on top and been none the wiser, until the next time.

"Lottie, you there?"

"Yes." She sounds like she's been deep in thought too.

"How will it work? You and me. Together. Trying to hold down a job. Given that I'm reinstated, a police officer's job?"

"Easy. We play to each other's strengths and cover each other's weaknesses. We need to both be there, all the time. The spontaneous stuff, acting on suspicion, staying cool in the heat of the moment will be for you while analytical, persuasion, long game stuff will be for me. We will both need personal space. We have our differences so we just need to talk to each other and be respectful. We could divide up certain responsibilities. For example, probably best if you take responsibility for keeping the body fit. In my hands, we would be four stone heavier in as many weeks."

She's probably right there. "Happy with that. In return, if you don't mind, the killings stop."

"That project will be completed, even if I have to go behind your back." Her voice has taken on that smooth convincingness again. In addition, I'm picking up her feelings. Anger came in there along with her words. Not just the way she said the words, the emotion itself welled up inside me. This is where she has me over a barrel. I'm a quick learner but she's lived this existence for years.

However, I'll give her a bloody good run for her money. She hasn't picked up on my thoughts of suicide or, if she has, she's not showing it. "I don't think it will be *if* we end up in prison; I think it will be *when* we end up in prison. I'll keep the body fit and you take everything else. The prison food, the aggression, the turf wars, the boredom."

"We will not end up in prison."

"We could end up in a prison of our own making. If we kill the wrong person."

"We will not kill the wrong person."

"Your verification process? Not good enough."

"What more do you want?"

"Nothing more. There is nothing more. We can't take it to police, the Child Exploitation lot. Links would be made with the Daventry and Pope killings and we'd be back in front of Homicide. DS French. He's good."

"So, we carry on."

"No. We stop."

* * *

Charlie is changing her tune, evidenced by the immediate denial, followed by the anger and now the bargaining. Wade will help her through the depression onto acceptance.

Wade will be here at four.

Charlie has nowhere to go and she knows it.

What will pull Charlie round is the impact it has already had on Ush and Zachery and the impact it will have on Eileen and Robert. The thing she must still figure out is the impact it will have on me.

How do I feel? Left out, is how I feel. I am dependent on the others to identify my abuser. Still nothing. I want to get there, be given the thumbs-down and plunge in the knife. Then, as he dies, I will tell him who I am. "…that little girl you…"

This will never happen if Charlie is not on board. Wade is my best hope but, in all honesty, I do not think she can be brought round. Very stubborn is our Charlie. She remains unconvinced by our identification process and she will only be convinced by being there.

Ah. Wade has turned up, early, with a takeaway curry.

"Charlie make it home alright?" he asks while unpacking the foil containers.

"I presume so."

"Don't you talk to one another?"

"We fight a lot."

"What can you possibly have to fight about?"

Such a tease. It is good that we can find humour in these circumstances. I have always liked Wade. Of Charlie's friends, Wade is the one with the ability to take all this in. Imagine Albert Lavender. "Friggin' 'ell, Charlie. You the government's plan to increase police numbers?" Kathy Bond. "Does that mean you can have sex with yourself without masturbating?" All of them would have some smart-arse comment. Not Wade though. "Charlie make it home alright?" Maybe it is smart-arse, but subtle and his quip comes from true affection. I still have no idea how he feels about me.

As we tuck into the curry, he says, "Your identification process is not sound."

"That is a matter of opinion," I say.

"No room for opinions in criminal law."

"Opinions disappear when actually there."

"I remain unconvinced."

"As the academic argument fails, you need to be there."

Wade was not expecting that and must think it through. This is why he fails as a copper on the streets. Time to think things through is a luxury he does not have when he has a suspect in front of him. Charlie will make the leap and arrest on suspicion, lawfully and well within her powers, and then search for further information. Witness statements, suspect interviews, physical forensics. Wade finds that leap difficult. People like him are needed in the Job, but a different part of the Job. Trouble is, to get there, he must get through his probation. To do that, he must make that leap. I like the point Sergeant Cantrell made about if he becomes a lawyer, he will benefit from the experience of making that leap. Not sure Sergeant Cantrell meant the kind of leap that will take him to thumbs-up or thumbs-down.

"It's the academic argument that's heard in court." Finally, he has found his voice and his response is pathetic.

"Wade, you and Charlie need to be able to judge for yourself and the only way you can do that, is by being there."

"My problem with what you've just said is the word *judge*." That is a better comment.

"Not your place to judge? Well, I think it is your place to judge. Because, if you choose not to, who will?"

Wade looks stumped. I cannot believe it was that easy.

Keep going. "We have located Eileen's abuser, Frank Amos. We have been working on the approach. I think you and Charlie should go on that one. Do the verification for Eileen, with Robert. Ush and Zachery will lay the alibis."

Shit. I was concentrating so hard on that exchange with Wade, I missed Charlie coming onto the *stage*.

"Excuse me," Charlie says barging me off the *spot*. "Who's Frank Amos?"

This is the difference between Wade and Charlie. "Eileen's abuser. Identified via Facebook. We know where he lives. We are working on his movements."

"Where does he work?"

Wade is looking like he cannot believe what he is hearing. Not sure I can. Is Charlie coming on board? Unlikely. What is she up to? "All we know is that he commutes daily. Train, Tonbridge to Charing Cross, and back."

"What's the problem with the approach?"

"Not secluded enough."

"Who does he live with?"

"Lives alone."

"Break in."

"Alarmed."

"Won't be alarmed when he's in."

Unbelievable. Wade's hair has dropped. Has Charlie just switched? No, she is playing with me but she is playing with Wade too.

"Lottie. Leave us. I want to speak with Wade. I don't want you listening in."

* * *

"I've been thinking. Seems to me…"

"Has Lottie gone?"

Wade's already interrupting. Jeez. "Yes. If you believe that, you'll believe anything."

"Sorry. You were thinking?"

"Lottie's going to do whatever she's going to do. I have two choices. I can join her or kill her."

Most people, on hearing something like that, drop their jaw. I reach up and sweep Wade's hair back behind his ear.

"You're joking."

"Not really. I don't think the gang will continue killing without Lottie galvanising them." I hope Lottie's listening. "Killing her involves committing to a degree of self-sacrifice I'm uncomfortable with. So, joining her it is. At least by joining her, I will have influence."

"What about persuading her to stop?"

"First step to that is joining her."

"With you. What about stopping her from taking the *spot*?"

"There'll be another incident, I'll go into emotional turmoil, she'll break out and it'll start over. Joining her means I'll have a say."

"So, what's your plan?"

Wade doesn't even see it coming. "Two parts. First, persuade them to beef up the identification and verification procedures so they become impossible to achieve. My greatest ally there will be Eileen."

"Part two?"

"Persuade you to step away."

"Persuade away."

"When this project is completed, given that I've not been imprisoned or institutionalised, and given that you're still free, we'll try again."

"I'm not leaving you."

This is killing me. All I want is to be scooped up by Wade and carried away. Mustn't let that show. Come on. They're only words. I must get them out. "You must. Because you're involved, it's not in your interest to dob us in. Getting more involved would be foolish."

Wade falters. He looks down at the mess the takeaway curry has become. His face has gone stony. He gathers the dishes together and starts washing up.

I lean on my fridge, it still has a few letters and numerals. Wade's movements are deliberate and precise. Whilst I know that turning his back on all this is the best thing for him, I don't want him to go. He's working his way through his argument for why he should stay. He's figuring out where and how I'll contradict him, and he's preparing his responses. He won't just launch in. If anyone can convince me that involvement in premeditated murder is a good idea, he can, and I so hope he will.

He dries his hands. His hair tucked neatly behind his ear.

"Everybody resents my Eton education. I went there because I have a rich mummy and daddy, not because I'm bright or intellectual. They sent me there so they could say, 'Wade's at Eton, of course.' I was side-lined while they flounced around the world presenting that English stiff upper lip, with nothing to offer but misplaced self-confidence. I was groomed to be shameless, to tell barefaced lies with confidence, to employ sophistry and bluster. Had I been able to tolerate the insincerity of it, I'm sure I'd have done very well."

Jeez. Where did all that come from? What the hell is sophistry? "Wade. You must step away."

"Must I? Maybe I'm just right for Lottie's little venture. Will anyone kick up a stink about a few paedophiles?"

He's angry. How can I be there for him when I'm not even there for myself?

The person I'm resisting is not Wade. It's me. "A significant part of Lottie's venture is to minimise the risk of the victims being linked to paedophilia. With that link comes the link to the children's home. With that link comes the link to me and Eileen, Ursula, Rob and Zach. You've met DS French. We wouldn't stand a chance."

Wade's eyes narrow. "With the link to paedophilia comes the link to the children's home. How so?"

I even have to explain this and every word is driving a wedge between us. "They've been going around showing dozens, if not hundreds, of people illicit images. Do you think none of those people have complained?"

Wade shakes his head. "I still don't see how they would be linked to the children's home."

"It just increases the risk. Then there's Travis Hendry." I can't hold my composure any longer, my eyes have filled with tears.

Wade's still looking baffled.

More words. Come on Charlie, get them out. "Peter Daventry and Vincent Pope may seem like normal people, nice photos in the press, unfortunate victims of senseless murder but, to other members of the paedophile ring, how do you think they look?"

"So alarm bells start ringing about who'll be the next victim."

"Yes, and what do you think they'll do?"

"They'll go to Travis Hendry because, from their perspective, he's the only person who knows who they are." Wade raises a finger. "Travis will use his videos to defend himself." Wade's nodding, finally cottoning on.

Just a few more words. "Yes. Travis will bring his videos out into the open and then it will all start to unravel. Homicide will form a squad with Child Exploitation and it won't be long before they're hammering down my door."

Wade's gone quiet.

There. It's done. I've said the words. I've silenced him. Or have I? "I thought you said you were well schooled in, what was the word? Something and bluster. Come on then. Let's see some."

"Sophistry and bluster. I can do better than that."

I don't understand.

He's carrying on. "You've come on quite a journey over the past six weeks, Charlie. You're discovering yourself. What you've discovered would be enough to drown the hardiest of people and you have the hardest bit yet to face. I feel privileged to know you and I feel privileged to be a part of this. I'm in for the long haul, no matter where it takes us."

The tears come streaming down my cheeks. The strain of it. The stress. Then on top of that, the emotion

Wade has just unleashed. It all comes flooding out and I can't stop myself laughing. It's not even funny, I'm stressed as hell, I'm drained, physically, mentally, emotionally. Totally spent and, here I am, laughing like a hyena.

Wade returns to the washing up. He understands my reaction, we see it often enough. He's even started laughing.

I take control of myself. "Wade, there's something you need to know. Something I've pieced together." Oh, god. Should I tell him this? I have no choice. I must let him in. "I have no memories from before I was six years old."

Wade's laughter evaporates. He's working out the implications. "Most people form sustainable memories from the age of three."

I nod.

He squeezes past me and sits down on the sofa. I follow but stay standing. He takes one very deep breath and sweeps his hair behind his ear.

I sit next to him. "When I was first called in for an interview about the Peter Daventry murder, I kept thinking why I wasn't coming clean and declaring memory issues brought on by the tanker incident."

Wade says nothing.

"I had that note, the note I wrote."

"You were working off a hunch. Something you're so good at."

"It was more than a hunch. I knew the route I'd taken to get there and home again. I knew I'd been to the Colombian Cockney. I knew about the Back Yard Cinema and that it had moved on."

"Lottie?"

"Must have been. The thing is, Wade, there's a stark difference between things I don't remember but recognise, and things I don't remember at all. I don't remember anything since before I was six."

"Your first memory being?"

I try to say it, but the words don't come. I swallow. "Pots and pans, Wade. Pots and pans."

Wade shakes his head, just ever so slightly.

"I think what I'm trying to tell you, is that, like Lottie, I'm an alter too."

CHAPTER THIRTY-SIX

It's 3am.

I can't feel Lottie. She must be in the *dressing room*.

Telling Wade I'm an alter, drove him away. I didn't feel snubbed. I think I know him well enough. He had to leave to get his head round it.

He feels privileged to know me. I intrigue him. I don't want to be an object of curiosity. I don't even know I want a relationship.

Lottie won't be persuaded. She's going to finish her *project*, behind my back if necessary. Three more killings and a fourth for me. I'm not dim. She's talking about Travis Hendry being my target. If his videos surface, Lottie's project will be exposed. If he's killed, the likelihood of those videos surfacing will increase. He needs dealing with, but the videos will need recovering first.

What then? Will she stop? If I do manage to keep us out of prison, will she want to stop?

There's only one way I can stop her and that's by ending her life which, of course, means ending mine. Anything else will leave us with a life not worth living.

I heave myself onto my side. These thoughts won't go away.

Up until the tanker incident, my life was going somewhere. Here I go again. Another grinding through the cycle of thoughts. Now, six weeks later, it's heading for a cul-de-sac. There's no hope. Even if Wade swept me off my feet and carried me into the sunset, there'd be a load of shit following. Two killings so far, a third in the pipeline. Then two more after that, possibly three. Will Lottie really stop there? The links between the victims will be found and when they are... I don't even want to think about it. So it's the life of a villain or no life at all.

How will I be able to form any kind of relationship with anyone? Even Wade?

And here I am, back at the beginning ready for another circuit.

I'm up and slipping on my running gear. No lights. That'll disturb Lottie down in the dressing room.

* * *

My knee's not hurting. Hope it holds out. I can't have it waking Lottie. I shield my eyes from vehicle headlights. Bright lights will wake Lottie too.

Running up Camberwell New Road, I can't believe how calm I feel. So much has changed. I'm not the only person to experience change. I know people who have faced physical life-changing conditions. Victims of car crashes, victims of crime. I don't know anyone who's faced a mental condition.

There's a lorry coming, brightly lit. I turn into a doorway, pressing my hands against my eyes.

After the lorry's passed, I stay still for a minute, checking the *wings*. Lottie's not there.

I pull the peak of my baseball cap lower over my eyes, step out of the doorway, leg's still good, and continue.

Another lorry. I turn my head away and angle the peak of my cap. The lorry passes. I wait. Nothing. I wait a bit more. Nothing.

The bus stop, where burning bodies were piled in mounds, stands lonely. The shopfront the flaming car reversed through has a dummy dressed in a fashionable red dress. The spot where the woman fell as her flames rose is indistinguishable. All those people died in awful circumstances and everything is back to normal.

The spot where the car stood and Madeleine pointed with her chin. The spot where Lavender dumped me on my arse, with Billy on my lap, and emptied a fire extinguisher over me.

How many of the people who were there, including us blue-light people, are suffering? Shouldn't I be trying to help them?

Nobody's helping me. I know Lottie was stifling any chance of meeting Doctor Slattery. What about Lavender? Kathy? Why did they diss me? Where is Cantrell? Only Wade has stood by me, and even now, I've frightened him away.

Whatever happens, I've got to deal with it myself. Kevan House looms above me. I'm checking continuously. No sign of Lottie.

Using the keys I pinched off the janitor, I'm in through the main door, up to the twentieth floor, through the maintenance door and out onto the roof.

This is my spot. I sit, cross-legged, my knee's good, and close my eyes. "Hello, Joel. I was here a few days back.

Seems a lifetime. There's been another murder. I was nicked but the detectives haven't got enough so I'm out on bail. Suspended. All these weird goings on. I've found out I've got Dishoshi… Jeez, can't even say it, Dissociative Identity Disorder. DID. It turns out that, like you, I was sexually abused as a kid. DID was my response. I have an alter called Lottie. How unimaginative is that? She took the abuse. I knew nothing of it. When the abuse stopped, she got trapped, down inside, somewhere, somehow. That tanker incident brought on the perfect storm. Gave her the chance to break out. She's bent on revenge, not doing the killing but organising those who are. All a bit iffy. Could easily be killing innocent people. The detectives have the right person, they just don't know it. They suspect, but they don't know. I'm trapped. Trapped with a life not lived. The only way I can see to escape is to do what you did. What's it like, Joel, when you run and launch yourself out there?"

* * *

This is early in the morning for Charlie to be talking.

I have not been able to sleep either. I cannot stop thinking about the Frank Amos confrontation. Should Charlie and Wade go along? If he gets a thumbs-up, it would be good to have Wade and Charlie there. Charlie will talk her way out. I hope he gets the thumbs-down. Eileen will take a thumbs-up worse than Robert. We are nowhere near identifying my abuser. Back to Frank Amos. How will Charlie and Wade react to a thumbs-down? That is what I am gambling on.

Well, Charlie is up and about. Might as well spend some time together.

Hang on, where is she? What? The roof. Highly emotional. Running. Towards the edge. I take the *spot* and drop her, let my legs go. Sprawled on the floor. She wants it back.

"Charlie. Stop. Stop."

Pushing hard.

"Charlie. You are too emotional. I will not let you back. You were going to throw us off."

Pushing, pushing.

"Charlie, calm down."

The door bangs open and someone pops out.

"Wade." Thank god. "Over here."

He grabs my shoulders. "Lottie?"

"Yes, it is me. Charlie was going to throw herself off. I caught her just in time."

"Let Charlie back onto the *spot*. I need to talk to her."

"Not sure about that."

"Come on, Lottie. You must let her back onto the *spot*. I'm holding her. You're perfectly safe."

* * *

Wade's here. What the hell? Lottie's moving aside. I push back onto the spot and run but I'm held, vice-like.

"Let me go. I want to be with Joel."

"Charlie. You must calm down."

"I must get away from you."

"Charlie."

He's too strong. I kick and punch but I'm too close.

And he's here. I twist and stamp, but he won't release. Won't release. Strong hands. And Wade's here.

"Come on, Charlie. Breathe. In for four, out for six."

Fuck breathing. What's Wade doing here? How?

I stop struggling and surrender to a warm hug, the warmest hug I've ever felt. "Wade. How did you know?" I'm blubbering into his jacket.

"I left to get my head straight. Figured I might have upset you so, couldn't sleep, instead of waiting till morning, I came back. You weren't answering the door. I telephoned you. I could hear your telephone ringing but you weren't picking up. Text. No response. I was close to kicking your door in. Then I remembered something Lottie said. You sometimes come up here when you're feeling lonely. By leaving like that, I must have made you feel so lonely. I rushed round here and pressed every bell until someone buzzed me in. Up the lift. Found the maintenance door open. Here I am."

I collapse in Wade's arms.

* * *

"Charlie is in danger."

Wade is holding me and looking closely. "Lottie."

"Yes. Charlie is so emotional she is in great danger."

Wade is still holding my shoulders, tightly. "Forgive me if I don't trust you."

"Wade. Charlie has gone down. She is probably the lowest she has ever been."

Wade will not let go of me. "Do you need to go after her?" he says.

"I do. Can you carry us home?"

"Yes. I have my car. I just need to…"

Wade's voice fades as I dart out through the *wings* to the *dressing room*. Charlie has gone farther. The *abyss*. I see her falling. Gently tumbling. I grab her and stop her descent. She struggles against me. I am better at this. On feeling safe, I look around. There is nothing, no one, just dark. I check again. No one. Just dark.

* * *

I'm tired of this pushing and shoving. Leave me be.

All I can see is Wade's worried face.

I'm in my flat.

How?

"Wade. Thank you. Please stay with us. I do not want to lose her."

"What can I do?"

"Just be here."

Voices. Wade's talking but not to me. Lottie.

"Charlie. I know you hear me and you know it is me. Do not leave me, not like that. I could not stand to be on my own. I need you."

Bitch. Intent on murder and says she needs me.

"We are unique. If we can keep this secret, think how strong we could be. What we could do. How far we could go."

"No. You're a killer. A psycho. You say you'll go behind my back. Well, that works both ways. The killing stops." I'm screaming. Wade's making soothing noises.

"Charlie, you are not angry with me. You are angry with the people who created the circumstances whereby the two of us exist."

"Don't go getting all fancy with me. Save it for the gang. What you're doing is wrong and you know it. I don't want to be imprisoned. I don't want to be institutionalised. I don't want it."

Wade moves to the window.

"Charlie. I do not want it either, nor do Zachery and Ush, nor Robert and Eileen but this is what we have. All we can do is make the best of it."

"Murder is not the best of it." I'm shouting again.

"We will not be handing this to police."

"Then let it drop."

"Not an option."

"Of course it's a bloody option. You've chosen to ignore it. You've…"

"Charlie. It is not just me. It is the rest of the gang and we have all been round the block on these options, several times, and we always come back to the same conclusion. No police. No court. Justice."

"That's nonsense."

"Charlie, the police and the courts will not lead to justice. Not for us. You have seen Zachery and Ush. Compare them to Robert and Eileen. Then there is me, how do you think I feel?"

I think that's the point. There's no way I can know how they feel. I've been on the receiving end of Travis Hendry's sadism but my experiences have been nothing like theirs. I ran away from that.

My hands are resting on my knees, scarred but comfortable. The skin sometimes feels taught. The salamander tattoo and the scars it hides. No. There is no way I can possibly know how they feel. "Lottie, who dragged the boy from the burning car?"

"You did."

"I couldn't have taken that pain."

"Okay, Charlie, I helped."

Wade is no longer staring out the window. He's turned and is leaning back against the sill.

"You took the pain. I put us in that position and you took the pain."

"Essentially."

"Lottie, basically, you took advantage of Charlie." Wade's still perched on the sill. "You used that situation to cause those injuries knowing you'd be able to capitalise on them."

Lottie's there but not answering.

"Charlie's an innocent victim…"

"Wade, stop. You're not being fair. We call it the *stage* and *wings* and so on. They're just names. They're places we've imagined into existence. It's a no-man's land. A limbo, all the time teetering on the edge of nothingness. I've been there. It would have been so easy for Lottie to just let go but she stayed, she hung on. Why?"

"Well, I don't know, but…"

"Wade, it's so much more than the boy in the burning car. I've been in a lot of scrapes, picked up injuries. Every time, I've felt this kind of, I don't know, out-of-body? I don't know, disconnected? Yes, disconnected. It was Lottie. Whenever I got myself into difficulty, Lottie would take the pain. That's why she's there. That's what she does. It's her *raison d'être*."

"Less than an hour ago, Charlie, you were trying to kill her."

"She saved me."

"She saved herself."

Lottie's still there, on the *stage*, watching, listening. She's emotional. She wants to speak but can't. It's down to me.

"No. Wade. She saved me. It's called a disorder. Dissociative Identity Disorder. When Travis Hendry's physical abuse got too much, *I* formed to take it. Amongst the pots and pans. Age six. I couldn't take the sexual abuse and Lottie formed to take that. Age eight. We are a multiple. This DID isn't a disorder. It's a defence."

"At some point you must have been a singleton."

"Yes. Let's call her Charlotte. If I formed when I was six years old, imagine what Charlotte must have been going through. I took the bullying and physical abuse that Travis Hendry meted out so that she didn't have to. Then, when the sexual abuse started Lottie formed and she took that so I didn't have to."

"I'm really trying to keep up with you but this is mind-blowing." Wade rubs his head, his hair all over the place. "Where's Charlotte?"

"I'm a part of Charlotte. Lottie's another part of Charlotte. When I was down in that limbo, in that no-man's land, I didn't feel alone."

"There are more of you?"

"I don't know, Wade. I don't know how to interpret these feelings."

"Isn't that what Doctor Slattery could do for you?"

"What Lottie's saying is that everybody wants to turn us back into a singleton."

"Integration."

"Yes. No. I don't know. Lottie saved me. Time is weird in that limbo. I felt like I was there for days. It was only the time it took you to carry us back here. I was drifting, getting lower, getting darker. If Lottie hadn't come for me, I'd still be there gradually fading. Lottie didn't need to come for me. She took a huge risk. All I want to do is give her a big hug, but how the hell do I do that?"

CHAPTER THIRTY-SEVEN

Tuesday 2nd February 2021 – a date to remember – the date I was reinstated after two-and-a-half weeks suspension. I was called in for a helpful chat with DS French from Homicide and DI Reeve from DPS. Lottie calls them Humpty and Dumpty. Insufficient evidence, DS French explained. Lottie was right. After the explanation, which took two-and-three-quarter minutes, the superintendent came in, handed me my warrant card and told me if I wasn't quick, I'd be late for parade. We had a good piss-up that night. Everyone was there, many more than just my team. All the awkwardness of the dissing because I was on bail was forgiven. Even Lavender showed contrition. Kathy couldn't stop crying and Cantrell made a bit of a speech. DS French turned up as well. Not like he wasn't welcome, but strange.

Thank god that was followed by a couple of rest days.

* * *

And here we are, Friday Early-Turn. I'm out with Lavender – again. It's quiet, he's quiet and so am I.

Frank Amos lives in Tonbridge. His house is in a cul-de-sac overlooked by several others.

Peter Daventry walked home from work through Primrose Hill. It was easy to catch him on his own. Ursula used a tablet to show Daventry a video of a man sexually assaulting a boy. That man looked like Daventry. The boy was Zach. Ursula watched Daventry's reaction and gave the thumbs-down. Zach, who'd crept up behind, stabbed Daventry under his left armpit. Whether Zach spoke to him as he died by the children's playground, only Zach and Ursula know. Zach withdrew the knife and they scarpered.

Vincent Pope lived on a quiet street in a house with a gravel drive. Neighbouring houses were over fifty yards away. Driving home, Pope encountered a dustbin blocking his drive. He got out and was confronted by Rob with a tablet showing child pornography featuring a man looking like Pope and a young Ursula. The way Pope reacted led to Rob giving the thumbs-down. Ursula, who'd crept up behind, stabbed Pope under his left armpit. Whether Ursula spoke to him as he died on his own drive, only Ursula and Rob know. Ursula removed the knife and they scarpered.

What Xavier Viceroy thought of three people in pantomime costume showing him illicit child porn, no one would know. "Would you tell anyone," Lottie had convinced the others, "that some lunatics had approached you, shown you awful child-porn and then run away?"

To understand that reaction, they'd shown the video clips to many people. Some of them would have reported the bizarre incident. Lottie would have engaged her most convincing tone of voice. "If you were a copper, would you believe them? Would you record it? Enter it on intelligence systems? Let's say you do. We conducted all those trials in different areas. If any incidents were recorded, would they be linked?"

"Possible," Eileen had said, "even probable."

"But is it likely?" Lottie had convinced.

I can just imagine Lottie's calm voice massaging away their fears, playing on their disrupted childhoods, offering salvation. Was that a false hope?

I saw Rob's despair and Eileen's heartfelt disappointment for him, as if transferring it onto herself. I saw the attitude of Zach and Ursula who'd had the *therapy*. Had it worked? They said it did. Were they making it up to help Rob and Eileen? To appease Lottie?

"You out with the friggin' fairies?" Lavender elbows me and points at the radio. "Answer the call."

I grab the handset. "Received by Mike-Three."

Lavender flicks on the blues-and-twos and eases us out of the line of traffic. I've no idea what or where the call is. Do I ask Lavender? Not a chance.

I check the mobile data, pulling up the last-assigned for Mike-Three. "This isn't urgent. It's kids playing football."

"Urgent enough to get us out of that friggin' traffic jam."

I return to my thoughts.

What about Lottie? What about her abuser? My abuser? I must start thinking of him like that. It's because of that abuse we now have this condition. In all our chatting, analysis and soul searching, we have worked out a way forward.

Wade and I are together, he pretty much lives at my place but he hasn't moved in. Too soon for anything like that. Lottie says she's fine with our intimacy, disappearing to the *dressing room*. Does she? Is she fine? I wonder if she can be. I've spoken with the others. All four of them have hang-ups. Zach and Ursula less so than Rob and Eileen, but one thing's for sure, they're all happy for me. Ursula said Lottie was happy for me too.

I've made my peace with Joel.

We've arrived. Six kids playing football, using a garage door as a goal. Every so often, above the shouting and screaming, there's a resounding boom as the ball hits the garage door. Must be driving the local residents nuts. Curtains are twitching. Lavender's stayed with the car, as usual. The ball escapes from the kids and rolls my way. I trap it under my foot. They stop. One of them is Jonny Frakes' kid. Explains why the locals called police rather that telling them to shut up.

"That's our ball," one of the kids shouts.

"Come and get it then," I say.

He rushes forward.

I switch the ball to my other foot.

Another lad goes for it.

I turn into them, protecting the ball with my body.

They start yelling as I break away, dribbling the ball around them and shoot for goal. A perfect shot and I'm surprised the garage door's still standing. The ball bounces back and I pick it up. "But you're a girl," one of them shouts.

"I'll pretend I didn't hear that," I say. "Now, listen. You're making a lot of noise and disturbing everyone.

The park's only over there."

"Great, we'll…"

"No. First, you'll tell your mums and dads where you're going and what you're doing."

One of them takes the ball and they all charge off home.

As I return to the car, Lavender's leaning against his door. "You could play for West friggin' Ham with a shot like that. You bent it."

"What the door?"

"Nah, the ball. You know, like Beckham."

I jump into the car and Lavender glides us off the estate. It's been a quiet morning and our Early Turn is gliding to an end. I resume my cogitating.

None of the gang have had any meaningful relationships. Ursula said she's thinking about it now. I told her about my patchy past with boys and that Wade's my first. What she said has stuck with me. "What happened to Lottie happened to you. The feelings you experienced were the same as Lottie's. You just didn't know why."

Nearly going-home time and Lavender's heading back to the Nick.

What about the Homicide detectives? They have two murders in quick succession. For each the cause was a stab wound under the left arm. Both were accompanied by a phone call to Crimestoppers implicating that 'hero cop' Charlie Quinlan. Caller's voice and my voice digitally identical. A detective like John French is never going to let that go. He'll be searching for the link between Peter Daventry and Vincent Pope. If he finds it…

Thank god Xavier Viceroy was a thumbs-up.

The method must change.

Then there's the other weakness. Travis Hendry and the paedophiles. These murders have had a high profile in the press. Travis Hendry may be piecing things together. Would Travis Hendry know the paedophiles? Would he recognise them from their media pictures? Do members of a paedophile ring know the identities of the others? Would they come forward?

I'm in because I have no choice. Lottie will push on regardless and there'll be no talking her down. If I'm in, I've got to have a positive role. I've taken it upon myself to keep us all out of prison.

Wade's in because of me. If he wasn't, he'd be another risk like Travis Hendry and the other members of the paedophile ring. After what happened at Kevan House, he's in for Lottie as much as for me.

The team are all together waiting for Cantrell to give the off. Kathy calls across. "We're going for a lunchtime drink. You coming?"

I look at Wade. He shakes his head. "No thanks."

"The love birds," Kathy can't help herself, "have better things to do."

Everybody laughs and it's friendly. It seems that hooking up with me has given Wade some status.

Their tune would change quick enough if they knew the real reason why we were declining a drink.

Cantrell comes in, asks if any of us dares have a report for her, which no one does, and she gives the off.

We file out.

In the locker room, Kathy can't stay quiet for long.

"You've really got to do something about your boyfriend's hair."

"Aw, Kathy. You jealous?"

"I'm pleased for you, Charlie. About time. Apart from the fact he's a complete dork, he's quite a dish."

I close my locker door. "You so much as look at him, I'll consider it theft."

"No intention to permanently deprive, darling."

I throw my arms around her and we hug. "It's been over a fortnight since I was suspended and I still feel I'm emerging from some awful quagmire. It's great to be back."

"It's great to have you back."

Yeah. Right. All forgiven, sure, but I'll never forget how you dissed me that time outside Morrisons. I give her another squeeze and leave the locker room, to re-immerse myself in that awful quagmire.

* * *

Wade and I have taken to riding our bikes everywhere. I still do my running and punchbag work but mostly it's cycling.

It's just turned February.

Tonight we approach Frank Amos. It's Eileen's kill. Rob, Wade and I will be there ready with our thumbs. Jeez, I feel like a Roman Emperor.

We've decided on the approach. We'll split up outside Tonbridge and meet at the copse we've recce'd. We'll change our clothing, leave what gear we don't need there and gather outside Amos's address. Then the *what-ifs* will start.

We've met up at Rob's place in Lewisham and Rob's leading us through our checklist.

Tablet – check.

Burners, batteries fully charged and removed – check.

All other mobile phones, Fitbits and anything digital left at home – check.

Everyday clothes – check.

Beanies – check.

Duct tape – check. "I still don't understand what that's about." Rob isn't scathing, just curious.

Wade explains. "Charlie and I have had our DNA added to the Contamination Elimination Database. If we leave any trace of ourselves at the scene, we'll be caught."

Rob shakes his head and looks at Eileen. "What about MI5 operatives?"

Eileen doesn't react to Rob's question but Wade covers it. "I don't know and there's no point asking." Eileen gives Wade a little smile and Rob gives up.

Black bin liners – check.

Ice-cream container – check.

Pizza box – check.

Boiled sweets – check.

Lights – check.

Tool kit – check. Hopefully none of us will get a puncture.

Chain and padlock – check.

Keys for the padlock – we all hold up our keys – check.

Red scarves and disguise – check.

Watches – analogue – check. We check the time.

Knife – check. Eileen's holding her paring knife. She shakes her head. "It's so…"

Rob deals with that. "A knife for peeling fruit? Seems small?" He takes the knife and holds it up to his chest. "In through the left armpit and the blade will easily reach the heart and, even if you miss the heart, there are so many large blood vessels around there, the kill's inevitable." He hands the knife back to Eileen.

I'm not sure that's what Eileen meant. A question hits me, what if she doesn't go through with it?

I ditch that thought. We can't have Eileen spooked. Not now.

Interesting choice of weapon. Lottie would have prompted that. Because it's small, it's less likely to get stuck or break and so minimises the risk of the weapon or part of it being left at the scene.

After that momentary lapse, Eileen's back on it, focussed and stuffing her backpack.

Not a good time to suggest changes but my job is to keep us out of prison. Wade will be with me and Eileen might be an ally too. Lottie's on the *stage*, watching and listening. "Maybe the surgical incision used for Daventry and Pope isn't right for this. If he gets the thumbs-down, we want it to look like he's disturbed burglars. A precise entry wound doesn't go with that."

"It's a good idea to change the *modus operandi*." Wade's come in on my side. "We don't want to start developing a pattern."

There's that rush. Lottie has bounded forward but stopped short of the *spot*.

"I suppose we have time," Rob says. "With Daventry and Pope, there was no chance to hang around. The attack had to be guaranteed fatal. With Amos, we'll be able to stand over him till we're sure he's dead."

Lottie moves back.

"Agreed," Eileen's relaxed. "A frenzied attack would be more appropriate."

Lottie settles back on the *stage*.

"Blood spatter will be the issue." This is Wade. "We do not go in there with any clothing we intend to keep. Everything we take in there, even our underwear, must be destroyed afterwards."

"Agreed," says Eileen.

"Sounds good," says Rob.

The ride to Tonbridge is twenty-five miles and includes up and over the North Downs. About two-and-a-half hours.

The time for the approach has been set at nine-thirty. Ursula and Zach have our debit cards. Zach will be doing Lewisham and Camberwell for Rob, Wade and me. Ursula will be in Harrow for Eileen.

"It's half-six, time to go." Rob clips his helmet strap under his chin. We're all ready.

"Before we set off, if you don't mind, I need a little more clarification." Wade has got some questions. Fair enough but, right now?

Eileen is visibly annoyed. Rob is all patience.

Wade is unperturbed by Eileen. "How did you find out Amos's routine?"

"Once we had his address, I followed him. That's how I know he orders pizza every evening."

A little wave of alarm passes through me. Following someone without showing out is not easy.

Wade continues. "What does Frank Amos look like? I mean, in comparison to the images of him in his abuse clip?"

This time, Rob looks at Eileen before answering. "Well, he's fifteen years older, obviously. Late thirties. He's filled out a bit. He goes to the gym every evening on the way home."

I close my eyes. Wade's onto something. Even Lottie has moved forward.

"He goes to the gym each day? So he's fit and strong." Wade keeps his voice calm and even.

Eileen's irritation has morphed into worry. She's now looking at Rob, eyes wide.

Okay, so he's going to be a handful and Eileen clearly wasn't aware of this. Much as I understand where Wade's coming from, I really don't need Eileen spooked.

"It's okay, Eileen," Wade says. "Charlie and I are well used to dealing with people like him. We're Hendon-trained."

* * *

Cycling to Tonbridge is uneventful apart from coming down Poll Hill. Scared the shit out of me.

We ride into Tonbridge separately and meet at the copse.

Rob arrives last. "Amos is finishing up at the gym. Bit of good news, I heard him on the phone ordering pizza."

Great.

Rob looks at Wade. "You made a good point. He's

built like a brick-shit-house."

Great.

Rob changes his clothing quickly as Wade and I help each other cover all the joints in our clothing with duct tape – wrists, ankles, waist. Rob holds up the pizza box. "We all ready?"

We all nod.

Rob continues. "We deliver the pizza just after he goes indoors. When he answers, Charlie and Wade, you go in. Keep him away from the panic-button. Door hinges on the left, panic-button's on the right."

I like that Rob's taken charge.

Wade holds up his empty ice-cream container to show he's ready.

Rob attaches a moustache to his upper lip, puts on a pair of thick-rimmed specs and, lastly, a blond wig.

We've all changed from our cycling gear into everyday clothes. Apart from Rob, each of us has a beanie we can pull down over our face. I hold up my red scarf. "Don't forget to put yours on."

Rob shakes his head. "Seems strange, wearing something that will make us so noticeable."

I've explained this already. Try again. "If he gets a thumbs-up he'll call police as we're legging it. If we're not wearing red scarves, he'll describe each of us individually. If we are wearing the scarves, his description of us will be four people wearing red scarves. Trust me on this."

Eileen shakes her head. Oh, god. What's up with her? "Seems strange," she says, "that a bloke who's so keen on physical fitness eats takeaway pizza."

Eileen's good.

It's an unpleasant night, not raining but there's a dampness in the air. It was uncomfortable changing. We chain our bikes and backpacks together and conceal them under leaves and broken branches. Each of us has a key for the hefty padlock. This is where the weather's doing us a favour. There won't be many people about. A dog would find them but there won't be many of them about either.

A thumbs-up will be an incident from which we will need to run like mad. A thumbs-down will be an incident from which we can retreat more leisurely.

What we're doing is wrong. I've decided that, no matter how it goes, Amos will be getting a thumbs-up. So, we'll be legging it.

* * *

Amos will be here soon. We spread out around the cul-de-sac. With better weather, this would have been impossible as we'd have attracted too much attention.

Amos comes into view. He's a big guy.

He's distracted, fumbling with his keys, keen to get indoors.

He's in. There's beeping. A light comes on. The beeping stops. Another light comes on. The door closes. Sliding metal as the chain goes on. A light goes out.

Rob's heading up the path.

Wade, Eileen and I pull down our beanies. Wade and I wrap the duct tape over the join between beanie and top. We follow Rob and fan out either side of the front door. As Rob knocks, I check the other houses. Nothing moving.

The door opens, thudding back against its chain.

"Pizza," Rob says.

The door closes, Wade moves round in front of Rob. Sliding metal. I move in right next to Wade and the door opens.

Wade kicks the door hard. He's in, ice-cream container over the panic-button. I'm in and onto Amos. He bats me away and lunges for the panic-button but Wade has it covered.

Amos is not cowed, he's going at Wade, all fists and snarling teeth.

I'm back at him. No room for kicks. Right hand – jab. Left hand – jab. Amos has become my punchbag. Wade's on him. Rob too and he's over-powered.

The bundle has taken us inside.

Eileen comes in and closes the door.

There's no hallway, the front door opens straight onto the living room.

Wade has Amos pinned down and nods. He's in control but we can't afford for Amos to break free. I take Rob's arm. "I need you to do something."

Rob's eager. I kneel down and lean on Amos's head. "All your weight on his head. Like this. Keep your fingers away from his mouth."

Rob takes over from me.

With his head pinned, Amos won't be able to cause problems for Wade.

I stand back. They're steady. Wade nods.

Kitchen's clear. Eileen and I are up the stairs. We know what we'll find, but it needs checking, even under beds and in cupboards. There's no one else in the house.

We rush round closing all curtains. The décor is dark.

Back down to Amos who Wade and Rob still have pinned to the floor.

Eileen stays back where Amos can't see her. We all have boiled sweets in our mouths.

Amos has stopped struggling. Wade has both his arms twisted up his back though, with the muscle-bulk, he's struggling to get Amos's wrists much higher than his belt.

I move round and kneel, positioning myself to see his face.

Wade indicates he's in control.

Rob releases Amos's head, opens his pizza box, removes the tablet and, seconds later, has the video playing.

It's him.

Lottie's right there with me, by the *spot*. I can feel her excitement.

I check out Wade. He's seen it too.

Rob has his hand up, ready to give the signal.

What is it we've seen? It was momentary and undeniable, but what was it?

Best I can say, it was a double-take. First came incomprehension and then came the recognition. He recognised himself. In less than a second, he covered the recognition over but it was there. The incomprehension was out of place, should have been disgust at seeing a grown man abusing a small girl. Where was the disgust? Two points of confirmation. This is the guy who abused Eileen over fifteen years ago. Verification – check. That's what the gang look for although they haven't been able to put it into words.

Rob's seen it. He's stopped the video, a freeze frame of Amos and Eileen, and given the thumbs-down.

Wade? Christ, he's given the thumbs-down too.

Lottie has seen it. She's pushing, banging, screaming. I can feel her. She's staying back though. So much is going through my head. It's him. We've got him. My intention was to let him go and pursue him lawfully but that won't work. Of course it won't work. This little incident will come up. What on earth was I thinking?

I still need more though.

I lean down so I'm right next to him. "Let me introduce you. That little girl," I say pointing at the frozen frame on Rob's tablet, "is standing behind you."

"You're female." Amos has a soft voice. "Get out of my face, you filthy slut."

He's talking. Good. "You have a problem with females."

He cranes his neck round to Rob. "Only if they're dirty."

My god. "Meaning?"

"Tell her," he's still directing what he's saying to Rob, "and the other one, to get their filthy bleeding apexes out of my house."

I look round at Eileen. She's pulled up her mask. Even if she hadn't, I'd be able to tell we're past thumbs-up-or-down. She walks round so she's in Amos's view. She doesn't even notice my thumbs-down.

"Frank Amos," she says, "you were a significant person in the forming of this woman who is going to kill you," she holds up her knife, "but this isn't right." Eileen walks out to the kitchen and comes back with a huge chef's knife. She turns the knife back and forth in front of Amos.

Amos is scared. He tries to free himself but Wade has him secured.

Eileen kneels down so Amos can see her more easily. "Here's the scenario, Frank. We were burgling your house when you came home and disturbed us. Big fight, during which you were stabbed with one of your own knives and died from your injuries." Eileen turns the knife and light flits across Amos's eyes. "So, given that scenario, where do you think you would be stabbed?"

Amos isn't speaking. He's struggling to free himself but, with his hands pinned behind his back, he's stuck. He does manage to get a knee up under his hip and he's lifting Wade. I stand quickly, kick his leg out straight and Wade's back in control.

Eileen continues. "Frank, where do you think you'd be stabbed? In the genitals? Seems appropriate. That's where you stabbed me when I was nine years old? How many other young girls have you stabbed in the genitals?"

Amos starts struggling again, but he's weakening.

Lottie's there. Still listening. Still watching. I wonder what she's thinking.

Amos turns to Rob, "Back then, she was pure."

Eileen is keeping her distance. How she's keeping from whirling into a frenzied knife attack is disturbing in itself. "Trouble is," she says, her voice calm, "in this scenario, you know, you disturbing burglars, you wouldn't really be lying down when you're stabbed. So you're going to have to stand up." She motions Wade to step away.

Is this a good idea?

Wade does step back. As he does so, Amos, his arms free, springs forward, but Wade knees him hard in his thigh.

With the force taken out of Amos's charge, Eileen allows him to fall onto the knife, which enters under his left collar bone. Any vestige of strength Amos still had, drains from him. He finishes on his knees, his arms draped around Eileen.

Rob pulls Amos back and I pull Eileen away. She's covered in blood. Her steely calm is cracking. She's sobbing. All I'm thinking is evidence. What's she leaving here? I pull her beanie back down over her face. She tries to stop me but I won't let her. She turns and buries her face into my neck, her arms around me, her sobbing growing. At least, whatever's coming out of her mouth, nose and eyes will be caught by her beanie and, if not, will be caught on my clothing.

I'm stroking the back of her head. She's calming.

Amos is lying face down on the floor, motionless, a pool of blood spreading from under his left shoulder. Rob is checking his pulse. Wade has moved across to Amos's computer desk.

"What are you thinking, Wade?" I say, still comforting Eileen and realising I, too, have some of Amos's blood on me.

"We don't want police linking him to paedophilia." Wade's pulling out the stack.

"You're not going to try hacking into his computer, are you?"

"No. I'm just thinking that, as this is supposed to be a burglary, it would be appropriate to take his computer."

"Wade, we can't. It's a desktop. We've got to cycle twenty-five miles in the dark, up a bloody steep hill. We've got enough kit of our own to carry."

"It's too good an opportunity. Amos lived alone. He's a complete perv. Imagine the information on this computer."

"Leave it to the local Old Bill."

"You, yourself, said we don't want police making the link with paedophilia and child exploitation. It just brings them one step closer to us."

"Can we smash it up?"

"Not reliably. All we have to do is take the computer." Wade's already unplugged it and pulled it out onto the floor. He's releasing the last few cables, the keyboard, monitor and phone line.

"It's still a big heavy chunk." I'm not happy. I think Wade's right, we should take it but how will we manage it?

"I've got a big enough backpack. If we could share my stuff between the three of you, I'll carry this."

"I think he's right." Eileen has recovered a little. "This is a burglary. We need to take something."

"Okay," I say. "If we don't take the computer, it will be forensically examined. You're right. If they find pervy stuff on there, they'll have a motive other than burglary-disturbed. Can we just take a piece of it?"

"We're disturbed burglars," Wade's gone out into the kitchen and is rummaging, "we're not going to be dismantling computer hardware." He comes back with a supermarket bag.

"We should have thought about this before." I'm shaking my head.

"We didn't. We're thinking about it now. What's the difference? We've still got to take it away with us." What a change. I never believed I'd hear this kind of decisiveness from Wade, especially in all this mayhem.

"Okay. You bring it. Rob, Eileen, this place must look like it's been burgled. Our point of entry is the kitchen door. We must break the door from the outside. Rob?"

"Okay."

Wade calls out. "Don't get too carried away. The pizza will be arriving soon."

Of course. I stand with my back to the front door. I can see Amos's legs and some of his blood which has spread across the white carpet. "Can we put together some sort of screen?"

Eileen and Rob shift the sofa.

"Bit farther."

They shift it more.

"That'll do."

"Come on, Eileen." I charge up the stairs. "No. Wait. You're covered in blood. Leave it to me." I have some blood on me but not much. Must be careful. Any blood upstairs would look weird.

I pull out a drawer from the chest and leave it. I open a cupboard, pull a couple of things off the top shelf and leave them where they land on the floor. Into the next room and a similar approach. Amos was tidy and organised. I'm half expecting to find things revealing his perverted and sordid life but there's nothing. Even the book on his bedside table is a fiction novel.

The doorbell sounds. I hear the door open against the chain. A voice saying, "Pizza." I hear the door closing and the chain sliding. Then I hear Rob's voice, "Thanks, all paid for, yeah?" "Yeah, no worries there, mate. Enjoy." "I will," says Rob. Then, exactly what I've been dreading. "Where's Frank?" A delay, then Rob's voice. "He's upstairs getting changed, do you want to speak to him?" "Nah. Just say hello for me. It's Jim." "Okay, Jim. Thanks for this. Really quick." The door closes and I haven't been breathing.

Shit. Now we have a witness. Jim. I work through what witness Jim will say. He'll describe Rob, white male, red scarf. He'll recount the conversation, not accurately, but good enough. The question is, what did he see?

I'm down the stairs. "Rob, how close did he get?"

Rob's opening the pizza box. He can't be thinking of eating it. "As close as he needed to hand me the pizza."

"How tall was he?"

"My height."

"Okay." I wait until I hear witness Jim drive away on his scooter, open the door and step outside. There's no one there and if anyone's watching, what will they say? I turn and face Rob. I can see the back of the sofa. I can't see Amos's legs. I can't see any sign of a disturbance. I step back inside pulling the door to.

I give Rob a pat on the shoulder. "Brilliant, Rob. Fucking brilliant. What you doing with that pizza?"

"Don't care. It's a peperoni feast. I'm veggie."

Vegetarian murderers. Jeez.

Rob heads off towards the back door. He's proving to be a gem. So calm.

Wade comes over, the computer in a carrier bag, and opens the cupboard by the front door. He's looking at the alarm.

"The police will be asking why the alarm wasn't activated."

"What I'm thinking," Wade says. "It's cheap and simple. Audible only. There's no record of when it was last set or cancelled or activated even. The police will think he forgot to set it. There's no neighbour to say they heard it go off because it never went off."

Eileen. She's not looking good. She's standing looking at Amos's body. She's lifted her beanie again.

I put my arm around her shoulder. "Eileen, you must keep this over your face." I gently ease the beanie down past her chin.

She adjusts it to properly align the eyeholes. "He's dead," she says, "and he knew why."

"Right now, we've got to get out of here," I say.

"But I'm not feeling it."

"Feeling what?"

"Free."

"When we get away from here, you will. You're in shock. We all are. We must keep going. We've got to get out of here."

A thud from the back door startles us. It's Rob. He's found a spade in the back garden and used it to prise open the back door.

He comes in and sees Eileen. He pulls her into a tight hug. "It's okay. You remember how Zach said he felt like this, how you're feeling now? It was a couple of days before he started to feel the release Lottie promised us. Ush felt the

352

release immediately. Different for each of us."

"I know." Eileen's still staring at Amos's body.

I feel Lottie pushing. I let her take the *spot*.

"Eileen. You will feel the release, I promise. Right now, we must go."

Eileen looks away from Amos and curls into Lottie. "Thank god you're here. It was only knowing you were here that I could go through with this."

"You did well, Eileen, you can move on but, right now, we must move on from here."

Eileen leaves through the back door with Rob. Lottie leaves through the front door with Wade. We're running. There's still no one on the street. I can't check windows and who might see us, Lottie's not looking up at them. There's bugger all we can do about it anyway. Probably better not to know.

Within minutes, we're back with our bikes. All our clothing comes off and is placed in a pile. We layer on our cycling gear. Lottie's the last to get her helmet on. We each have a black bin liner in our backpacks. Lottie, Rob and Eileen split the clothes between them. It will all be destroyed. Wade fits the computer into his backpack.

We're ready. Lights on and we're off.

"May I," Lottie says, "leave the cycling to you?"

She's talking to me. I look at Wade who's slipped in beside me.

"Lottie left you to it?" he asks.

"I have my uses," I say.

THE END

DIAMOND
CRIME

Passionate about the crime/mystery/thriller books it publishes

Follow
Facebook:
@diamondcrimepublishing

Instagram
@diamond_crime_publishing

Web
diamondbooks.co.uk

Printed in Great Britain
by Amazon